SUPERIOR RUN

A Novel

By

Tom Wells

SUPERIOR RUN

First Edition

Copyright © 2011 by Tom Wells

Background for front cover art:
"Storm Clouds on the Ocean Horizon"
Sam Mugraby (Photos8.com)

ISBN-13: 978-1463719012

Acknowledgements

First and foremost, this book is dedicated to my wife and lifelong sailing partner, Sandy. Without her support and encouragement, it could never have come to light.

Our longtime friend Lorri Shurtleff helped us to weed out the inevitable typos and other errors in the initial drafts after waiting very patiently for the final chapters.

Finally, our thanks go to our friends Karen Larson and Jerry Powlas of *Good Old Boat* magazine. Their expert editorial assistance and technical input were vital in making this book a reality. Through them, we have found ourselves more deeply involved in the world of sailing and boats than we ever thought possible, and we are most grateful.

PROLOGUE

July 23, 4:37 p.m. CDT

Under a clear blue afternoon sky that was mirrored in the cold waters of Lake Superior, a single sailboat stood out against the horizon. A solitary figure sat in the cockpit, one foot braced against the heeling of the boat. Tall and wiry, he had the face of a mariner, with wrinkles about his deep blue eyes and weatherworn features topped off with an unruly shock of graying hair. He wore a yellow foul weather jacket in the cool breeze. An inflatable life vest/harness combination with a tether clipped securely to a beefy padeye kept him securely on board, though in all his years of sailing he had yet to need them. He held a cup of coffee in one hand, while the other absently caressed an idle winch mounted on the coaming. This sublime experience represented beauty, joy and contentment for him. The rush and hiss of the bow wave added to the aura of elation as the boat surged through the mild chop. Between the calms and the fierce storms, Superior could be like this; he savored the moment.

Paul Findlay had owned *Pipe Dream* for the past nineteen years. She served as his home, his lifestyle, and his first love. She was 37 feet of fiberglass, teak and assorted metals, but to him she was alive. Over the years a very subtle language had evolved between Paul and the boat. When sail trim was not proper or if anything else was not as it should be, she told him. Likewise, if he wanted that extra half-knot of speed or a little smoother ride through the chop, he would tell her. Each responded in kind, in a strange symbiosis of flesh and sailcloth, of bone and fiberglass. Paul knew beyond a doubt that *Pipe Dream* had a soul. No amount of logical assessment would convince him otherwise.

She and her 485 sisters started in the mind of the owner of Tartan Yachts and were brought to life as Sparkman & Stephens design number 2253. S&S had risen to the top among yacht designers in the 20th century, beginning with a series of legendary classics, such as *Dorade,* and continuing into the fiberglass era. *Pipe Dream's* elegant lines, her manners under sail, and her excellent performance were evidence of her pedigree.

Paul would normally be reveling in these qualities as he sailed westward, but today other matters intruded. This passage was being made because of a cryptic wire message from an old acquaintance. It arrived for him via Western Union, forwarded through the Marine Post Office at Sault Ste. Marie, as he prepared to depart for the North Channel on Lake Huron. He had intended to revisit some favorite anchorages there and work on his latest novel, but now those plans had been put on hold. Instead, he traversed the famed locks and headed west across Lake Superior's vast expanse.

The wire was from his college roommate, Richard Perry, a man he hadn't seen in several years. He smiled a bit is he recalled his old friend. They had been close at school and had stayed in touch for years following graduation, but that closeness was broken when Rich's wife died. Paul's own wife had left him as well; she'd been unable to adapt to sailing as a way of life. Without the influence of the two women, Paul and Rich had simply fallen out of the habit of frequent contact, and eventually there was no contact at all. He shook himself back to the present, and pulled the folded yellow message from his pocket to read it once more. The terse note read, simply:

Paul,

Will be in Bayfield WI starting July 23. Understand you are somewhere on Superior. Urgently need to see you if possible. Staying Rittenhouse. Please come.

Rich

P.S. Please do not call my phone. Very important you do not.

There was no address or phone number, and no clue as to the need. It was just like Rich. He had always been unpredictable and more than a little undependable, but he was a good friend. That was all Paul had needed to make a change in his plans and set a westward course.

Paul went below as the autopilot kept *Pipe Dream* on her course. He should be in sight of Stannard Rock Light in just a while, and it was time to log his dead reckoning entries on the chart and verify his position using GPS. He sat at the nav station, gnawing on the blunt end of his pencil. His brow furrowed as he pondered the message, especially the curious comment about the phone. Then he laid the thought aside and concentrated on his navigation. *Pipe Dream* pushed on toward the lowering sun.

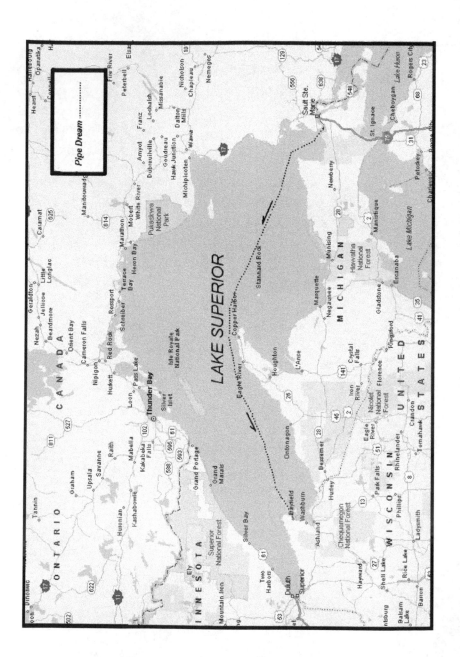

Pipe Dream ....

Chapter 1

BAYFIELD

July 23, 6:46 p.m. CDT

Bayfield, Wisconsin, is a beautiful village on the shore of Chequamegon Bay. Here, Lake Superior's temper is muted somewhat by the Apostle Islands. The islands themselves, with the exception of Madeline Island, are a part of a National Lakeshore and are a magnet for recreational boaters, sea kayakers, and backpackers. Several charter sailing fleets in the area assure the islands are packed with sailors during the summer. The village is careful not to allow franchise restaurants and other development; such establishments would spoil its wonderful character.

Up the hill from the downtown area of Bayfield along Rittenhouse Avenue stands the Old Rittenhouse Inn. The inn is a large, beautiful, ornate structure, built in the days when gingerbread and long front porches constituted the height of architectural fashion. Its many rooms are finished in period style, and its sumptuous common rooms and excellent cuisine make it a preferred lodging.

On this late July day, a green Toyota Camry pulled into a vacant parking spot hidden behind the inn. The driver got out, carrying only a soiled sport jacket. He draped the jacket over his left arm and walked quickly around the building to the entrance. His eyes darted nervously about, as if trying to take in more than could be seen in a casual glance. He was tall, with the slight paunch of middle age. A receding brownish gray hairline was evident over his darting eyes and rimless aviator spectacles. He took a last look at the surroundings, then entered the inn.

The desk clerk greeted him warmly: "Good evening, sir." Her pleasant smile did not seem to put him at ease. "May I help you?"

"Uhhh, y-yes . . ." he stammered slightly, forgetting for a moment what he was about to say. "I believe you're holding a reservation for me. The name's, uh, Pearson. Robert Pearson."

The clerk checked her papers. "Yes, Mr. Pearson, we show you staying with us for the next five days." She handed him a registration form and instructed him on the proper entries, then left for a moment, saying, "I'll be right back to finish checking you in." He watched her disappear around the corner, then turned to the paperwork. He had purchased traveler's checks in Chicago, and he had purposefully made the signature scrawled and hard to read so anyone might believe the name was Robert Pearson. He hoped she would not ask for any further identification.

When the clerk returned, she asked for a credit card; he mumbled, "Don't carry 'em. I prefer to use these." He laid his traveler's checks on the counter.

The clerk looked at them, frowned slightly, then looked back up. "Without a credit card, we'll need a deposit in case there are incidental charges."

"Uh-huh, that's okay. Can I cash these for the deposit?"

"Yes, sir. You're here for five days, so a $100 deposit should do over and above your room charges. You'll get back anything that isn't used. Oh," she continued, "and I'll need to see your I.D."

He hoped the cold sweat didn't show. He reached back and pulled out his wallet, then flipped it open. His Illinois license was in its plastic sleeve; he moved his thumb to cover the last part of his last name, then held it in front of him. The clerk looked down at it and as she did, he let the sport jacket slip to the floor. "Oops! Clumsy…" he said, stooping to get the jacket and pulling his wallet back with the motion. He stood back up, the wallet in his hand but just half open. "Sorry. Are we all set?"

She regarded him for a moment, then smiled and turned the registration slip back toward him. "If you'll just sign this and put your car information here, we will be."

He felt the relief but tried not to show it. He quickly filled out the form, stopping only to ask if he could return with the car license number. The clerk finished the check-in process, then showed him to his room.

He had asked for a room with an outside exit. Most rooms in the inn did not have that luxury, but his was on the main floor near the inn's entrance and it had doors to the inn and to the outside. He looked around the room, noting the large brass bed and the Jacuzzi. Satisfied, he went to the outside door, opened it, and paused to look around. Then he quickly walked around the rear of the inn to the Toyota to get his bag.

July 23, 6:54 p.m. CDT

Two hundred thirty miles to the east, *Pipe Dream* was passing the Stannard Rock Light.

July 24, 8:07 a.m. CDT

Morning found the Rittenhouse Inn buzzing with activity. While it was a Wednesday, it was still high season in Bayfield and the inn was full. The clink of tableware and the aroma of a well-prepared breakfast came from the main dining room. As guests shared coffee and conversation, they looked out on a brilliant summer morning. One guest was not in the mix.

Robert Pearson, actually Richard Perry, slipped quietly out of his exterior door and walked away from the main flow of traffic on Rittenhouse Avenue, instead going North to Washington Street. He then turned east and walked down the hill along Washington street, past the city park and its old wrought-iron railroad bridge, crossed Highway 13 and found himself at the shore of the bay. He stood by a long wooden building on an old pier, next to the ferry docks where passage could be made to Madeline Island. Past the ferry docks, he could see the concrete municipal docks inside their breakwater. Still farther south he could see the forest of masts in the Apostle Islands Marina. He had no idea what to look for, except that it was a sailboat and her name was *Pipe Dream*. That much he had gotten from a mutual acquaintance as he was trying to locate Paul Findlay.

He walked quickly to Front Street, which ran along the harbor. He stopped, his eyes darting about as they had before, and then walked to the south toward the City Dock past the small bed-and-breakfast lodgings and souvenir shops. At the end of the street was another city park, with a small gazebo overlooking the harbor. To his right, he saw the windows of the Pier Restaurant as its patrons enjoyed their breakfast with a harbor view. To his left stood a large barrel-roofed building at the land end of the City Dock. The building was used to house exhibits, host reunions, and hold meetings and gatherings of all kinds.

He turned east again and walked out onto the wide concrete expanse of the City Dock. Ahead, a red tanker truck was fueling the idle Apostle Islands excursion boat. There were several sailboats tied up alongside the pier in the joint municipal/ferry harbor to his left, and a mix of charter fishing boats and sailboats in slips to his right, to landward of the excursion boat. He walked quickly, nervously, looking for the name on each boat or a familiar face that would tell him he had found his old friend. Finding neither, he retraced his steps to the park gazebo and walked a paved path along the harbor leading south toward the Apostle Islands Marina.

The marina lay inside a second breakwater to the south. It consisted of wooden piers and slip fingers, with the larger boats on the northernmost pier and many more boats on more piers to the south. He stepped onto the first pier, walking with purpose now, to keep from drawing attention. He wanted to look as if he belonged on the docks.

One by one, he inspected the boats on each of the piers, but he found no sign of either *Pipe Dream* or her owner. He disappeared down a side street and took a circuitous route back to the Rittenhouse Inn. He entered through his outside door, locked it, and fell back onto the brass bed.

July 24, 8:46 a.m. CDT

About 140 miles away, Paul was nearing Eagle Harbor along the coast of Michigan's Keweenaw Peninsula. He checked his charts and verified his position. *Pipe Dream* was close reaching at almost 7 knots in a good breeze. If these conditions held, he could be in Bayfield the next morning. He had kept a singlehander's offshore night watch, catching catnaps and relying on the race timer alarm in the boat's instrument package to rouse him every thirty minutes or so. He would then reset the alarm, check the course and the trim of the sails, check his position, look for shipping traffic, check the NOAA weather station for updates, and sit in the cockpit until his eyelids began to droop again. Now, with morning and fresh coffee to energize him, he tried to imagine what Rich wanted, and how he'd been doing since he saw him last. Their last contact had been at a funeral, and Paul hoped this would be a more positive meeting.

July 24, 10:20 a.m. CDT

A solitary figure walked through a parking garage below a Chicago hotel. The short *bee-beep* of an electronic lock being activated came from a black Ford Explorer parked in a dark corner. The figure approached the Explorer and opened the driver's door. The glare of the dome light revealed a short, athletic man in a dark business suit. He hefted a large briefcase over the front seat, placing it on the rear seat before entering and starting the Explorer. He sat for a time with the door slightly ajar and the engine idling, unfolding a Wisconsin map. His finger traced a northerly route, leading through Milwaukee and then west away from Lake Michigan toward Madison, then northward again. The finger stopped, finally, on Bayfield. He refolded the map, laid it on the passenger's seat, and closed the door. The Explorer began to move, turning slowly out of its parking space, then proceeding up the ramps toward the street.

Exiting the garage into the glare of the late morning sunlight, he sought the turns that would take him to the Edens Expressway. The strong light made his features clear; the close-cropped brown hair and square jaw gave him a tough, competent appearance. He reached for his sunglasses and hid his alert, dark eyes. The package he had received last evening provided all he needed to proceed with the assignment. There was to be little further contact until the job was done and then only through a pre-arranged safe-deposit box. That is where the other half of his fee would be left for him.

To his clients he was known only as Jack. That wasn't his real name, of course, but in his line of work it didn't pay to publicize. He was the best and also the most expensive, but to those with a very specialized need he was well worth the price. This time, the price was a cool half-million. The target was unimportant; that his client wanted the target eliminated was the only thing that mattered. He had reached the freeway now and he smoothly accelerated and merged into the northbound traffic.

July 24, 6:26 p.m. CDT

Afternoon in Bayfield gave way to evening as Richard Perry arose from a fitful sleep. His mind was racing with fears, hopes, and a search for options. He was alone with his thoughts, and those thoughts provided no comfort. His mind drifted back over the twisted sequence of events that had brought him to this place and this situation. He still found it hard to believe. His employer, his longtime friend, was no longer either. Rich now found himself an unwitting player in a deadly game, all because of his work ethic. Unbidden, the memories came flooding back . . .

July 19, 1:46 p.m. CDT

Ted Mansfield asked Rich Perry to return some books and ledgers to a safe-deposit box during his lunch break. Rich took the books in their sealed folder, along with the box key and instructions to call in when they were safely locked away. This had not been an unusual thing over the years; Mansfield had a number of clients who kept their records very closely guarded. He placed the folder beside him as he drove toward the bank.

His windows were open to take advantage of the favorable weather and it was an enjoyable drive, at least until the accident. He was normally a very cautious driver, but on that day he did not check the cross traffic as carefully as he usually did before proceeding on the green light. The hurtling cab trying to beat the yellow light was too late. It struck Rich's Lexus just forward of the passenger door. The impact slung the Lexus around, and, as its wheels struck the curb, its momentum carried it onto its side, driver's door down, on the sidewalk. Rich was stunned for a moment, then quickly unbuckled his seat belt. Ignoring the pain in his left shoulder, he pushed aside the deflating air bag and clambered out through the open passenger side window. He fell to the street, then stood, shaking, on the sidewalk next to his ruined car.

Things became a blur for Rich: the arrival

of the Chicago police, the jabbering of the cabbie in broken English, and the paramedics checking everybody over. When they wanted to send him to the hospital to check his shoulder, he refused. It wasn't more than a bruise, and he had to call Mansfield and tell him what happened. He thought of the folder, but the police were keeping everybody away until the tow trucks could remove the vehicles.

He asked an officer if he could retrieve his belongings. The officer was polite, but told him to wait until the vehicle was righted. He used the time to call Mansfield from a nearby pay phone. The receptionist, Sherry, was upset when he told her about the accident. When she put him through, Mansfield was blunt: whatever happened, Rich was to make certain that the folder got to the safe-deposit box as soon as possible. That was it. No concern over Rich's condition or any expression of relief that he was all right.

After Rich hung up the phone, he went back to the accident scene to find his car had been pulled upright. A police officer stooped to the gutter by the driver's door, then stood with a sodden handful of books and papers. The folder had been thrown across the car and out the open window during the accident, spewing its contents into the gutter. Motor oil and anti-freeze had drenched everything, including Rich's cell phone. The officer handed the soggy mess to Rich with a comment about it not being Rich's day.

Once he had finished with the police and the

tow truck at the accident scene, Rich stopped a cab. He took the documents home with him to clean them up before taking them to the bank. He reasoned that if they were all legible, he would clean and blot them dry. Then he'd put them in the safe-deposit box; if they were illegible he would have to take them back to Mansfield for instructions.

Back in his apartment, Rich wiped down his cell phone and confirmed that it still worked. Then he sat down and worked carefully to separate page upon page of the messy papers, carefully blotting them with paper towels. He had gotten into the third book, a blue-covered ledger, when he saw it. He stopped and carefully looked over the entries on the page, not believing what he was reading. He then turned to the next page, blotted it, and read on. As he continued, his stomach tightened into a knot and beads of cold sweat appeared on his brow.

July 24, 8:19 p.m. CDT

Rich shook himself out of the unpleasant memories and walked across his room. The Rittenhouse Inn was quiet now, with the dinner hour over and dusk descending on Bayfield. He opened his outside door, looked around quickly, and headed for Washington Street. He was going to check the Harbor again. He thought as he walked, "God, please let Paul be there."

The evening solitude allowed his mind to wander and he soon found himself thinking about the long history he shared with Paul Findlay. By pure chance he and Paul had been assigned to the same college dorm room. They could not have been more different. Paul had been a serious, studious young man, majoring in engineering, while Rich had been something of a loose cannon. He'd majored in business because he couldn't decide what he really wanted to do. In spite of their differences they had hit it off famously, each finding something in the other to make himself better. Some of Paul's dedication to his studies had rubbed off on Rich, and likewise Rich's more gregarious nature began to bring Paul's social skills to the surface. Later, when dorm life soured and off-campus living called, they'd gotten an apartment together. They had remained close after graduation and Rich had served as best man when Paul married Gina. Paul had returned the favor two years later when Rich had wed his Meg. Meg . . . the thought of her brought a lump to his throat. Memories of the policemen at his door with the news of her accident came unbidden and with them came a renewal of the deep sense of loss. The day of her funeral had been the last time he'd seen Paul. Rich now felt a stab of anxiety. How would Paul react to this new situation?

July 24, 10:43 p.m. CDT

The Black Explorer pulled into a parking space behind the motel on U.S. 2 in Ashland. Its driver had taken his time; there was no need to hurry. The target would still be there tomorrow, and Bayfield was not far away: just westward on U.S. 2 to the foot of the bay, then north on Highway

13 through Washburn. A short trip, an easy mark, and it would be done. Time now for a good night's sleep. Jack took his briefcase and a hanging bag from the Explorer and made his way to his room. He unlocked the door, entered, and closed the door behind him. Leaving the single light on, he laid the hanging bag on the bed and placed the briefcase on the table near the TV. He thought to himself how naive people were when they tried to be secretive. Perry had used his ATM card to get money from his bank accounts. Jack surmised that Perry would quickly leave town, so he had visited the travel agencies around The Loop, passing himself off as a cop. He had only worked through a half a dozen agencies when he found it. The agent had recognized the picture he showed her, but she told him she had not made any reservations in the name of Richard Perry. The man in the picture had called himself Robert Pearson, and she had booked him into the Rittenhouse Inn at Bayfield, Wisconsin. There had been no travel tickets, meaning he had probably rented a car. Easy to check, easier to find. Tomorrow or the next day, the job would be done and Jack would be on his way back to Chicago to pick up the other $250 grand. Richard Perry, or Robert Pearson, would cease to be a problem for his client.

July 24, 10.57 p.m. CDT

As the man from Chicago sat in his room and thought about his assignment, Paul and *Pipe Dream* were less than 60 miles out. Paul set his course to make the Apostles on the west side of

Outer Island and began his night watch routine. The cold breeze stayed steady out of the northwest and *Pipe Dream* was flying along easily. Morning would find him nearing Bayfield.

July 25, 12.05 a.m. CDT

The late trip to the waterfront had been fruitless. Rich returned to his room, where he spent several hours staring into the darkness, his thoughts racing. What if Paul didn't come? What if he had never received the message? As it stood, unless Paul arrived, he would be all alone. He was fairly certain they didn't know where to find him yet, but with time they would be on his trail. He would have to move on soon, trying his best to stay low and be invisible. He wasn't accustomed to it, and he felt the cold fingers of panic clutching at his throat. Forcing the worries away, he tried to think of better times and gradually drifted into a restless sleep.

July 25, 7:46 a.m. CDT

Pipe Dream had ridden the favorable northerly into the islands early in the morning, leaving Outer Island to starboard. Paul then set his course to pass between Michigan and Stockton Islands, and finally, with the long expanse of Madeline Island to port, through the broad channel that separated it from Hermit and Basswood Islands. Past the southern tip of Basswood Island, Paul could make out the Madeline Island Ferries as they shuttled back and forth. At the western end of the ferry route he could see the Village of Bayfield.

He thought about calling the Apostle Islands Marina to check for a transient slip, then thought the better of it. He would try to find space at the City Dock. There were no public showers there, but he could shower aboard, and besides the rates were right. The breeze was waning, and with the harbor in sight, he released the sheets and hauled on the furling line. The big genoa disappeared as it rolled obediently around the forestay. He secured the furling line and both sheets, then turned and started the Westerbeke diesel. The hum of the diesel split the quiet morning. Paul looked over the stern to assure himself that cooling water was being discharged through the exhaust. After a minute of warm-up he raised the shift lever, gave the throttle a slight boost, switched the autopilot to standby, and swung the bow into the wind. Locking the wheel, he centered the traveler, pulled in the mainsheet, adjusted the topping lift, and released the sheet stopper to drop the mainsail. It fell obediently onto the boom, restrained by a set of lazy-jacks. Soon, the cover was secured over the main. He opened his cockpit locker and retrieved a set of docklines, took one forward and secured it to the cleat and through the bow chock. He brought the line back to the port side boarding gate and tied it off to the stanchion. He repeated the exercise with a stern line and put out fenders on the port side. He then unlocked the wheel, turned toward the harbor and pushed the throttle forward. *Pipe Dream* hummed along at 5 knots toward the green marker at the City Dock entrance.

He had to slow down and wait while the *Island Queen,* one of the Madeline Island ferries, made her approach and entry. He then powered past the end of the rock-and-concrete breakwater and idled into the City Dock area. He found a spot on the outer arm of the dock, between a large power cruiser and a small trailerable sailboat. He angled the bow to port and in toward the dock and swung *Pipe Dream* gently into the space. As he brought the wheel back to starboard, he shifted to reverse and boosted the throttle. The boat stopped as the prop walk brought her stern in and the fenders gently touched the dock. Paul idled the diesel, shifted to neutral, and then went quickly to the boarding gate, retrieving his docklines and stepping to the dock. He made the lines fast to the large cleats, then went back aboard to find two more lines. He set these as spring lines from each cleat to a point amidships to keep the boat from moving back and forth at the pier. Finally, he stepped back aboard and bent to the engine panel on the port side next to the wheel, found the kill switch, and pulled it up. The kill switch stopped the flow of fuel to the diesel, and there was quiet. It was 8:07 in the morning, and he had made it to Bayfield.

Chapter 2

THE MEETING

July 25, 7:46 a.m. CDT

Squinting against the low early morning sun, Rich was once again making his way down Washington Street toward the harbor. He heard the gulls cry and looked up as they wheeled and turned, making their way toward the water and food. He felt somewhat better after a few hours' sleep, but he still carried with him the air of a desperate man. His eyes darted about quickly as his active mind conjured up a threat behind every bush and around every corner. He wanted to blend in with the surroundings and just watch, but he had to go on.

The bay was a deep blue, peaceful and so beautiful. At any other time, Rich would have allowed himself the simple pleasure of stopping to enjoy the view, but on this morning he continued on his urgent downhill way. A ferry returning from La Pointe was approaching the northern breakwater entry, with a few lone gulls circling nearby.

He heard the rumble of the ferry's engines as it reversed to slow its progress toward the dock. He made out the name *Island Queen* on her side. The ferries had become familiar to him during the past two days. The *Madeline* and the *Island Queen* ran nearly all the time, while the smaller ferry, the *Nichevo*, spent much of her time idle. He supposed she was reserved for peak times and possibly for special transport. He absently watched as the ferry tied up, then began walking down Front Street.

Glancing at the breakwater, he saw a graceful sailboat entering the City Dock area. She was sleek and low, with four portlights along her cabin trunk and a navy cove stripe below her teak toerails. He saw only one man aboard at the helm, wearing a yellow foul weather jacket. Even from this distance, he thought he recognized the form. He stopped and watched as the boat turned away from him toward an open space on the outer arm of the dock. As her stern came into view, he could make out the name: *Pipe Dream.* He felt a surge of excitement; Paul had come! Perhaps now there was some hope. His pace quickened as he hurried down the street toward the Pier Restaurant and the landward end of the City Dock.

July 25, 7:51 a.m. CDT

In his motel room in Ashland, Jack was using a cotton cloth to carefully wipe down anything he might have touched. Satisfied, he put on his sunglasses, straightened his tie, and picked up his briefcase and luggage. Looking around the room a last time, he walked to the door, wiped down the doorknobs on both sides, walked out, and closed the door. He put the cotton cloth in his pocket, placed his bags in the Explorer, and retrieved a pair of driving gloves from the passenger seat. Slipping them on, he walked to the motel office to check out. By the end of the day his work should be done and he'd be a wealthier man.

July 25, 8:10 a.m. CDT

Paul had stepped back aboard to check his panel and assure himself there were no unnecessary systems operating. He would worry about a shore power connection in a few minutes. He had just gone below when he heard the voice on the pier. "Paul? Paul Findlay?"

Paul stepped up through the companionway and turned to the dock to see his old friend. He could find some of the young Rich in the middle-aged man before him, but there was now weariness where there had been energy and the face that had most often worn a friendly grin was now lined with worry. Paul jumped to the side deck and then to the pier, extending his hand. "Rich," he said, searching for the right words, "good to see you. I got your message when I reached the Soo." The hand was grasped, firmly, almost urgently, and he searched his friend's eyes for clues to the urgency. Rich looked past Paul, then up and down the pier, before returning his gaze.

"Let's find a place where we can talk," Rich said, releasing Paul's hand and turning to walk toward the shore.

"How about below? I'll put on some coffee," Paul replied. It would be private, he thought, since it appeared that the last thing Rich wanted was prying eyes or ears. Rich turned back and followed Paul aboard, and then down the companionway.

Below decks, *Pipe Dream* was all traditional. Her joinerwork was teak throughout, with a teak-and-holly sole underfoot and white Formica-like headliner panels overhead between transverse teak battens. Her portlights and overhead saloon hatch admitted ample light but did not take away from the dark richness of the space. Unlike the newer boats with their open spaces and expanses of white plastic, she had been built when the craftsman's touch brought out the warmth of the wood and melded it with the form of the boat.

Paul moved forward to the bulkhead just to port of the keel-stepped mast and lowered a hinged teak table from the wall. He fixed its leg in its socket on the sole and motioned to Rich to have a seat. As Rich slumped into the settee at the table, Paul turned aft to the galley and filled a teakettle. The buzz of the water pump startled Rich for a moment, but Paul finished filling the kettle, activated the propane safety system, and lit one of the burners on the stove. Placing the kettle on the burner, he moved back to the saloon and sat opposite his friend on the starboard settee. For a few moments there was silence, as both men seemed to ponder their shoelaces; then Paul spoke.

"It's been a long time. How did you find me?"

"Gina. I thought if anyone would know, she would. The last I had heard, you were still sailing the lakes, probably eastern Superior or maybe the

North Channel. She gave me the boat name, and told me to wire the marine post offices along the lakes."

Gina. Paul felt a moment's pain, replaced quickly by the familiar sense of loss. She had been so much of his life, but she couldn't take the isolation of life on a boat. He had made a choice; still, he often wondered if he had made the right one. He shook himself out of the haze of memory. "I assume this is more than just a 'glad to see you'."

Rich sighed. "I don't know where to start . . . it's happened so fast, and I'm not even sure myself what . . . I mean . . . "

Paul cut him off. "Take your time. I'm in no hurry and the coffee will be ready soon. Now take a deep breath, and tell me what's got you so excited."

Rich again stared at his feet, then looked up at Paul. "What I'm going to tell you may put you in danger. I don't want to do that but, frankly, I have nobody else to turn to." He shifted on the settee, then continued, "If you'd rather I'd stop now, I'll leave and you can forget I was here."

Paul shook his head, waving a hand in front of his face, "No, tell me what's up. I came this far, and you look like a man who needs a friend."

Rich sighed again, this time deeply, and seemed to relax a bit. He looked at Paul with a thank-you written in the glance, and then he began to speak. Paul listened with interest, then alarm, as Rich told him about Mansfield, the crash, and the oil-soaked books. When the teakettle whistled, Paul turned off the burner and they ignored the coffee as Rich continued and the morning slipped by. Though the sun was shining, Paul felt the day growing darker as the details tumbled out.

July 25, 9:02 a.m. CDT

On Highway 13, the black Ford Explorer was passing through Washburn. To his left, Jack glanced at an earth contact structure marked by an overhead sign as the world's first "underground Dairy Queen." He drove northward past the rest of Washburn's shops and museums, then accelerated as the highway left the town and continued north through the Wisconsin greenery. He went over the process in his mind: locate the Rittenhouse, stake it out, and wait. Once he had spotted the target, he could wait for the best time and place. He got out the folder with the picture and glanced at it as he drove, reinforcing the memory of the features.

July 25, 9:25 a.m. CDT

All was silent aboard *Pipe Dream*. Paul's mind was racing, trying to run through all the permutations and possibilities. He stood, let out his breath slowly, and wordlessly went to the galley. He re-lit the burner under the teakettle; they would need that coffee now. He turned back to Rich, saying, "You always had a talent for finding trouble. Looks like this time, it found you."

Rich grinned for the first time since they had met. He seemed somehow more at ease, having told his story. "I'm afraid it's found you, too, if they ever figure out I told you." His face went dark again at the thought.

"Let me make sure I have this straight." Paul looked directly at Rich. "The entries in the book show that your boss, this guy Macefield . . . "

"Mansfield."

"Yeah, Mansfield. That he's been laundering drug money through an offshore bank? And serving as a front for the dealers?"

"That, and the payoffs. The names in the book are ones you'd know if you lived in Chicago. You'd hear them on the news all the time. Powerful people who are willing to let this go on. For a price, that is."

"How certain are you that you've reached the right conclusion?"

Rich looked up, directly into Paul's eyes. The look was a look of pain. "That's the part I haven't told you yet." And slowly, he began to speak again as the memories came flooding back.

July 19, 3:32 p.m. CDT

Rich went back through the soggy pages to assure himself of what he had seen. How was he supposed to tell Mansfield? He would know or at least suspect that the book was compromised. Rich had worked for Ted Mansfield for the last nine years. He knew his boss was ambitious, driven, and sometimes even a bit ruthless, but this . . . it was unbelievable.

He got a pen and paper and began to write down the names. Alderman Scianno, Police Captain Mays, the Mayor's aide Rzepa . . . it read like a Who's Who *of powerful people. Other names, he recognized from the news. Drug lords and gang chieftains appeared on the incoming side of the entries. They were sending Mansfield the money and he was banking it in the Cayman Islands under the name of a dummy corporation. Millions upon millions of dollars. Proceeds from "stock transactions". Then, with an internal bank transfer to accounts of a second corporation, payments were issued for purchase of imaginary goods from a third corporation. The payments were cashed out, then deposited as returns on investment into accounts held by the "stockholders" in that third corporation . . . the names in the book. It was all handled offshore, hence no IRS records or involvement. Most of the money went to the drug lords, but a fair percentage found its way into the accounts of the powerful people on the list. It was all too clear. Mansfield was the launderer, the middle man in a flow of dirty money; he was as dirty as they come.*

He had set the whole thing up and the book was a safety valve, a way to cut a deal with the authorities if it all came down. If some of the names on either list knew the book existed, Mansfield would be a dead man. Rich continued writing, now detailing the flow of the money, the accounts, the fake companies. This list was going to be his own insurance policy.

Finished, he sat with his head in his hands, staring down at the information he had copied from the book. The ring of the telephone interrupted his sudden cold sweat. He let it ring, once, twice, three times . . . the answering machine kicked in with his short message, then the tone. It was Mansfield. "Perry. Call me immediately." Then the click and the silence.

He sat for a few minutes, his stomach turning over. What would he tell Mansfield? Would he know? Best perhaps to play dumb, let Mansfield lead the conversation. He reached for the phone.

One ring, immediately answered. "M&L Investments." It was Sherry.

He tried to sound as normal as possible. "Hi, Sherry . . . Rich. Can you put me through to the boss?"

"Jeez, Rich. Where are you now? Are you okay?"

"Still a little shaken up. I'd better talk to Ted."

"He's been looking for you. I'll put you right through. Are you coming back today?"

"Uhhh, yeah, I guess . . . I might stop and see a doctor first. Nothing serious, just a couple bruises."

"Are you sure you're okay? Do you need me to come get you?"

"No, I'm home. Just put me through."

"You got it. Hope you're really all right." The click of the hold button, then Mansfield's voice.

"Where have you been? You were supposed to call from the bank."

"I had to go home to get some clean clothes."

"The folder?"

"It's here. I'll drop by the bank and put it in the box on the way back in."

"See that you do, and call me as soon as it's done." Click. Silence.

Rich put the phone down, then went to the bathroom, removing his shirt. An ugly purple bruise covered his upper left arm, mirroring the dull throbbing in his shoulder. He was pretty sure it wasn't broken, because he could move it without more pain, but he would probably go in and have it checked over. Right now, though, he needed clean clothes and a ride. He washed up quickly, changed clothes and went back to the table. He looked at the books and the folder, then checked them over. He had wiped away most of the fluids, but what was left wouldn't be hard to spot. Sooner or later, Mansfield would know he'd seen them. He would have to convince the boss that he simply cleaned them up and put them away without actually reading through anything. He put all of them back into the folder and closed the flap. Then he picked up his handwritten list, put it in the pocket of his soiled sport jacket, and hung it in the hallway closet. It would stay there until he returned. He would have time then to consider what he would do with it.

After the cab arrived, Rich went to the bank and instructed the cabbie to wait. He replaced the soiled folder and its contents in the safe-deposit box, then called Mansfield. The boss was short and to the point. "Good. Get back here NOW." Click. Silence.

The ride to the office was too short. His mind racing, Rich was imagining different scenarios, and none of them were good. He stepped out of the cab and paid the driver, squared his shoulders and walked through the revolving doors. He went to the elevator and pushed 16, then

*watched the lights advance up the scale, too fast.
The door hissed open and he was staring across the
hallway to the oak door with gold letters spelling
out "M&L Investments." He hesitated, then had to
put his hand out to stop the elevator doors from
closing. He crossed to the door and opened it.*

*Sherry was sitting at her desk, but her face
told him things were in an uproar. "He wants me
to send you in right away." Her eyes would not
meet his, and her voice had the tone of a sibling
sending her brother to the woodshed to have a talk
with Dad. This wasn't good.*

July 25, 10:20 a.m. CDT

Rich sighed deeply again and took another
sip of coffee, then shifted his weight on the settee.
He lifted his gaze to Paul. "It's hard to talk through
all this. I still can't believe how quickly things can
change. I mean, one minute I'm an anonymous
bean counter in an office on The Loop, the next I'm
trying to stay out of sight because somebody is
trying to 'cash my check.' "

Paul was still pondering what he had heard
so far. "How did it get to this point? You could
have gone to the authorities. They have safe
houses, the witness protection program . . . "

"I tried! I went to the cops, and just made it
out of there when one of them tried to put
Mansfield's people on me. Remember the names
in the book? A lot of them were cops, and a couple

were Feds. I could never be certain I wouldn't be talking to somebody who was involved."

"Not even going directly to the top?"

"After what happened, I can't take that risk. I don't know how high this goes. I have to think. . ."

"Okay, so where do I come in? We haven't talked since Meg's funeral. I'm really sorry about that, but it's a fact. I don't know what you . . . "

"That's what makes you my safest bet. All my other friends . . . they have homes, families, and my stuff is full of addresses and phone numbers. If I went to any of them, I'd be easy to find. You don't have a home . . . "

Paul smiled. "You're sitting in her."

"Right. Sorry . . . I mean you have no permanent address. Besides, like you said, it's been so long, even if they tumble to your name looking through my stuff it won't mean anything to them."

"Let's hope not. So, you're sure what happened when you talked to Mansfield?"

"Like I told you, he was cold. Really cold. Just sat across that big desk, sizing me up like I was a piece of meat. Then he told me point blank that I looked at the books. I told him that some oil got on them during the accident and I just wiped it off with a rag, but I didn't look at anything. He just sat there and waited, and then his phone buzzed, and Sherry told him he had a call. He picked up the phone and listened, and then hung up. He told me to wait and left the room."

"That's all?"

"No . . . this is where it all got out of hand." He began describing what had happened next . . .

July 19, 4:53 p.m. CDT

Rich watched Mansfield leave the office and close the door behind him. His mind raced. What was happening? He had never seen Mansfield so grim. He wanted to go back to this morning, walk to the bank instead of driving, put the folder safely away, and not know what was in it. Damn . . .

Mansfield walked back into the office. He motioned to Rich to come with him, then turned and went back out the door. He followed the boss down the hallway, then into a windowless conference room. A third man appeared from the corner of the room, and went behind them to close the door. He was an unfamiliar face, a heavyset man in street clothes. He looked hard, tough.

Mansfield motioned to a chair, "Sit." The command was given as if to a bad dog.

Rich sat, palms sweating, the creeping sensation of fear crawling up his spine. Mansfield sat opposite him. Rich felt the presence of the third man standing behind him, to his right.

Mansfield gave him a long, hard stare, then spoke. "I sent one of my associates to the bank to make sure you replaced the folder. After you left I had the folder pulled and checked. It was full of oil, all right, but somebody had wiped down all of the pages in the books. You saw them." It was a statement, not a question. Mansfield went on. "This gentleman is going to take you back to your apartment. You are going to help him look for anything you may have relating to those books."

Rich swallowed hard. "Ted, I didn't . . . "

"Now." Mansfield rose, walked to the door and left the room without further comment.

The heavyset man who had been behind Rich now stood by the door. His dark hair was unruly and seemed to cascade over the soiled white collar of his too-tight dress shirt. "Let's go." He said, following the command with a motion of his hand toward the door.

Rich sat, shaking now. Cold logic told him they would not let him live after he had seen the books. He knew with an awful certainty what awaited him after the return to his apartment. How would they do it? A trip to the roof, followed by a quicker trip to the sidewalk? A forged note, perhaps left on his computer?

A heavy hand grasped his arm. "Like the

37

boss said, NOW!" He was pulled rudely from the
chair. He shook the hand loose, but it immediately
clamped back down, with a growled "Hard way or
easy way. Your choice."

Escorted by the heavyset man, Rich left
M&L Investments for the last time, by the back
door. He wondered if Sherry would realize he
hadn't come back out?

He was taken to the garage and hustled into
a waiting car for a short, miserable trip from the
office back to his apartment. His keeper had been
joined by another man, a tall, thin Germanic type,
who now sat next to him in the back seat of the car.
The back doors were locked; he was certain they
could only be opened from the outside. He sat
silently, cold sweat beading his forehead and
dampening his palms, as the car made its way into
the parking garage beneath his building. The thin
man growled, "Where's your spot?" Rich didn't
answer quickly enough to suit him. "I said, where
is it?" The thin man had grabbed Rich by the neck,
his face close. Rich could smell stale tobacco,
could feel the fingers tightening. He shook himself
away; delay wasn't going to work.

"It's, uhh, in the back. Next to that BMW."
The heavy man swung the car into the slot, turned
off the engine and got out. He came around to the
passenger's side and opened the rear door. Rich
found himself being pushed from the back seat,
nearly falling as he scrambled out. The heavy man
took him roughly by one arm as the thin man got

out and closed the car door.

His apartment was three flights up. They took him roughly up the stairs, one pushing and the other leading the way. When they reached his door, Rich made a show of fumbling for his keys, again trying to stall for time, hoping a neighbor would come by. The sharp slap across the back of his head was followed by the heavy man's threatening voice. "Quit stalling. You're gonna make it harder."

Reluctantly, he retrieved his keys and opened the door. They pushed him roughly into his apartment, where the heavy man threw him into a chair like a rag doll, then sat across from him, saying nothing and watching him intently with cold, hard eyes. The thin man began "tossing" the apartment, looking for anything connected with Mansfield's books. The big man at last spoke. "You might as well tell us if you copied anything. We'll find it sooner or later, and the longer we have to hunt for it, the madder I'm gonna get. Why not make it easy?"

Rich swallowed hard. "You wouldn't believe me anyway. I didn't . . ." His statement was cut off by a hard slap, open-palmed, to the side of his head. It knocked him sideways off the chair, and his glasses went spinning across the room onto the floor. He almost blacked out.

He regained his senses, then looked back to the man. "Okay . . . I . . . I'll find it. Can I get my glasses?" The man motioned toward the glasses, but stayed where he sat. Rich slowly rose, crossed the room and retrieved the glasses. The bows were slightly bent, but the lenses were intact. He straightened the bows as best he could, and put the glasses on.

The big man rose, saying, "Okay, it's showtime. Anything to do with those books, let's have it."

Rich stammered, his mind racing. "I . . . can I use the toilet?"

"Make it snappy. I'll be right here, so don't try anything."

Rich walked to the bathroom. It was down a dead-end hallway. No hope of escape that way, but maybe... He closed the door, not all the way. He didn't want to arouse suspicion. He looked in the mirror, seeing the red side of his face, then raised the lid and urinated. He finished, then turned out of habit to wash his hands. A dead wasp lay in the sink . . .

His heart raced. There might be some hope, if he had left it here. Under the sink, leaving the faucet running to mask noise . . . yes! The wasp spray! It was advertised to shoot 20 feet, to knock them out of the air. If he could use it on those two men . . .

He turned the water all the way to hot.

Steam began to rise from the sink. He removed the liner from the wastebasket, then tilted the empty wastebasket under the tap. Damned shallow sink! It wouldn't be much, but it would be all he had.

"Hurry up in there!" The voice growled, coming down the hallway toward him. It was now or never. Rich placed the wasp spray on the vanity beside him, turned off the water and held the hot wastebasket, ready.

He heard the heavy footsteps. "Quit stalling! I'm gonna . . . " As the door swung open, Rich tensed. When the face appeared, he threw the hot water full at it. Screaming, the big man clutched at his face, then turned back toward Rich, fists bunched. Rich dropped the wastebasket, picked up the wasp spray and aimed it into the man's face. It had the desired effect. Blinded and in pain, the man fell to the floor. Rich leaped through the door and over the thug, then into the living room. The other man was rounding the corner.

"What the hell . . . " The exclamation was cut off by the sudden hiss as Rich sprayed the wasp killer directly into his eyes. The thin man fell to the floor, clawing at his face and cursing. Leaving Mansfield's hired muscle writhing on his carpet, Rich ran to the hallway. His hands found the heavy brass hat rack with its weighted base. He ran back toward the thin man, who was rising. Swinging the hat rack with its base outward, Rich felt the impact as it struck the man's knee and he slumped back to

41

the floor. Rich brought the base back down to strike the side of the man's head, collapsing him into a heap.

He turned as he heard the grunt; the larger man had recovered and was coming for him. Waiting, waiting, the footsteps down the hall . . . now! He swung the hat rack with all the force he could muster.

It caught the heavyset man high on the shoulder, causing a yelp of pain and surprise and sending a metallic object sailing across the room and into the wall. The man fell, then recovered quickly, using his remaining good arm to lever himself up. "You asshole...you're gonna suffer before you die!" He lumbered across the room toward the metallic object. Rich saw it then, the unmistakable glint of the handgun on the carpet. He swung the hat rack again, knocking the man down. A foot lashed out, tripping Rich and making him stumble across the floor.

The heavyset man was rising again, intent on the gun. Rich picked up a heavy stone piece, a stylized horse, and flung it at the man, who ducked to evade it. The statuette whizzed over the man's head, thudded into the wall and fell to the floor behind him. He stood and glared at Rich, then at the gun. With surprising speed for an injured man, he sprang for it.

Rich barreled into him as he had done to the high-school tackling dummies all those years ago.

He took the man across the room and into the wall, then backed up and hit him again, knocking him down. Rich ran to the gun and picked it up. Its weight was unpleasant, unfamiliar. Shaking, he steadied the gun with both hands and aimed it at the man, who was rising. "Stop!" It was shrill, high pitched, but the gun gave his voice authority.

The man stood, his right arm hanging limply, a look of pure venom on his features. "You haven't got the balls. You little shit! Even if you shoot me, you're dead!" He took a step toward Rich.

Rich thumbed the revolver's hammer back with an audible click. The man stopped, still glaring, and waited. "You're going to sit down now," said Rich, "and I'm going to call the cops."

The man smirked, then slowly turned away and began to walk toward the doorway. Rich had no intention of letting the man walk out, but he couldn't shoot him. He bent to retrieve the hat rack, then said, sharply, "Stop. Face the wall." Slowly, the thug halted, then turned to the wall.

The growling voice was almost mocking now, speaking as he faced the wall: "I'm gonna enjoy peeling your hide off bit by . . . " The sudden impact of the hat rack base halted him in mid-sentence, and he slumped to the floor. Rich knelt and checked; almost with regret, he felt a pulse. He went to the thin man, who lay unconscious with a trickle of blood running from the gash in his scalp. Again he stooped and checked. There it was. The pulse told him he had not killed this day, had not become like them.

He stood for a moment, feeling the shaking start. Calming his breathing, he forced down the quivering, then quickly found a gym bag, filling it at random with clothing, toiletries, what he would need on the run. He went to his desk, opened the side drawer and retrieved two bank cards, an address book, and his passport. The gun . . . he stuffed it into the bag, then carefully pulled it back out and slowly released the hammer. He replaced it and finished packing, stopping often to check on the men, but both remained unconscious. He felt for his cell phone; where had he put it? He would be needing it.

He hefted the bag and headed for the door, but made a final stop in his hallway closet, grabbing his soiled sport jacket as he passed. In the left pocket were the notes they were after, the notes that might be his only hope. He was relieved to find that the right pocket still held his cell phone. He ran out the door, not even pausing by the elevator as he fled down the hallway to the stairs, listening for any sounds of pursuit. He made his way quickly down the stairway, pausing only when he neared the bottom. Silence. Continuing, he reached street level, put on the sport jacket and walked quickly out and away from the building, taking the first side street. He was thinking quickly now, trying to decide where to go, who to call . . .

After much soul-searching, Rich decided to seek protective police custody. He felt exposed, in danger on the streets, and his first impulse to run was giving way to his need for security. Several blocks of quick-paced walking found him at a precinct station, but as he approached the entrance he noticed the sign prohibiting weapons; that gun in his bag would get him arrested and maybe worse. He continued walking past the station and down the block, mulling over his options. If he could find a place to hide the bag, someplace nobody would think to look . . .

He needed to get off the street and think. He ducked into a little storefront coffee shop a half block from the station, ordered a small cup of black coffee and walked to a table near the rear of the room. As he pulled out the chair to sit, the unisex restroom door opened and a young, very sour-looking young man came out. He was evidently an employee. He was wearing a white apron, and his head sported a white paper hat with the coffee shop logo on one side. He was carrying a large plastic trash bag. He walked to the corner and opened the rear exit door, disappearing through it as he took the trash bag to the dumpster in the alley.

As Rich sipped his coffee and thought about his options, the young man returned from the alley. He walked to a closet, retrieved a new trash bag, and then walked back to the restroom door. He knocked sharply, saying "Anybody in there?" Hearing no answer, he opened the door and disappeared into the restroom for a moment.

Rich could hear the sound of a plastic lid being shuffled aside, the rustle of the bag, and then a hollow thunk as the lid was replaced. That was followed by the sound of running water; Rich made note of that, thinking, 'At least the kid knows enough to wash his hands.' The water stopped, replaced by the sound of a paper towel being pulled from a dispenser and then by a slight flapping sound as the towel was deposited into the trash. Rich's eyes raised suddenly to the restroom door. The trash!

He waited until the kid had come out of the restroom and had returned to the front counter. Then he quietly rose, taking the bag with him, went into the restroom , closed the door and pulled the sliding barrel bolt to lock it. He looked at the large trash barrel and saw that it had the typical double-sided lid with swinging doors. The new trash bag edge was visible, pulled over the barrel beneath the lid edges. He pushed the swinging door in and peered down into the barrel; the single paper towel the kid had used lay alone at the bottom of the bag. It would be hours before they changed the trash bag again.

Rich put his bag on the floor by the barrel, and then carefully, quietly lifted the lid and set it aside on the sink. He bent and unzipped the bag, then removed his passport, papers, and bank cards and put them in the sport jacket's right pocket with the phone. He closed the bag's zipper over the gun and clothing, picked it up, and slowly lowered it *into the bottom of the barrel. As he placed it on the bottom, the doorknob rattled; somebody wanted in. "Just a minute!" he said, turning and reaching across to flush the stool.*

Moving deliberately now, he retrieved the lid from the sink and carefully placed it back on the barrel; then he turned on the faucet, let it run for a few seconds, and turned it off. He pulled three paper towels from the dispenser, lifted the trashcan lid slightly, and placed the towels over the top of his bag. Then he lowered the lid back in place, straightened the sport jacket, checked the floor around him, and slid back the barrel bolt. He opened the door to find an elderly black man waiting patiently. "All yours!" he said, forcing a smile.

He walked to his table, picked up the cup and drained the remaining coffee, and walked to the front door. The young man who'd changed the trash bag didn't even look up, but the woman who had served him smiled and waved, offering a practiced, "Please come again!" Rich waved back and left the shop, then walked the half-block back to the station. He made his way up the steps and to the security area, and after a brief delay there he found himself explaining his situation to the desk sergeant.

He was ushered upstairs into a small office, evidently used as an interview room. There was a single narrow window overlooking the street and a glass panel in the door. He took a seat at the small oak table near the window. Why did this feel like he was a suspect rather than someone looking for help? He swallowed hard and adjusted his breathing, telling himself to calm down. This was the right thing to do. It had to be.

A middle-aged, slightly heavy man entered. His nondescript suit and half-loosened tie belied a sharpness in his eye as he sized Rich up. "Mr. Perry," he said as he extended his hand, "I'm Detective Purnell."

Rich rose and took the proffered hand, and the detective's firm handshake put Rich at ease. Purnell then took the chair opposite as Rich sat down. He looked at Rich, looked down for a moment, then clasped his hands on the table in front of him. "That's a pretty wild story you gave the desk." His gaze returned to lock with Rich's.

"I wish that it was my imagination, but it's not." Rich replied. "It's a waking nightmare. Those guys were going to kill me."

The detective paused, then said, "Okay, let me get this straight: Your boss is into some dirty business, and you stumbled onto it? That's why these people were after you?"

"In a nutshell, yes." Rich wanted to tell the whole story, to purge it from his system. He reached inside his sport jacket and brought out his notes. "The books contained these entries. I copied them down, but if you check this stuff you'll find it's all true. The names are pretty well known."

The detective took the notes and scanned them quickly. "Could be anything. What's so special about this stuff?"

"It's the names and accounts. To put it as simply as possible, they make a neat chain, leading right back to a lot of dirty money. My boss and a lot of other very big names are mixed up in this whole scheme. Did you ever wonder to yourself how some politicians get so wealthy so quickly? This is how some of these people afford the big homes, the fancy cars, the high life. What I know can bring it and them all down, which is why they want me dead. I have to get this information to the authorities, and then I'll need your help staying alive."

Detective Purnell had listened carefully, staring at the notes and nodding all the while. He whistled, low and soft, then shook his head. "If this is what you say it is, you're on to some amazing shit," he said as he leaned over and put his hand on Rich's shoulder. "Wait here. I'll get things rolling, but you stay in here until we're ready to move you." He stood and dropped Rich's notes on the table, then left the room and closed the door.

Rich stared at the door for a moment, and then reached across the table and retrieved the notes. He returned them to the sport coat pocket. He looked at his watch; it was almost 7:00. For several minutes he sat, lost in a myriad of thoughts. Jesus . . . it had been such a beautiful day, and now he was in hell. It seemed like years ago, but it was only a few hours . . .

Ten more minutes went by, and the detective had not returned. A nagging doubt was growing in Rich's mind; still, no names like "Purnell" had been in the book. Shaking the thought, he rose to stretch his legs. His shoulder still hurt from the accident; he gingerly worked the shoulder joint as he paced the small room. He stopped near the door. Through the glass, he could see Purnell, sitting on the corner of a desk, talking animatedly on the phone. Purnell's back was to the door, but something in his posture made Rich feel uneasy.

Rich went back to the table to sit, but stopped to look out the small window to the street. A car pulled up, double-parked, and two men got out. One was thin, with close-cropped hair . . . limping. The other, a heavy man, was holding his shoulder as they headed for the station door . . . The realization struck him like an electric shock: "Christ, Mansfield's goons!" There was no time for thought. Purnell had called someone, all right, and Rich knew who. There was no time to spare. He came out of the interview room, and Purnell immediately met him, motioning him back. "You'd better stay put until we get this sorted out."

"Uhhh . . . just need a restroom," Rich said, trying to look at ease. He didn't feel that it was working very well; nevertheless, Purnell pointed down the hall and went into the interview room to wait.

Rich headed down the hall, risking a quick glance back over his shoulder. *Good! Purnell had disappeared into the room.* Past the men's room door was a stairwell entry, and Rich took it, heading quickly downstairs. He went to the bottom of the stairwell, knowing that the main floor would not be safe. As he exited the stairwell, he found himself in a long hallway. The paint was peeling from the old walls and it smelled of stale humid air and mildew. A whistling custodian was pushing a trash bin down the hall away from him, and Rich followed.

The custodian banged the trash bin through a set of double doors. Rich waited until the doors swung shut behind the man, then carefully went through them. He found himself in an underground service garage. There were patrol cars everywhere, some being serviced, some parked and awaiting their assigned patrol officers. As he stood and wondered which way to go, he was startled by a voice from behind. "Are you lost?" He turned quickly. The voice came from a young, attractive policewoman. *God, he wanted to tell her everything, get this off his back . . . but it would just get referred to the higher-ups and he knew where that path would lead.*

"I guess I am," he lied, "I was on the second floor and took the stairs . . . thought they'd get me to the street." The officer nodded, looking him over. He felt uncomfortable.

"Well, this isn't the way." She said. "This is the service garage, and you're not supposed to be here."

"I'm really sorry." He replied, looking down the long bay toward the traffic exit. "Okay if I head on out that way?"

She looked at the exit, then looked at Rich again. She seemed to ponder for a moment, then smiled. "Go ahead . . . you don't look like the hardened criminal type to me."

"Thank you!" he responded, meaning it. He walked quickly to bottom of the traffic ramp, then waited while a patrol car made its way in. The officers in the car didn't give him a second look; he imagined they were cycling off shift and were more concerned about getting home. He then strode quickly up the ramp to the side street, looked quickly for any sign of the thugs, and then turned right and ducked into the alley. It was time to find the back door to the coffee shop and pick up the trash.

July 25, 10:57 a.m. CDT

"Shit, Rich . . . no wonder you're so shook." Paul was thinking out loud now, involved for sure and not liking it at all. "So why not just go to the press . . . break the whole damned mess?"

"Same reason the cops aren't safe. Detective Purnell's name wasn't in the book, but he

was obviously aware of it and probably a part of it."
Rich shifted on the settee, then continued. "I
thought about the media, but there were some
names in the book with media connections. I had no
idea who would be safe to talk to."

"So you ended up here?"

"Yeah, that's another leap. I didn't know
where to turn, and I was thinking of who I could
call. Just a lot of dead ends, and then I remembered
reading one of your articles. Hell, I don't even sail,
but I saw your name on a magazine cover and
leafed through it at the newsstand a couple of weeks
back. I remembered you wrote about the North
Channel, and said you'd be heading up here this
year. Your picture was there and everything."

"Paul smiled thinly. "Notoriety. Just when
I needed it." He glanced up quickly, noting the
pained expression crossing Rich's face. "Sorry . . . I
didn't mean it that way."

"I know," Rich said, "but I hope you know I
wish nobody else was involved in this. I even
hesitated calling Gina, but . . . "

Paul's quick rage cut Rich off. "Shit, that's
right. Now you've brought her into this!" He rose
and went to the companionway, looking out at the
harbor and trying to regain control. His fingers dug
into the teak grabrails on either side of the steps.
He waited until his breathing slowed, then turned
back to Rich. "Goddammit. If anything happens to

her . . . well, she had better be safe." He glared at Rich for a second, then sat back down.

Rich was silent for a few seconds, then raised his eyes to meet Paul's. He spoke slowly, deliberately. "I called information and got her number in Minnesota. She told me you were in this area someplace and she suggested I try the marine operators, but I lied and told her it wasn't all that important. I didn't want any radio conversations anybody could listen in on. That's when she said I could send a blanket wire to the marine post offices." He took a breath, swallowed hard and continued. "After I talked to her, I decided to head up here. I knew there was a good harbor, a lot of sailboats . . . I used my ATM card to withdraw a bunch of cash. I took a cab clear across town for that. Then I figured I didn't want to use credit, and I.D. for a hotel would also be a problem, so I used some of the cash to get some traveler's checks for that. I screwed up my signature enough that the only things clear were the R and the P. Then went to a travel agent downtown to book a reservation. They recommended the Rittenhouse . . . I took 5 days. They helped with my car rental. I figured with so many travel agents downtown, they'd have a hard time finding out where I went."

"I wouldn't bet on that." Paul's brow was furrowed now, his concern growing. "The cops can track stuff like that pretty easily. If they're in on this . . . then the crooks have some real pros working on their side of the street."

Rich sighed. "I know . . . I thought about that all the way up. I shouldn't have made any reservations, just headed up here. I guess I was worried that it was high season, and without a reservation I'd be out of luck. But I did use the name Robert Pearson."

Paul looked at Rich, then down at his shoes. He rested his elbows on his knees and clasped his hands. "I'll bet they've run your picture past everybody in town. How long do you think it'll take them to figure out who Robert Pearson is? Jeezus, Rich . . . you used the same initials!"

"I never was good at planning ahead. The initials made it easy for me to remember who I was supposed to be. So that's all water over the dam. I sent the wire for you, and then got a cheap motel on the north side to catch some sleep. I had to make another ATM withdrawal in the morning, and didn't want it tracked anywhere but Chicago. Damned daily limit. I didn't get much sleep that night. Every noise sounded like those creeps coming for me. Next day I made the withdrawal and started heading up here."

Paul stood and turned to look aft through the open companionway. His senses were alive, and he could feel the hair on the back of his neck stand up. Rich was in deep shit, that was certain, and now he'd bought into it. "Rich," he said, turning back to face him. "You aren't in Chicago any more. Call the local police, the FBI, anyone. With all the different players and the offshore involvement, it's bound to fall under federal jurisdiction."

"You don't know these guys." Rich's voice rose. "There are all kinds of ways to get to me, if they know the right people. And they do. I figure they've got some Federal people on the payroll, so if I contact the Feds and go under protection, they'll still get to me. With all the legal delays, they'll have the time, and with all the leaks . . . and they know that without me to testify where it came from, the stuff I wrote down is meaningless. What I have to do is get the list, the account numbers . . . the whole story . . . to the national media. Once it breaks, they'll be busy covering their tracks. If I can cool my heels outside the country, I might be fairly safe. But I have to get there without anyone knowing where I've gone."

"And that's where I come in?"

"That's where you come in."

Paul changed the subject. "So what about Gina? Goddammit, they'll figure out you called her!" His face grew red at the thought, his anger returning.

Rich swallowed hard, then said, "No. I don't even have her name in my address book. Yours is there, but it's an old address and phone. Back when you still had a foot on dry land. It'll be a dead end for them."

"What about phone records?"

56

"I used my cell. That's an unpublished number and even if they tumble onto it, it isn't like getting the records from a local provider. Anyway, it'll look like a business call."

"Not since you made that call after all the shit hit the fan."

"That's the thing!" said Rich. "Even if they get that number, how do they make the connection? The last thing I wanted was to get Gina in any kind of trouble."

Paul thought for a second, then answered, "It's a little late for that. I'll call her after a while and tell her to go someplace for a few days. She'll be pissed, but she'll do it." Paul stopped talking for a minute, then shrugged. "Okay, let's say I can get you out of the country. There's still the matter of customs, passports, identification . . . little things like that."

"I'll risk using my name and my passport at a Canadian customs office in a harbor. I was hoping you could get me to Thunder Bay. I figure they'll be watching all the border crossings."

Paul thought it over. He'd made that passage before. From here past the western tip of Isle Royale, then on into Thunder Bay . . . it was around 150 miles, and with the prevailing winds you usually didn't have to go to weather. With a good breeze, it would be a full day's run. If they left this afternoon, they could be in the port city of Thunder Bay late tomorrow. Even without favorable conditions, it'd be a couple of days at the worst. "I can do that, but I'll need to check weather, get some provisions . . . "

Rich smiled for the first time since he'd come aboard. "You don't know what this means to me," he said, assuming a more relaxed slouch.

"This is what I'm going to suggest. You said you were staying at the Rittenhouse?"

"Right."

"By this time, I wouldn't be too sure these people don't know where you are."

Rich said, "I'm not registered under my own name."

"I already told you what a lame deal this "Robert Pearson" alias is. I think you should stay here."

"But . . . "

"No buts. If they do know where you are, they'll be watching the Rittenhouse for you. I'll take your key and go back to get your things."

Rich turned in his seat and reached into his pocket. He withdrew a bronze key. "There's an outside entrance to the room. It's the door just north of the main registration entrance. I asked for it, so I could come and go without being noticed by the management or the other guests."

"Is there another door to the inside?"

"Yeah, it's past the desk, then around the corner to your right."

Paul thought for a moment, then went forward past Rich, disappearing past the teak bulkhead. He lifted the cushion on the V-berth and opened a hatch to a compartment below, withdrawing a brown duffel bag. "I'll take this." he said, returning to the saloon. He opened a side compartment behind the starboard settee back and began removing old shirts and rags, stuffing them into the bag. "I can leave this crap in your room and put your stuff in the bag."

"You don't need to use your clothes . . ."

Paul cut him off. "This old junk is what I use when I'm working on the diesel. It's not much good for anything else. I go in with a full bag, come out with a full bag. That way, if anybody does see me go in, I come out carrying the same thing. I'll use the inside door."

"The people at the inn will know it isn't me."

"How's this?" replied Paul. Rich watched as Paul reached into a hanging locker, withdrew and donned a worn khaki jacket and turned up the collar, then pulled a black watch cap over his head. He slouched into the jacket, his face all but disappearing. "You and I are about the same height. The jacket and cap hide everything else."

"I guess it'll work. Just make sure you get my passport. It's with the papers on the table by the phone."

July 25, 11:42 a.m. CDT

The Ford Explorer sat parked on the up-slope of Rittenhouse Avenue near Washington Street. Through the windshield, Jack could see the Rittenhouse Inn and observe the comings and goings of its guests. He had quickly noted the main entry, as well as the ornate porch with its chairs and lounges, but so far there was no sign of Perry. Patience was called for, and patience was a part of the job. Plan, execute, and disappear . . . it was the same every time, if you took out the details.

His head was tilted back against the headrest as he watched the inn through slitted eyes. It was a practiced art, almost sleeping while alert. He had learned this technique all those years ago when he had been "on the other side." He thought about his time on the force. Long, dangerous hours and minimal return . . . this was far better, and the guilt had ended long ago. He had learned to consider the facts . . . that if somebody wanted them dead, his targets must not be very good people in the first place. He sipped lukewarm coffee from a plastic cup and checked his watch . . . 11:45.

His eyes strayed to the passenger-side mirror. A figure was coming up the hill along the sidewalk. Concentrating now, he quickly took in the details: A man, middle aged, but apparently fit. Black knit cap. Tanned . . . outdoor type. Carrying a small duffel. Looks like a seaman who's come ashore. Not his target. The man walked on, past the Explorer and purposefully across the intersection, then up the walk to the Rittenhouse. He paused to hold the door for an elderly couple, then adjusted the jacket collar as he entered.

Jack's eyes went back to their careful study of the inn and its surroundings. He could wait. He had seen the rental car in back of the Inn. He had checked the register for "Robert Pearson," telling the clerk he was an old friend, in town for a reunion. She had told him that Mr. Pearson was not in and offered to leave a message. No, he had said, it was to be a surprise. She had grinned conspiratorially and assured him she would keep the secret. He had left the inn and phoned Chicago, telling his associate to notify the client that "Pearson" had been found. He would be back. It was just a matter of time.

Ten minutes passed before motion at the inn entrance caught his eye. The man he had seen earlier was coming back out. He still carried the duffel. He came down the walk to the intersection, this time pausing and looking around, then continuing across Rittenhouse Avenue in front of the Explorer and down the sidewalk on the south side of the street. Jack watched him in the driver's side mirror as he paused again in front of a small shop, then entered. The cold eyes left the mirror and returned their gaze to the inn.

Paul stood in the corner of the gift shop, apparently pondering a purchase. He was actually looking out the window and back up the hill toward the Rittenhouse. He was probably being over-cautious, but after what Rich had told him, what he had seen was suspicious. The black 4-wheel drive sport utility parked near the inn, with Illinois plates, was not in itself alarming. The fact that the driver had been there when he went to the inn and was still there when he came out, was. The man was not dressed like a tourist. Add to that the uncomfortable sixth-sense feeling of being watched. It was all too coincidental. He decided to wander back to the boat as if he had no particular timetable. He would have to tell Rich what he had seen and then they might find more security for the time being out among the islands.

Chapter 3

CHICAGO

July 25, 12:31 p.m. CDT

Ted Mansfield was still seething. He loathed incompetence, and he had seen enough in the past two days to last a lifetime. Now, there had been no word from the "specialist" sent to take care of the problem.

He turned in his chair to look out the window, picking up a squat glass and sipping Dewar's straight up, raging inside as he drank. Damn them! Two "professionals" who couldn't handle a middle-aged accountant. And that dumb ass cop, Purnell . . . all he had to do was grab the list and hold Perry. Bastard's nothing but a waste of a shitty suit.

He turned the chair back to the desk and hit the intercom. "Sherry, did the mail come in yet?" He lifted his hand and waited.

"About ten minutes ago." Her voice crackled through the speaker.

His hand descended again as he instructed, "Bring it in." He turned back to the window, his jaw working, his gaze intent. He was staring at the skyline as he took another sip of Scotch.

There was a soft knock on the door; Sherry

walked in with the stack of mail. She laid it on the broad oak desk and turned to leave, then stopped. She turned around and stood, waiting. Mansfield turned to look at the mail, and then looked sharply back at Sherry. "Is there something else?" he said.

She shuffled her feet, not meeting his eye. "Uh, well, actually, I was wondering when Rich would be back. I haven't seen him in the last few days. It's not like him not to even call."

"You won't have to worry about him any more. We let him go."

She had been afraid of this, but usually when someone was fired there was lots of office gossip. Not this time; the subject seemed taboo. Nobody knew what had gone on between Rich and the Boss, and the subject was quickly changed if it came up at all. Sherry swallowed, then asked, "Should I get his forms in order? I mean the COBRA for his health insurance, resolution of his accounts . . . I can call him to get . . . "

Mansfield cut her off with a wave of his hand. "Already taken care of. He's gone, and you have nothing more to do in that regard."

She thought about pressing the question, but the steely expression on the boss's face put an end to the idea. She replied, "Yes, sir," then turned and walked to the door, letting herself out and closing it behind her.

Mansfield picked up the stack of mail and rifled quickly through it, tossing the unwanted items away and placing the rest in a pile on his right. He stopped when he retrieved a postcard. He put down what was left of the stack.

The postcard had no postage, no postmark. It had been slipped into the mail stack. Someone had come to the office . . . The front of the card showed a Chicago harbor scene, probably Grant Park. Boats on moorings. At the bottom it read, "Peaceful evening." He turned it over to see that it was addressed simply to "Ted." He read the printed message:

Having a good time in Bayfield, Wisconsin. Found what you asked for. Have not purchased yet but sure it will be in hand soon.

J

Mansfield put down the card and turned back to the window. He had been told there would be a message if Perry was found and another when it was done. Bayfield . . . if he'd had to guess he would never have thought Perry would stop anyplace that close. A stroke of luck — soon it would be over.

He picked up the glass and downed the rest of the Dewar's, replaced the glass on the desk, then stood and walked to the door. He closed a deadbolt lock, then crossed the room to a second door, opened another deadbolt, and let himself out. He turned and closed the door, fished out a set of keys and reset the deadbolt. He was standing in a dark stairwell off the main hallway. He looked around, then descended the stairs to the floor below. He walked down a long hallway to a service elevator, boarded it and punched "B." He waited as the door closed, then idly stared at the lighted numbers as they descended . . . 15, 14, 12, 11, 10 . . . he looked at his watch, a jeweled Rolex. 6, 5, 4 . . . he shifted his weight, cleared his throat. 1, L, B. The deceleration, as he braced his knees, then the slight jog and the "ding" of the hollow-sounding bell. The door hissed open and Ted Mansfield walked out of the elevator into the underground parking garage.

July 25, 12:34 p.m. CDT

At the Bayfield City dock, the figure in the khaki jacket walked slowly toward *Pipe Dream*. He stopped, apparently to look at another boat, but his glance strayed back up the dock toward the gazebo and the town. No sign of the black Explorer. He turned and finished his way to the boat.

Below, Rich tensed as he felt the boat shift slightly and heard the footsteps on deck. He stood and reached over the low bulkhead to a shelf over the nav station and grabbed a large flashlight. It wasn't much, but it was heavy. He pulled the flashlight back, ready. Somebody in the cockpit now . . . The companionway hatch slid open and Paul appeared, framed in the opening against the light. Rich lowered the flashlight and let out a long breath as Paul came down the steps, lurched into the Starboard settee, and tossed him the duffel. "I only took your papers and what I could cram in the bag. If you need them, I've got some extra clothes."

"Did you get that old sports jacket?"

"Yeah, why?"

"It's got all my notes in it. In the pocket." He started to stand. "I thought I'd walk up the street and pick up a few shirts, maybe some underwear . . . "

Paul cut him off. "Wouldn't advise it. I'm not sure, but I think the inn is being watched. That could mean they've already figured out you're in Bayfield."

"How . . . already? Goddamn Mansfield!" The oath sounded resigned more than angry. Are you sure?"

"Like I said, I don't know . . . but there's a black SUV with Illinois plates parked on the street down the hill from the inn. The driver was there when I went in and when I came out. He could have been waiting while his wife shopped, but he didn't look like a family man. Black suit, driving gloves, and shades. I crossed right in front of him to get a look."

"Then he saw you."

"Of course he did . . . that's the point. It wasn't you he saw, so hopefully he'll stay there. We're leaving. Now."

"Can we pick up some things? I need . . . "

"You need to be away from here as soon as possible. I expect when you don't return to the inn, he'll eventually go inside and start asking questions. Then he'll tumble to me. If we're already out in the islands, he'll have a hell of a time finding us. Hopefully, nobody will connect me with the boat."

"Okay, but you'll need gas. Let me buy you a tank."

Paul gave him a patient clap on the shoulder. "In the first place, it's a diesel. In the second place, we won't be using it much; she's a sailboat. That's a 50-gallon tank and it only took 20 gallons when I topped it off at the Soo. Now you stay below and out of sight while I get us out of here." He reached for the VHF radio and tuned it to the weather channel. As Rich started to speak, Paul put up his hand. Rich held the thought.

The digitally rendered voice droned with the near-shore forecast: " . . . winds northwest at 10 to 15 knots, waves 2 feet . . . " Paul pushed the priority button and the radio was reset to Channel 16. Before Rich could pick up his thought and carry on, Paul had vanished through the companionway. He reappeared in a moment, tossing an inflatable life vest/harness combination to Rich. "Put that on." he

68

said, disappearing again. The diesel thrummed to life, and Rich could hear Paul moving about on deck, preparing to get underway.

Paul, already in his own life vest/harness, moved quickly and efficiently, but no faster than usual. He didn't want to seem hurried to anyone observing him. He secured his forward hatch, which had been left open for ventilation. He checked his running rigging to be certain everything was as it should be. Then, casting an eye toward the town, he stepped to the pier. The boat rocked ever so slightly as his weight came off the deck. He uncleated the springlines, leaving *Pipe Dream* secured only at the bow and stern. Next, he went forward and retrieved the bow line from the huge cleat on the pier, coiled it and tossed it carefully to the foredeck, making certain it would not fall into the water and become entangled in the prop. Moving back to the stern, he uncleated the stern line and left a single loop around the cleat. Holding on to the bitter end of the stern line, he stepped back aboard the boat and behind the wheel.

He bent to check his gauges in their alcove next to the wheel, observing with satisfaction the proper oil pressure and amp readings. He straightened and took a long moment to check the waterfront one last time. No sign of the black Explorer, or of its curious driver. Time to cast off.

He heaved on the stern line, still rounding its dockside cleat, and *Pipe Dream's* stern swung gently toward the pier as her bow swung out. As soon as the bow was clear of the boat ahead, Paul released the bitter end of the dockline, picked up its loop from the stern cleat, and pulled it around the dock cleat and into the cockpit. Once the line was safely aboard, he worked the shift lever, feeling the "clunk" as the transmission engaged and the prop began to turn. He applied a slight amount of throttle. As *Pipe Dream* began to move, he brought the wheel sharply around. She answered by turning to starboard, out into the protected area between the dock and the shore. The turn continued until she was heading toward the entrance.

Paul checked quickly for ferry traffic and other boats, then boosted the throttle a bit as he straightened the helm. Reaching the entrance, he turned again slightly to starboard and passed the end of the breakwater with its green light and marker.

The ritual was automatic: Coil and stow the docklines; Pull in the fenders and stow them in the cockpit locker; check the lifeline boarding gates to assure the pelican hooks are firmly engaged; put the boat nose-to-wind, idling forward; connect the main halyard, free the mainsail from its cover and ties, raise it, and tension the luff; ease the lazy-jacks and turn off the wind to allow gravity and breeze to shape the main; shift to neutral, then a slight bit of throttle before lifting the kill switch to stop the flow of fuel and shut off the engine; shift into reverse to prevent the prop from free-wheeling; and finally on course, unfurl the genoa, sheet it in and feel *Pipe Dream* surge ahead. Setting a course of 60 degrees magnetic, Paul switched on the autopilot, took a last look about him for boat traffic and obstructions, and went below.

"That was quick!" marveled Rich. "It looks like you've been doing this awhile."

"Yeah, a year or two." Paul was grinning at the thought. He had been "doing this" longer than he cared to remember. "You develop a routine, and after a time it gets to be second nature. What were you going to say before we left?"

Rich looked pensive. "When you went to the room, did you notice the chair by the bed? I had one of those yellow maps the National Park Service gives out. You know, about the islands. I think I left it laying in the chair."

"And? "

"If he . . . whoever he is . . . sees the map, he might figure out where I've gone."

"There are 23 islands, and lots of boats. Even if he thinks you've gone out, he won't have any idea where, or on which boat." Paul turned to go back up the companionway ladder.

Rich stared at Paul's retreating back for a moment, then said, "I still wonder. Like I said, you don't know Mansfield. He's a piece of work. Knowing what I know, he's probably got somebody after me who is very good at what he does. Maybe more than one."

Mansfield drove home, thinking along the way about getting some "insurance." What if the bastard slipped away? Jack had come highly recommended, but so had the two idiots who were supposed to take care of Perry in the first place. By the time he reached his driveway, he had made up his mind. This was too critical, and there were too many powerful people involved. Jack was getting some help, whether he wanted it or not. He pulled the silver Lincoln to a stop in the circle drive and shut off the engine, impatiently throwing open the door and heaving himself out of the car.

He stood for a moment in the glare of the early afternoon sun, his shadow falling over the walk and almost reaching the marble steps at the door. Ted was a big man, all the better to intimidate underlings. He cared little for what others thought of him and of his methods. He'd come to Langdon Investments as a young and very aggressive broker and his quick success had caught the aging Bruce Langdon's eye. Before two years had gone by he was a junior partner. It was around that time that he'd started investigating ways of accumulating wealth that were at the very least outside the law. His power and influence had grown astronomically. Years later when the old man died, the board of directors had offered Ted the top spot. He'd agreed only after the board also consented to change the company name to Mansfield & Langdon Investments.

He had long ago concluded that it was his place to lead, and the trails he blazed had not always been on the legal side of the road. They had, however, always guided him to the money. That was what mattered, and from which all other benefits and power derived. As far as Ted was concerned, you could lead, follow, or get the hell out of the way. Perry was in his way now, and Ted viewed him as just another obstruction to be shoved aside.

He stepped to the door and keyed a code into the lighted entry pad. There was a series of three quick beeps, and the door latch clicked open. He let himself in and turned to the security panel on the wall next to the entry closet, and began entering a second code. LCD numbers on the panel were counting down . . . 22, 21, 20 . . . as he entered the last number of the code. The numbers went blank and an intermittent red light on the panel ceased its flashing and turned to green. He turned away from the panel and removed his suit coat, draping it over his arm, then began to loosen his tie. He walked quickly through the hallway to a paneled sitting room next to the kitchen, and threw the light switch at his right.

Heavy drapes were drawn over the windows, shutting out the daylight; Indirect fixtures reflected their soft light on the ceiling and bathed the room in a gentle glow. He hung his suit coat on a waiting rack, then crossed the room to a small bar and opened a low set of double doors to retrieve a half-empty bottle of Dewar's. He reached over the bar to open a sliding glass door and pulled out a squat tumbler, then slid aside a bar top panel and dipped the glass full of ice cubes, opened the Dewar's and splashed some over the ice. He left the bottle on the bar and crossed the room to a leather chair by an ornate maple desk. Taking a sip and rolling it about in his mouth, he slumped into the chair and stared at the bookshelf behind the desk.

Ten minutes, staring at the wall, with an occasional sip . . . then he picked up the phone and punched in a number. He leaned back in the chair, waiting for the answer. One ring, two . . . at five rings there was an audible click, then the hum and the recorded voice: "You have reached the office of Chicago Aldermen Vincent Scianno. If you are calling concerning City business, please press "0" for Mr. Scianno's assistant. If you wish to leave a message . . . "

Ted held the phone away from his ear until he heard the message end with an audible "beep", then spoke: "Cut the bullshit, Vince. I know you're there. You never leave the damn place. Now pick up the phone." Silence, then another click and an answer.

"Ted? What the hell is this? We agreed you wouldn't call me here."

"Things change. I'm worried about our problem."

"Jack will take care of it. Has the problem

been found?"

"Your contact says so . . . I don't know. I won't breathe easy until I know he's done it. I want to send some help."

"Christ, Ted . . . I had to call in a lot of markers to get Jack without any questions being asked. I can't go back and tell them . . . "

"Just remember, buddy, your ass is on the line as much as mine is. I don't want any more slip-ups."

"He's found him, it'll be done today. He won't screw this up."

Mansfield leaned forward in the chair, his face reddening. His voice rose in volume. "Like those two pros you sent me? They weren't worth a shit!"

"Take it easy, Ted. They were just street muscle. This Jack, he's the best there is."

Mansfield thought for a minute, then sighed; a long, audible exhalation. He slumped back against the chair back. "Okay, I'll give it a chance on your say-so. But one thing: if this guy doesn't get it done damn soon, we'll be talking again." He hung up before Scianno could reply.

July 25, 2:14 p.m. CDT

At the other end of the severed connection, Vincent Scianno slowly lowered the telephone handset and replaced it in its cradle. His brow was furrowed in thought beneath the dark hair that swept down and across the high forehead. He was often mistaken for a younger man, and he was proud of the fact that he had very little gray hair although he was nearly 60. He was short but powerfully built, with a shape that had earned him the nickname "fireplug" in his college days. He hadn't let the years get to him, running each day and visiting the gym three times a week. A prominent and popular politician, he was now beginning a campaign for the mayor's office. He was in shape, successful, and admired. Until recently he had been confident and self-assured. The last few days had changed all that.

He turned and looked at the mirror behind his desk. The face that stared back was starting to look its age. Worry lines were replacing the light wrinkles that his ready grin had produced in his features; this situation had to end.

He stood, looking now at nothing as he recalled how it had started. He had been younger, foolish perhaps, but freshly elected and flushed with victory. He had been open to all constituents, and believed he was above the corruption that was rampant in city politics. He had befriended a number of up-and-coming businessmen, and among them had been a younger Ted Mansfield.

Mansfield had been quick to hitch his wagon to Vincent's rising star, and through the first couple of campaigns thereafter, Ted had been a stalwart supporter and good friend. No under-the-table dealings were ever discussed. During the third re-election push, when a vigorous challenger arose and the campaign was faltering, the opposition appeared poised to oust Vincent from office. He and Ted had been commiserating over a beer when it came. Ted had asked him point blank what the election was worth to him. The conversation had continued far into the night, and when all was said and done, Vince had reluctantly agreed to let Ted help him. The "connections" he gained in that midnight counseling session had turned the tide. Legitimately or not, Vincent Scianno had been firmly entrenched in office ever since. The problem was, he now knew too much of what went on behind the scenes. He owed favors to people with whom he would never want to be seen, and the money which had helped him roll up his impressive election victories was tainted. Until recently, he had pushed the unpleasant thoughts aside, reasoning that this was how the big game was played. But now he couldn't stop the thoughts. They were with him day and night, so much so that he hadn't slept since Ted had first called him about the "situation."

Just six short days back, he had been in his office, enjoying what had been a very good run of luck. Two of his pet projects had received good committee recommendations and were poised to move ahead, and his stock for the upcoming mayoral race was on the rise. When his receptionist had told him Mr. Mansfield was on the line, he had answered quickly, happily: "Ted! Just who I want to talk to! We're going to the top, buddy . . . I can feel it!"

Mansfield had been urgent, curt: "All that can wait. We have a problem. Come to my office right away."

"Ted, I can't just drop everything . . . "

"Yes, you can. You have to. Come now." The click on the other end of the line signaled an abrupt end to the conversation. Vincent had felt the beginnings of a churning stomach then, and he had chewed on a couple of antacid tablets to quiet it down. He had no idea what Ted was all upset about, but something in the tone of the call told him he had better go and find out.

He had gone to meet Ted, at first curious, then angry himself as Mansfield described the compromised records and Perry's involvement. He was quick to recognize the impact that the release of those records would have on his career; ouster from office and probable prison time did not figure into his plans. At Mansfield's insistence, he had made a quick call to someone he pretended publicly not to know. Some heated conversation and some promises of quid pro quo, plus a half-hour of waiting, delivered the two "hired hands" to Mansfield's office. Per instructions, they came in through the rear entrance. With his part done, or so he thought, Vincent had excused himself. He hadn't wanted to know what was going to happen next.

He had thought it was over, until Mansfield called him again. Ted had been almost acidic, the vitriol in his voice making chills run up Vincent's spine. Perry had somehow gotten away, and left two very messed up thugs behind him. "Twice . . . at the apartment, then at the cop shop!" Mansfield had shouted. "A middle-aged bean counter . . . Jesus, what a mess!"

Vincent had assured Ted he could handle this, but he would need to write a lot of political I.O.U.s to pull it off. For the second time that day, he had found himself on the phone, talking in vague terms to people he wished he did not know. The promises he had made effectively erased any last vestige of the ethical public service a younger Vince had embraced, but the deed was done. The man they would send was known only as Jack, and in certain levels of society the name brought averted gazes and looks over the shoulder. If he was as good as his reputation . . .

A clock chimed in the hallway; the sound brought Vincent back to the present. He looked down at the pile of paperwork he'd been pushing through, and it suddenly seemed insignificant. The mayor's chair would certainly not be his; that had become the least of his concerns. He stood and squared his shoulders, exhaled slowly, turned, and walked to the window. He stared ruefully out at the City he loved, the City for which he'd sold his soul.

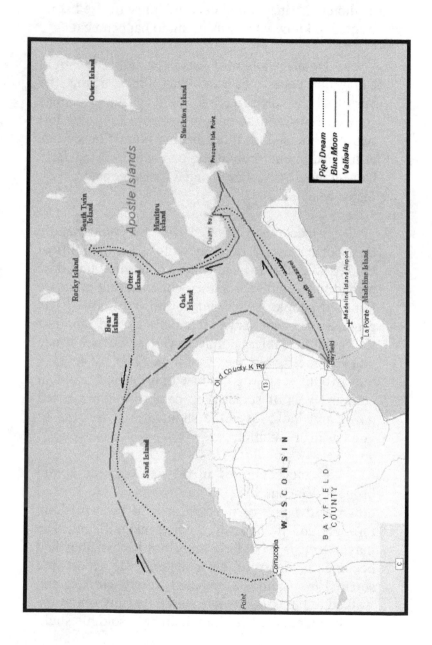

Chapter 4

HEADING OUT

July 25, 4:12 p.m. CDT

Stockton Island was a popular sailing and hiking destination. A quarry on its southern end had yielded much of the brownstone that went into landmark buildings in the great midwestern cities. Now, the quarry itself was overgrown and returning to nature. The remaining evidence of the quarry, in the form of the great gaps in the rock and the remains of tools and hoists, was now a popular stop in the Apostle Islands National Lakeshore. The anchorage at Quarry Bay was protected except from the southeast. Today it was deserted save for a small power cruiser and a single white sailboat. The name on the sailboat's transom was *Pipe Dream.*

Paul and Rich had found the west wind ideal as they broad reached up the North Channel. They had overtaken some smaller sailboats and had seen two gill-net fishing boats, on their way back to Bayfield after a hard day's work. The clouds of seagulls following them told Paul that the catch was being cleaned on the way in.

As they had neared Stockton Island at around 3:30, Paul knew that most boats would be heading for the popular breakwater at Presque Isle Point. When they drew abeam of Quarry Bay and found it almost empty, his decision was made. The genoa was furled, the diesel started, and the main dropped and neatly flaked on the boom. Paul had introduced Rich to the helm and instructed him on what they were going to do to anchor in the bay. Although he had been nervous, Rich soon found himself reveling in the experience. He had followed Paul's instructions to a T, and now they swung gently in around 18 feet of water, the big CQR anchor firmly embedded in the sand bottom. They were well off the power cruiser swinging at anchor near the dock. As they looked to the cruiser, they could see nobody on deck.

Now, sitting in the cockpit and absently watching the shoreline, Paul began to think about the coming run across the lake to Thunder Bay. He looked at the sky and felt the air, then rose to go below. Rich rose behind him. "Stay put," Paul told him, "I'm gonna get a weather check."

"Anything I can do?" Rich was still nervous; Paul recognized the edge in his voice. Time to get him to relax.

"Okay, for starters there's some booze in the middle section cabinet. Port side. Pour me a couple of fingers of that Black Bush. Fix yourself whatever you'd like. There's pop in the fridge if you want a mixed drink."

"It's still early . . . I'd rather just have water or maybe a Coke . . . "

"Bullshit. After what you've been through, you need something stronger than that."

Rich thought for a minute; then with a small half-grin he followed Paul below. "Twisted my arm. Okay, what's the port side . . . "

"Left. Easy to remember. Port and left each have four letters."

As Rich aimed for the liquor, Paul tucked himself into the nav station seat. He thumbed his way through the VHF channels to the weather band and stopped at 3. The droning voice was mechanical, disembodied. "Damn technology," he thought to himself. "Weather by machine." Paul was not comfortable with the new format, which used voice synthesizers to repeat weather messages endlessly. At least the information was the same, so he settled in to listen. The drone continued: " . . . near shore forecast for western Lake Superior: winds south to southwest at 5 to 10 knots, becoming south 10 to 15 knots by nightfall. Waves 1 to 3 feet. Tonight, winds becoming southeasterly 10 to 20 knots, waves building to 2 to 4 feet. Winds increasing through . . . "

Paul's brow wrinkled as he listened. A low-pressure center was pushing across the area, heading down from Canada but passing just south of the lake. The winds would follow the circulation, and build as they swung to head back and come out of the east over the north side of the low. He knew that by tomorrow, the main lake would be kicking up and a crossing wouldn't be prudent . . .

His thoughts were interrupted as Rich handed him a glass. "Black Bush, two fingers. And I have fat fingers." Rich was actually sporting a small grin.

Paul reached up and pushed the priority button on the VHF, switching it back to Channel 16. The robotic drone of the synthesized weather mercifully stopped. He regarded the glass and took a slow sip, holding the Irish whiskey on his tongue, then swallowed. Rich had turned back to find himself a drink, and Paul spoke to his back. "We'll need to move this afternoon. It's going to swing around and drive the seas right into this anchorage."

Rich stood, turning to reveal a glass in his hand. He had decided to try the Black Bush, a premium Irish whiskey from the Bushmills distillery. He raised the glass to his lips, took a sip and grimaced, then swallowed. "Whooboy!" His sharp exhalation blurred the expression. "That's some powerful stuff! Very good though."

"Grows on you." Paul pulled a laminated place mat from beneath the nav station. It contained a chart of the Apostle Islands, with the notation "NOT FOR NAVIGATION" printed on it. Many people used these anyway. Full-sized charts were too cumbersome and these little place mats were simply handy reductions and weather resistant as well. The lawyers made the souvenir companies put the note on each to avoid lawsuits in case of navigational errors.

As Paul laid the little chart on the navigation table, Rich leaned over to look. Paul pointed to Stockton Island and Quarry Bay. "This is where we are now. When the wind shifts, it'll drive in like this." He moved his finger to the right edge of the chart, then back left directly at the bay.

"So that means . . . " Rich's question hung in the air.

"It means we'll rock and roll all night in here. We need to be someplace like . . . here." His finger pointed to a pair of islands, north and west of Stockton Island. "At Rocky and South Twin, you have an anchorage you can move around in. When the wind is out of the southeast or east, we can tuck in to the lee of South Twin."

"How far is that? I mean, is there someplace closer?"

"Sure. Presque Isle Point's right around the corner. Here." He showed Rich the dumbbell-shaped projection running southeast from the main body of Stockton Island. The formation was called a "Tombolo", produced when a smaller island next to the main island was joined to it by sand over eons of wave action. "On the west side of the point, right here, there's a nice little harbor. Even has a breakwater and nice restrooms ashore."

"So why don't we go there?"

"Because everybody else does. That includes water taxis and tour boats. It's a busy place, and if anybody's looking, we'll be easy to spot."

Rich took another sip, this time savoring it a bit. "Somebody will be looking. I just hope we were inconspicuous back in Bayfield . . . "

July 25, 4:15 p.m. CDT

In the black Explorer, Jack had kept his vigil all afternoon. No sign of Perry....where was the bastard? Tourists walking up and down the streets, in and out of the shops, but no sign of his quarry. He was used to long waits, and had developed his patience to an extreme level, but this particular wait didn't seem right.

The only recent traffic in and out of the Rittenhouse had consisted of two older couples and a family with three kids. Uncharacteristically, he grew impatient. "Damn!" The oath and the slap of the dashboard came at the same instant. He checked the position of his pistol, then opened the door and got out, smoothing his sport jacket to make sure nothing showed. He closed the door and walked slowly toward the inn.

The couple with the kids was coming down the walk. The mother was clutching the little girl's hand and imploring the two energetic boys to settle down, the father trying his best to ignore them. One of the boys stopped in front of the man in the dark suit, looking up at him. The boy's smile turned suddenly to a look of fear, and he ran after his brother. His voice could be heard as the family walked down the hill toward the shops, "That man was weird . . . "

"God, I hate kids," Jack said to himself. He had seen it before. "Can't fool them."

He reached the door and went in, putting on his best smile. The clerk was busy behind the desk, but recognized him from their prior conversation. She returned the smile. "I'm sorry . . . Mr. Pearson hasn't come back yet."

"I'm not gonna be able to wait for him much longer." Jack decided it was time to check the room. "Could I ask a favor? I really wanted to surprise him, and I can still do that if you'll help."

"I dunno," she said, "it depends on what you want me to do."

Thinking quickly now, Jack pressed on. "Our crowd had a way of communicating back in the old days. We used to leave a shirt or jacket on a chair, folded a certain way. Everybody had their own particular way of folding. It was a sign to show who was trying to reach you. If I can do that, it'll drive him nuts and he'll come looking for me. I just need to get one of his shirts and do the folding."

"I'll get in trouble if I let you go into a guest's room." She was clearly nervous.

Jack turned on the charm. He reached out and patted her hand, smiling, and continued. "I wouldn't expect to be in there alone. You'd be with me, watching every second. And you can leave the door wide open. Please . . . I just want to surprise my friend."

She thought for a moment, then glanced around, still nervous. "Well . . . just for a minute. I suppose if you're not alone in there . . . " She reached back and took a key out of a slot, and motioned him to follow. The door she led him to was just past the desk, right there on the first floor. Working the key in the lock, she opened the door and went in ahead of him. As he followed her in, she turned back and put her hand up toward him. "Now, like I said, just for a minute. I'll get in trouble for this if anything happens."

He smiled again. "Sure . . . it won't take long at all." She stepped aside as he moved into the room. He glanced around quickly, taking a mental inventory. The room had a beautiful brass bed near the door, and at the far end was a Jacuzzi. A second door, probably to the outside, was in the wall to the right. A side chair next to the small desk had a yellow paper in it. "I'll just be a second."

He went quickly to the closet and looked inside. "Damn! No clothes!" he said to himself as he turned again, still searching. There! On the bed was a pile of what looked like dirty laundry. An old sweatshirt, a couple of tees, and what looked like old rags used for painting. He walked to the bed and picked up the pile. Strange, oily odor to the rags. It didn't seem like what an accountant like Perry would have with him.

He noticed that the clerk was fidgeting, nervous. He separated the sweatshirt from the pile, dumping the rest back on the bed. "This'll do!" He took the shirt and went to the desk, picking up the yellow paper from the chair and casually laying it on the desk as he sat down. As he did so he read it quickly. It was a small, crudely done map of the Apostle Islands National Lakeshore with a numbered list of attractions. Probably available all over Bayfield.

The clerk was growing more nervous by the second, her eyes darting to the door. He quickly folded the sweatshirt, placing one sleeve doubled back on itself and the other brought up and tucked into the neck. He carefully laid the oddly folded sweatshirt on the desk. "That'll get him thinking," he said, giving the clerk a reassuring smile. He rose and left the room. She quickly followed him out and locked the door behind her.

She was visibly relieved as she put the key back into its slot. "I hope he finds you."

"You can be sure we'll make connections now. You've been a great help." Jack gave her a final smile as he turned and left the inn. He was pondering the map and the pile of clothes. What was that odor on those rags? There weren't any other signs of his target in the room. He would have expected clothes in the closet . . .

As he returned to the Explorer and got in, a large truck labored its way up the hill beside him, spewing diesel smoke and fumes . . . The odor! It was diesel fuel. Like on the rags . . . Jack thought quickly now, recalling everybody who had gone either in or out of the Rittenhouse. The guy in the cap, with the duffel . . . shit! It had to be him. He must have pulled a switch for Perry, got his stuff. Jack remembered thinking the guy looked like a seaman. The diesel smell. Boats. The map. It all fit together. Perry was trying to make a run for it by water.

Chapter 5

ISLAND PURSUIT

July 25, 4:51 p.m. CDT

Paul stood at the bow, his foot on the switch activating the windlass. He watched carefully as first nylon anchor rode, then chain, was pulled in by the windlass and deposited belowdecks. As the big CQR anchor rose to the surface, he worked the windlass until the shank began to pass over the bow roller. He stopped and pulled it in the rest of the way by hand, then leaned over the pulpit and locked it in place with a pin and key. He tapped the windlass until the remaining chain was just slack, then went aft to the cockpit. Rich was moving aside to make room for Paul behind the wheel.

Paul slipped behind the helm, shifted into forward gear, and gave the idling diesel some throttle. "Let's go!" he said, more to *Pipe Dream* than to Rich. "We want to be at South Twin before this kicks up much more." The boat surged forward under power, making her way out of Quarry Bay and turning to starboard to head for the passage at the south end of Stockton Island.

July 25, 5:32 p.m. CDT

Jack talked to a lot of people around the docks, trying to avoid obvious tourists. The chances they would know anything were slim. It was the regulars, the locals, who would notice anything out of the ordinary. He walked along the line of boats at the city pier, stopping to talk to an old man at work over something on his cabintop.

"A lot of boats go out this morning?" Jack was putting on his best tourist face, making small talk with the old man, who busily sanded away on his teak grabrails. The sailboat was an older model with classic lines. if Jack had known anything about boats he would have recognized her as a Bristol.

The old man looked up from his sanding. A four-day growth of whiskers and the wrinkles about his eyes gave him the very fitting look of a weathered sailor. "Not hardly any. One or two this mornin' . . . but you oughta see the place on a Friday."

"Oh, well, I just thought maybe you saw my friends. I was going to see them off, but they may have left early."

"There was one left around 1:30 or so. Didn't see the name."

"A sailboat?"

"Yeah, pretty one, white hull with flag blue stripe. Tartan, I think. Mighta been a 37, or maybe one of the newer 34s. They both got the same lines. Longer, though . . . prob'ly the 37."

"With two men aboard?"

"Naw, I think he was a singlehander. At least I only saw one guy."

Jack held his hand at about six feet. "About this tall, khaki jacket and one of those black knit caps that pulls down . . . "

"Watch cap. Yeah, that sounds like him. If there was two the other one musta been below. Woulda expected him to be on deck helpin' with the lines." The old man scowled, leaned over and cleared his nasal passages, then delivered a spitball gift to the water alongside the boat. He clearly thought anybody who didn't help didn't belong on a boat.

"They were going out among the islands for a few days. Where do you suppose they'd head for first?"

"Stockton. Unless they been up here a lot. First-timers always wanna go to Stockton." He paused, scratched, then continued. "It's got a breakwater and all. Park Service put in new johns out there a few years back."

Jack turned to leave. "Thanks, you've been a big help." As he walked away from the old man and his Bristol, Jack was looking for something else now. He'd need a fast powerboat and somebody who knew the islands.

Nearer the land along the wide concrete pier that jutted out to meet the breakwater, a line of smaller powerboats displayed various signs offering charter service. Many were for fishing, some for diving on the old shipwrecks which littered the islands. Jack looked them each over as he passed, then stopped near a blue and white boat with a large cabin and flying bridge. The sign on the rail read:

Blue Moon charter fishing
G. L. "Skip" Meyer,
Captain
½ day or all-day charters
Lake Trout/Salmon

A hatch at the stern was open; the broad-shouldered man holding the hatch rim was finishing an engine check. Jack took a chance it was the owner.

"Captain Meyer?"

"Skip." he said, not looking up as he lowered the hatch into place. He took a moment to secure the hatch, stretching the black rubber retainers into their clips. Then he stood, pulled on a battered tan cap, and faced Jack, appraising him as he did so. He saw the suit and street shoes, and concluded that this was probably not a fisherman. Finally he offered, "Can I help you?"

Jack put on the practiced smile. "The sign says you take half-day charters. Are you available today?"

"You don't exactly look ready to go, and it's

already past five.   You'll wanna wait 'til tomorrow."   Skip looked at the sky and thought maybe tomorrow wouldn't be so good. "Or the next day if the weather comes in."

Jack was insistent.   "I've got to leave tomorrow, and I had my heart set on going out tonight. Just a couple hours is all. I can pay cash if that's a problem."

"Not at all. This time of year we still have about three hours of daylight, if you really wanna go out. Just basically a run up a little way and then come back after dark. Sorry . . . you just didn't look like somebody who planned on going right away."

Jack was ready with his response. "I didn't know if anybody would still be willing to go, but I thought I'd take a chance. I can be back here in about 20 minutes ready to go."

Skip thought a minute, then looked at his watch. "It's your money. It'll be after six, and I'll be coming back here no later than nine or nine-thirty. I'll have to charge you for a half-day charter. You got a fishing license, Mister . . . "

"Weaver." Jack used one of his many alter egos . . . he had documents to go with the names. "Fred Weaver. And no, I need a license. Where do I go?"

"I can do the paperwork right here. Cost you ten bucks for a two-day Wisconsin tag. And the charter fee for half a day is pretty steep. $450, but usually there's at least 4 people sharing the cost." Skip turned, then turned back. "And a $40 fuel surcharge. Prices have been high."

Jack looked at Skip for along moment. He saw a man in fairly good shape and he knew he'd need some leverage. "No problem," he said. "Be right back."

Four slips toward the shore from *Blue Moon*, he saw another charter skipper helping his customers offload their tackle. Jack turned and walked over to him. "Hello," he said, "I'm reviewing the various services here in Bayfield. I was just talking to Skip Meyer," he gestured toward *Blue Moon*, "but my magazine likes to get the family perspective. They like to hear from the wives and kids without coaching from the main subjects, if you know what I mean. How do I reach his wife?"

The skipper regarded him for a moment, then squinted a bit as he thought. "Char, that's her name. Must be Charlotte or something. She spends most of the summer down in Ashland with her sister. Skip's gone a lot and she don't like bein' alone. Skip'll know her sister's phone number if you want to call her."

"Thanks, I'll ask him when I come back." Jack had all the information he needed. He turned and broke into an easy jog as he thought about the coming hours.

July 25, 5:57 p.m. CDT

Mansfield had stewed all morning and all afternoon, waiting for word that didn't come. Scianno was weak, pliable, all-in-all somebody good to have in city government if you wanted influence . . . but no damn good in this situation. He drained the last of the Dewar's and stood, then picked up the phone. He dialed quickly, and as the call was answered, the walls heard the one-sided conversation. "Brad, Ted . . . Skip all the pleasantries. I need you to handle something for me . . . Whaddya mean 'it depends'? Remember who this is, and what you and I both know . . . That's better. Now listen: I need some people who can make a problem disappear. It's a very troublesome problem, for you and a lot of others . . . You know exactly what I mean . . . Yeah, they sent someone, one guy, but so far no dice. Your guys'll be insurance . . . Why you? because you're already in the neighborhood, you dumb shit!" As Mansfield listened, his face reddened and he spoke again, this time with anger. "You hang up now, your high life is done. Count on it!" There was another pause as he listened intently, and then he spoke again. "That's better. Now listen: The problem is in some podunk berg called Bayfield, up in northern Wisconsin. You get some people there, and I'll find a way to get this local guy in touch with them . . . You know the place? That's even better. I'm going up myself, and I'll need a place to stay . . . Good. So how do I get this condo of yours? . . . All right, just make sure they have your key. So who are these people and how do we get them together with . . . "

97

Mansfield stopped talking, grabbing a pen and pad from atop the bar. He wrote quickly, then read back what he wrote. "Okay, I got it. Bruno, Mike, and Sam. Those their real names? . . . no shit? Sounds like fake names to me. Driving a white SUV. What make?" He listened and wrote again, then continued. "Okay, Ford Expedition. So where is this 'Pier?' What's the street address? . . . Humor me. I know it's a small town, but . . . Well, you better be right . . . Sonafabitch just calls himself Jack. He'll be there. If he doesn't show, the problem might already be gone."

He listened for a few more seconds, then hung up the phone without any further comment. He stared at the floor, then smoothed back his hair and picked up the phone again. He dialed, listened to Scianno's familiar message, and then spoke. "Get your ass over to my office. Forty five minutes. I'm heading back there now. Don't make me wait."

He broke the connection, then dialed again. When Sherry answered, he spoke quickly. "Go back to the office. Pull that travel bag I keep out of storage and leave it in my chair. And pull some cash from the safe. 10 large for now. If I need more I'll tell you. Got it?" He paused as she repeated his instructions. "A couple of days. Flying out from Palwaukee . . . No, just say I'm out. They don't need to know where I am. Neither do you." He hung up, quickly walked toward the kitchen, and grabbed the suit coat from the rack as he passed. He strode through the kitchen and then to the entry door, opening it. He paused and entered another code at the alarm panel. The light changed from steady green to steady red, and Ted slammed the door shut behind him as he left. His home was secure, but he felt anything but secure at the moment. "Damned incompetents. Want something done right, you do it yourself." He spoke aloud as he slung himself into the big Lincoln.

July 25, 6: 03 p.m. CDT

Pipe Dream was heading northwest, passing through the channel between Oak Island and Manitou Island. Paul was at the wheel, Rich on the port side. The boat was running wing-and-wing, the main played out to port and the big genoa well out to starboard. Paul had instructed Rich how to rig a preventer to keep the boom from flying across in case of an accidental jibe; that was not only tough on the rig, but potentially dangerous or even deadly to crew. Paul was making slight corrections at the helm to account for the following seas and to keep the headsail filled. Rich could see it took a lot of practice, a lot of skill.

Paul watched Rich stare at the big headsail, reading his thoughts. "If I was by myself and going farther, I'd have the whisker pole run out. It just didn't seem worth it, 'cause we'll be changing course as soon as we pass little Manitou." He gestured to a small navigation marker on what appeared to be a lone rock, well ahead and off to starboard.

"Little Manitou?" Rich was puzzled. "I thought that whole island over there was Manitou."

Paul allowed himself a smile. "It is. But between that rock and the island, it's too shallow to pass safely. They put up the nav-aid, and had to call the rock something. Technically, it IS an island."

Rich changed the subject. "You fit in here. You look like a man who's found what he needs. And it's a far cry from the whole engineering and technical route you were following back in college."

"Yeah, I guess you'd say I was born to it. It didn't come without a high price."

"Gina?"

Paul's brief smile quickly fled. "She tried, you know. She just felt too isolated, and she needed other people around. I just needed her. It didn't work that way, and I guess we both had it figured out after that first year."

"She went with you, as I recall. We got postcards for a while."

"From her, not me. I never was good at writing . . .at least to other people. Funny how that's what I do for a living now." Paul shifted in his seat. "Like I said, we both knew. She knew I had to keep sailing, and I knew she couldn't be with me if I did. She was good at it, you know."

"At what?"

"Sailing. Hell, I'd trust her more than anybody but myself to handle this boat. She knows sail trim better than most, and she could even sail solo if she had to." The smile had returned.

Rich was silent for awhile, then looked up. "At least you've done something interesting. Aside from my current mess, about the most exciting thing that happens in my life is when the toast pops up."

Paul looked at his old friend, visualizing the Rich he knew before. "That's hard for me to believe. You were always the one in and out of trouble.'

"Yeah, as a student, maybe, but life was different. Right out of school I got what I thought was my dream job, working in investments. I had to pour myself into the job, because . . . well, you get the idea what Mansfield was like as a boss, but I thought it was all worth it." Rich was pensive now, looking down. "Then after Meg's accident . . . "

As Rich went on about his late wife, Paul thought back. It was the last time he had seen Rich, at Meg's funeral. He remembered how all the life seemed to have gone out of his friend, and how worried he had been. He felt like kicking himself for not staying in touch. As Rich finished, he thought that it was fortunate that Rich and Meg hadn't had any kids. "Rich, I've always meant to call, you know that. It just never felt like the right time." He looked over at Little Manitou, now abeam. Sailing was going to change this unpleasant subject for him. "Time to bring the jenny over."

Paul pulled the sheet from the starboard winch jaws, keeping it in his hands and applying tension to keep the turns from running on the drum. Rich loaded the port winch as Paul turned the wheel and brought the bow to starboard. The Genoa began to backwind, and he called out to Rich to haul in the sheet. He pulled the sheet in his hand upward and off the starboard winch. As Rich hauled in on the port sheet, the Genoa came through the foretriangle and filled on the port side. Rich kept hauling until he needed mechanical help, then he locked the tail of the sheet in the winch jaws and cranked it in until Paul told him to stop.

Paul told Rich to grab the wheel and stepped forward to release the preventer and haul in the mainsheet. Looking at the trim of both sails, he made a few fine adjustments and sat, leaving Rich at the wheel. "Take 'er for awhile. She'll show you what she's got."

Rich could feel the power in the rig and through the hull as *Pipe Dream* heeled and surged ahead. The rush of the water flying past and the wind steady on the right side of his face gave him a sensation of speed well in excess of the six to seven knots he was traveling. He let out a yell. "Whoooo-eeee! No wonder you love this!"

Sailing was therapeutic, Paul knew, and if anyone needed it today it was Rich. The boat pushed on to the northeast now, up the channel between Manitou and Otter Islands, as the two men aboard her shared an exhilarating communion with nature.

July 25, 6:12 p.m. CDT

Skip was cleaning up loose ends aboard *Blue Moon* when Jack returned. Jack was carrying a very new-looking tacklebox, and a rod and reel that looked like they were just off the shelf. He wore all new clothing, including a very white pair of tennis shoes and a sweatshirt that sported a lake map and the logo "Lake Superior shipwrecks." He also carried a slim briefcase. Strange combination, Skip thought. Oh well . . . his money. He can spend it however he wants to. He helped Jack aboard, taking the tacklebox and putting it down on deck. It felt very light. He reached for the briefcase, but Jack put it down beside him and reached into his pocket, pulling out a roll of bills. He peeled off six new hundred-dollar notes.

"Here's your payment." He handed the money to Skip.

Skip took the bills, peeled one off and handed it back. "It comes to five hundred, not six."

"Consider it an advance tip." Jack was again using the practiced smile.

Skip shoved the bill into Jack's hand. "You hang on to this, Mr. Weaver. If you're happy when we get back, you can tip me then."

"Fair enough. Let's go." Jack — "Fred Weaver" — followed Skip to the flying bridge.

Skip turned on a switch marked "blower" and the hum of a small electric motor could be heard from somewhere aft. He was explaining as he prepared the boat for departure. "This is a gasoline-powered boat. The blower makes sure no gas fumes are hangin' around when you start. There have been some pretty nasty explosions that way." He continued to stow things and at one point he reached into a locker and threw Jack a life vest. "Put this on. No exceptions, everybody on this boat wears one."

Jack put on the vest, not liking it and what it did to his mobility. He listened as Skip explained how he wanted the aft mooring line brought in. When Skip at last adjusted the throttle and started the big V-8, Jack went to the stern, stepped to the dock and took the line from the cleat, then stepped back aboard. Skip removed the springline and then went to the bowline and did the same.

"Okay." Skip was back on the flying bridge, putting the shift in reverse and giving the throttle a bump. *Blue Moon* eased aft away from the pier, and when he knew he had enough room, Skip shifted back to neutral, then forward, and turned the wheel hard to the right. The stern slid to port and bow swung over obediently, clearing the stern of the boat in front. Her course straightened as she idled toward the entry. "Bring them fenders in over the rail. You can leave 'em tied off."

Jack lifted the round plastic fenders over the rail and laid them along the inside, then climbed to the flying bridge. He stood behind Skip as they cleared the entry, and when Skip applied power the stern squatted and the boat began to pick up speed. Skip pointed to a plastic chart taped below the spray glass. "See this? You can't fish just anywhere. Restricted areas are marked...we'll head just east of this one. They're catchin' em pretty good there the last few days."

Jack stood silently behind Skip, his mind on things other than fishing. He looked ahead up the channel between Basswood Island and the larger Madeline Island. There was no conversation for several minutes, until they had pulled abeam of the southern tip of Basswood Island.

Skip was watching ahead as he spoke. "We get a little further out, I'll put 'er on autopilot and we can get your license taken care of. I'll need your I.D. for that."

It was time. Jack pulled the slim Beretta from his waistband, fumbling a bit under the life jacket. Damn thing has to go, he thought. He pulled the action to chamber a round, and Skip turned at the sound only to look down the waiting barrel.

"Wha . . ."

"Just shut up and listen. You won't get hurt if you follow instructions." Jack lied, like a dozen times before. Skip was already dead; he just didn't know it yet.

"I knew you weren't right, with your suit and . . ."

A hard, open-handed slap across the face stopped him in mid-sentence. Jack was glaring at him now, his voice hard. "I said shut up. Now think. I'm looking for a sailboat. A Tartan, probably, a 37-footer or maybe a 34-footer. White hull and some kind of blue stripe. Where is Stockton Island?" Skip stood in silent shock, *Blue Moon* still keeping her course up the channel.

July 25, 6:47 p.m. CDT

In the air-conditioned elevator car, Vincent Scianno was sweating. It wasn't the kind of sweat that comes with exertion, nor was it the uncomfortable clammy sweat that appears on a hot, muggy evening. It was the nervous, "what's going to happen" variety, and he didn't like it. As the chime signaled the impending stop at Mansfield's floor, he squared his shoulders and nervously cleared his throat. He noted the slight change in force against his feet as the car slowed and stopped; then the doors slid open and he found himself wishing he could just stay in the car and go back down. He stood for several seconds, his feet rooted to the car floor. The doors began to slide shut, and he put out his hand to hit the safety stop. The doors stopped and reversed, and he walked out of the elevator and into the reception area of M&L Investments. He was surprised to see Sherry at her desk at this late hour. She flashed a quick, nervous smile as she saw him. She started to rise to greet him, but something in his manner made her sit back down. This looked like another one of those things she would be told to ignore.

The door to Mansfield's office was closed. Vince stopped, wondering if he should go in; Ted's message had been insistent that Vince come immediately. Ted's voice had been, as usual for the past several days, irate.

Vince swallowed hard, straightened his tie and tapped on the door. It opened immediately, and Vince saw that Mansfield was sitting across the large office at his desk. He was hanging up the phone, and he motioned Vince to the chair opposite him, almost snarling, "About damn time. I said forty-five minutes."

As Vince crossed the room, he felt, rather than saw, behind him the man who had opened the door. It was a very uncomfortable sensation. As he sat in the proffered chair, he heard the door close. He swallowed again, looked at his watch, then put on his best confrontational façade. "So it was forty-eight minutes. What's this about, Ted? I thought we agreed it was all handled."

"Handled, my ass." Mansfield rose and leaned across the desk, hands on the edge, towering over the sitting Vince. "One goddam postcard and no word since. What the hell kind of pros are you hiring? The little shit should've been history a day ago."

"You can't expect him to do it that quickly. It's gonna take a little time, but he'll do it right." Vince stood, walked to the window and looked out over the Chicago skyline. He turned and faced Ted. "Trust me, he'll get it done."

Mansfield glared at Vince, his anger rising. "When? I don't HAVE time! The longer he's out there with what he knows, the more chance there is it gets to the wrong people. That's why your guy is going to get help, whether he wants it or not! As for you, you're going to tell me how I get in touch with this Jack."

"That's not how it works. He only makes contact one way and that's it. I sure as hell can't just call him."

"Then however you do it, you contact him and tell him I want him working with my guys."

"Your guys?" Vince turned. "Your guys? I told you, he doesn't work with anybody. He insists on it. His contact made that very clear. If I try to get around that . . . "

"You'll get around that or yours will be the

ass in the sling tonight." Mansfield was speaking now in low, measured tones, far too calmly, and the effect was chilling. "You'll contact him, however you can, and tell him to meet three of my people. They'll be coming into Bayfield later tonight. If he hasn't done the job by then, they will. Now write this down: They go by the names Bruno, Mike, and Sam. They're driving a . . . "

"I told you I can't do that. Don't mess with me, Ted. The people who got me Jack will be on your ass if I tell them . . . "

"I'm on YOUR ass, you dumb shit!" roared Mansfield, slamming his fist onto the desk. A pen set and a framed picture jumped with the impact. "I'm the one you better worry about! Now like I said, write this down!" He gave a sharp motion with his left hand, and the man who had closed the door appeared at Vince's side. He held out a pen and a spiral-bound notepad.

Vince looked at the man, sizing him up. There was no hesitation in the set of the jaw, and the sport jacket he wore wasn't tight at the shoulders because of any padding; it was all muscle. Vince knew the type. He took the pen and the pad and sat back down.

Mansfield picked up where he had left off. "Bruno, Mike, and Sam. Got it? They're in a white Ford Expedition, big-ass SUV. Minnesota plates. They'll wait for this guy at a place called The Pier, whatever the hell that is. They said it's about the only place everybody knows. Some restaurant or something. Make sure this goes down just like I told you. I want this taken care of, and these guys are my insurance policy."

Vince finished writing, then sat staring alternately at the floor and at the pad in his lap. Mansfield picked up the phone and dialed a number, giving terse instructions to someone on the other end. Vince heard the words and realized Ted was making arrangements for a flight out of Palwaukee. Mansfield hung up and left the office without a glance at Vince. The muscle left behind him, carrying a travel bag.

Vince knew that it was over. All the favors, the payoffs, the special favors over the years had come home to roost. He would do as he was told, but he was done in politics, no matter what else happened. He knew too much now, and he was likely to be next on Mansfield's list. He sighed deeply, then stood and ripped off the top page, stuffing it in his coat pocket. He turned and walked out of M&L Investments for the last time, into a world he no longer cared for.

July 25, 7: 31 p.m. CDT

In the calmer water between Rocky and South Twin Islands, *Pipe Dream's* diesel hummed to life as Paul pressed the start button. At Paul's instruction, Rich was already hauling in on the furling line, wrapping the big genoa around the forestay. Paul locked the wheel once he had brought the boat head-to-wind, then stepped to the front of the cockpit and released the line stopper that held the main halyard. The mainsail obediently parked itself atop the boom, contained once again by the lazy-jacks.

As he moved back to the wheel and turned the boat to port, Paul pointed to the L-shaped wooden dock on the South Twin Island shore to the northeast. "We'll Med moor there," he said. "If it kicks up a little, we don't want to be side-to on that dock. We'd beat the toerail all to hell, fenders or not."

Rich stopped hauling on the line, with the Genoa now completely furled. "What's 'Med moor?' I never heard of it."

"Normally, it's a space saver. You set a bow anchor out a good way, and then back down until you can get stern lines to the dock. Once you're made fast at the stern, you take up the slack on the anchor rode and it holds you just slightly off. You can get a lot more boats at a dock that way, and it originated in the Med. Hence the name. We could go in side-to, but like I said any chop'll have us riding up under that high dock."

"Okay, so we set anchor like we did before?"

"I'm gonna have you up on the foredeck. Backing down to a dock is tricky until you get used to it. Besides, I'll need to snag one of the cleats, and I've done it before." They were nearing the dock, and Paul motioned Rich forward. "There's a retainer pin at the anchor roller. Remove it . . . it's got a lanyard, so you won't lose it overboard."

"What about the anchor?"

"That's a free-fall windlass. I'll need you to pull out some chain at the windlass when I tell you, then hang the anchor off the roller. I'll tell you when to let go."

Rich went forward and did as he'd been told. Paul brought *Pipe Dream* in parallel with the dock, then turned her to port and idled forward away from the dock until he knew the distance was about right. He gave the wheel a slight turn to port, and as the bow began to swing, he shifted to neutral, then to reverse. He gave the diesel a fair amount of throttle, and the boat slowed and stopped, then began to back. He yelled to Rich to let go the anchor, and as the big CQR slid into the water, it was followed by chain and then by nylon rode. The prop walk began to take the stern back to port, but Paul dropped the throttle to idle speed as the boat gained steerageway, and *Pipe Dream* backed straight toward the dock.

As the stern neared the wooden pier, Paul picked up a telescoping boathook and extended it until it was nearly twelve feet long. He placed the eye-spliced end loop of a dockline on the hook, and then shifted from reverse to neutral. He eyed the dock as it approached, then shifted to forward and gave the throttle a quick burst to bring *Pipe Dream* to a stop. Then he shifted back to neutral. He reached over the stern with the boathook and dropped the loop over a cleat, and yelled to Rich. "Take up the slack in that anchor line!" At the same time, he pulled the boathook back into the cockpit, leaving the loop over the cleat, and hauled on the dockline until the stern was only a couple of feet from the pier. He secured the dockline to a stern cleat aboard the boat.

It took several more minutes, but at last *Pipe Dream* was secured, with two docklines and the anchor holding her away from the dock and yet near enough so they could go ashore if necessary. The two men sat in the cockpit, silent for awhile, and then Rich spoke. "I always figured you for a crazy man. I never realized how great this could be! It almost made me forget my problems. Almost . . ." his voice trailed off and the troubled look returned to his face. "Shit."

Paul leaned forward a little. "Need to talk about it?"

"No . . . you already know the most of it. I'm just sorry I dragged you into this."

"Hey, I was in it the day we became friends. Not to be melodramatic, but you'd do the same for me."

"I'm not that sure I would have. I'd like to think so, but I've never been all that noble. Now, with these people after me . . ."

Paul raised a hand, stopping Rich in mid-sentence. "I just said the guy LOOKED suspicious. It doesn't mean he was after you."

"If it isn't him it'll be someone else. I know Mansfield. He's totally without a conscience, and he would think no more of killing somebody in his way than you or I would think about swatting a fly. Speaking of which . . . " Rich stopped speaking and flattened a blackfly that had been crawling on his pants leg.

Paul didn't answer. He was thinking about the Explorer, the Illinois plates... it all fit together with what Rich was telling him. "Well," he sighed, "at least we're out where we'll be tough to find. We need to get some rest, so we'll do it in watches. You go below and get a couple hours rest, then spell me. We'll keep that schedule tonight, then figure out our plans after we check on the weather in the morning. It's already kickin' up a little." He stared south between the islands; the sun was low, almost to the trees on Rocky Island. The long summer daylight was winding down.

July 25, 7:38 p.m. CDT

Skip throttled back to slow *Blue Moon* as she neared the breakwater at Presque Isle Point on Stockton Island. His unwanted passenger stood behind him and slightly to the side, the Beretta at the ready. There were several boats within the breakwater area, both sail and power. Three more sailboats swung at anchor in the bay off to port.

Jack — "Fred Weaver" to Skip — looked toward the anchored boats, and gestured with his free hand. "Well?"

"Well what?" Skip wasn't about to volunteer anything. If this bastard expected cooperation he was barking up the wrong tree.

Jack's voice lowered to near a whisper. "Look, I don't give a shit if I have to drive this pig and look for 'em myself. It's all the same to me, but if you want to stay alive, don't give me any more crap."

Skip glared back at Jack. "Bullshit. You're probably gonna kill me anyway. Why the hell should I help you find some other poor bastard?"

"Have it your way. Just tell me one thing: How do you want me to kill Char and her sister down in Ashland when I'm done with you?"

Skip was stunned. "How in hell did you . . . "

"Never mind how. Just cooperate and I'll leave them alone."

Skip swallowed hard — he was left with no choice. "Okay, none of those are Tartans."

"You sure? They all look the same to me."

"No, there's differences. Different lines for different builders. Tartans have their own look, and there's none over there."

Jack looked hard at Skip, then shrugged. He turned and nodded toward the breakwater. "Okay, then what about those?"

"Dunno . . . we'll have to go in and check it out." He felt a small surge of hope. Perhaps if he could get someone's attention . . .

Jack's voice lowered again. "You make one wrong move, one word out of place, and you're dead now. Maybe some of them, too . . . " Skip saw that there were people on the docks and breakwater, aboard the boats and ashore. Kids. He felt the hope drain away as he throttled back to an idle and began a slow approach into the small sheltered harbor.

The National Park Service had greatly improved this popular destination in the islands, and it now featured a long, L-shaped concrete dock extending to the southwest from a timbered shore. The second, older dock left the same shore about 100 yards to the right, extending past the end of the other L and then turning slightly to form a sheltered entry. The result was a fully protected, tiny harbor, and cruisers loved it. New wooden walkways extended up into the forested area, where several newer buildings stood. These housed a small interpretive center with exhibits, and restroom facilities. In the summer, there was also full-time park staff on duty. Excursion boats and water taxis brought campers and casual visitors from time to time; Presque Isle Point could be a busy place. Today was one of those times.

As *Blue Moon* swung to starboard into the entry past the end of the longer dock, Skip made up his mind. He would have to go along. He couldn't be responsible for any of these people getting hurt. There would be time to try something else. He idled the engine and shifted into reverse, then applied a quick burst to bring *Blue Moon* to a near stop. He looked at the sailboats inside the breakwater. There were five Med moored at the newer L-shaped dock, stern-to with anchors set well out from the bow, and three more tied side-to on the other dock.

Jack jabbed the Beretta into Skip's ribs. "Any Tartans?"

"One. That black-hulled one over there." He pointed to one of the five med-moored boats. "That's a Tartan 33. You said you were looking for a white-hulled boat."

"Yeah, but let's wait a minute. I want to see who's around that one."

"I can't just float around out here in the middle . . . "

Jack cut him off. "No need. Look."

Skip looked back toward the Tartan 33. An attractive woman in her early 30s had come on deck from below, followed by two children in life vests. He looked back to Jack. "Okay, so what now?"

"So where's the nearest place they could've gone?"

Skip hated answering, but the sonofabitch knew where to find Char. "That'd be Quarry Bay. Over there." He pointed to the southwest along the shore of the Island.

Jack squinted, looking along Skip's arm. "I don't see anything."

"That's because it's in a cove. There's a wooden dock in there and anchorage space too."

"Okay, let's go. Now." He jabbed Skip's ribs again for emphasis.

Skip throttled up a little and swung around to idle back out. This is getting old, he thought — this bastard is going to get . . . there was another, sharper jab. "Ouch! Dammit, what now?"

" I said, let's GO!"

"I have to get clear of the area before I throttle up. I'll throw a big wake and . . . "

"I don't give a shit about your wake. Get this thing moving!"

Skip half turned to face Jack. "Look," he said, "the last thing you want is to draw a lot of attention. That's a sure way to do it. I throw a big wake inside here, they're all up in arms and some of them might even call the Coast Guard or the Park Service. You really want me to do that?"

"Okay, you're right. Just get us out of here." Jack backed away a little.

Skip idled *Blue Moon* out past the end of the breakwater and swung her to port a little, When he had cleared everything, he throttled up a little, gaining speed until he felt he was far enough out. Then he gave the engine its head, and the stern settled in as the bow rose and *Blue Moon* sped away toward the south end of the island. The chop was building, and the ride was a bit rough, but Jack didn't seem to care. Skip saw that he was still standing, gripping the rail with one hand and holding the Beretta steady with the other.

July 25, 7:50 p.m. CDT

The wind was increasing now, and whitecaps were building in the open water south of where *Pipe Dream* rode by the South Twin dock. In the cockpit, Paul shifted his position for comfort and somberly scanned the sky; this was turning into a fairly good southeast blow. He looked across the gap between South Twin and Rocky Island. He could see that fairly good-sized waves were running through the Rocky Island anchorage and breaking on the shore near the dock. He spoke softly to *Pipe Dream,* "We wouldn't want to be over there."

Below, Rich had been tossing on the settee, trying without much success to get some rest. He had drifted in and out of sleep for a minute or two, but it seemed that every noise, every motion of the boat brought him back awake. He wished he could just go to sleep, then wake up and find it had all been a nightmare. This wasn't working. He sat up and swung his legs over the side of the settee.

Paul heard the motion and looked at his watch. He called to Rich, "Stay put. I've got the watch."

Rich had already reached the companionway. "It's no good. I can't sleep at all. Between the motion and my little problem, I just can't relax."

Paul regarded Rich for a brief time, then rubbed his hands together against the chill northern air. "Fire up the stove and put on some water to boil. I could use a cup of hot tea."

"Anything in it?" Rich was smiling, holding up the bottle of Black Bush.

"Uhhh . . . no, I think we might want to stay alert. But it was a good idea." Paul returned Rich's smile. Good sign, he thought to himself.

Rich put the whiskey down, then turned

back to Paul. "I can really see now why this appeals to you so much. You used to talk about buying a boat and doing this when we were in college."

Paul shifted has weight and faced Rich directly. "Yeah, I always thought it would be great to live like this. You never thought I'd do it, but you know something? You named this boat."

"I did what?"

"You named the boat. It was when we were getting shit-faced over a bottle of Canadian Club — I think it was after second term finals, junior year — and I was going on about sailing all over the world and writing about it. Remember what you said?"

"I could hardly remember my own name after that night. What was it I said?"

"You said, and I quote: 'Findlay, that's nothing but a stupid pipe dream.' I never forgot that, and when I got the boat, it just fit."

"I'll be damned! Guess I was good for something."

"More than you know," replied Paul. "More than you know."

July 25, 8:06 p.m. CDT

It had been a short, rough ride in the

building seas, but *Blue Moon* was now idling into the anchorage at Quarry Bay. Skip was relieved; there were no sailboats at all in the anchorage. He hadn't seen any as they passed earlier on their way to Presque Isle Point, but you never knew. The only boat there was a small power cruiser, anchored fairly close to the wooden dock.

"Let's talk to this guy." Jack was standing directly behind Skip's right shoulder, the pistol at Skip's back.

Skip balked. "He's not going to know a thing. He probably wouldn't recognize a Tartan if he saw one. Most powerboaters don't pay much attention to the rag hangers."

"Let me be the judge of that." Jack's voice was cold, very low.

"Okay, but don't hurt anybody. I'll play along, just leave 'em be after we talk." Skip turned the wheel and idled toward the cruiser. There was a single man on the bridge, lighting a cigar. He waved to them and Skip waved back. "Wave," he said to Jack. "Everybody does."

Jack shrugged and shifted the Beretta to his left hand, then raised his right hand and smiled. "That good enough for you?"

Skip ignored the comment. *Blue Moon* was within easy talking distance of the cruiser, so he shifted into reverse to bring her to a standstill alongside and about twenty feet off. He waved again to the man on the cruiser, hailing him as he did so. "Looks like it'll be kickin' up soon."

The man stood, waved back and replied, "Yeah, I'm gonna pull the hook and beat it back to LaPointe." He recognized *Blue Moon* as a charter fishing boat and went on. "You're out late. Been catchin' any?"

Skip started to answer, but Jack interrupted. "No, we aren't out for fish this trip. We're looking for some friends of ours. They said they were going to be on a sailboat, a white Tartan, maybe 34 to 37 feet. Have you seen anything like that?"

"Yeah," came the reply from the cruiser, "There was a T-37 in here a couple hours back. Didn't stay long. I don't know if that was your friends. Two guys. I didn't see anybody else."

"Sounds like 'em." Jack was intent now. "What was the boat name?"

"Dunno — I didn't pay much attention." The cruiser skipper looked down for minute, thinking, then looked back at *Blue Moon*. "Started with a 'P', I think . . . Maybe Pepper something or Piper something."

Jack pressed for more information. "Did they say where they were headed?"

"No. They didn't talk to me. They lit out of

here headed south, but that could take 'em anywhere."

Jack was about to shout something back when Skip whispered to him, "He doesn't know. You have what you wanted, so leave him alone. Please."

Jack thought for a moment, looked at the cruiser and then at the Beretta in his left hand. He whispered, "His lucky day," to Skip. He waved to the cruiser with his free right hand, shouting a thank you. "Okay," he said to Skip, "Let's move. Get us going and then you tell me where you think they're headed."

Skip pushed the throttle forward, and once again *Blue Moon* raised her bow and began to accelerate, leaving the cruiser rocking in the wake behind them. He hoped against hope that the discourtesy would raise doubts in the man's mind, but the realist in him knew the most the guy would do would be to utter an obscenity and go below. Maybe another way to deal with this . . . "Listen,' he started, "with this weather closing in I'd bet they headed back to Bayfield, or maybe LaPointe. If we . . . " The sudden blow along his right cheek made his ear ring like a bell; he staggered and fell as Jack grabbed the wheel.

"No more delays!" Jack was shouting now, angry. "You look at your goddam map and tell me where you think he went! And no more shit!"

Skip pulled himself up, standing unsteadily as his head cleared. He felt his cheek . . . sore, but wet . . . he looked at his hand and saw the blood along his fingers where he had touched the gash. Damn, he thought — bastard smacked me with that gun. "Okay," he said aloud, "just a second." He bent to look at the chart beneath the spray glass. He'd have to make a guess and hope it was wrong. He really hoped the skipper on that Tartan had balls of steel and was headed out on the big lake. The boat could take it, he knew, and that would sure get them out of this bastard's reach. Finally, his finger settled on the narrow gap between Rocky Island and South Twin Island. "Here," he said, "That's where I'd go."

Jack looked at Skip, then out at the building seas. "Better be right." He settled in behind Skip, dropping to take a seat, the Beretta aimed dead at Skip's back. "I'd hate to have to take this boat in someplace by myself."

Blue Moon continued around the south tip of Stockton Island and headed west-northwest toward Manitou. Skip switched on the running lights as the setting sun grew low.

Chapter 6

CONTACT

July 25, 8:14 p.m. CDT

The big Ford SUV cruised along the streets of Bayfield, the three men inside looking intently at the parked cars. The driver was a heavy, broad-shouldered man with unkempt brown hair framing a blocky face, the nose red and off-center from one too many brawls. The short collar of his black leather jacket was turned slightly up on one side, but he obviously didn't care. At his right sat a second big man, this one not as muscular. His size was due to a fondness for pasta and other high carbohydrate foods. He was balding, but wisps of graying black hair were combed over from the sides in an attempt to hide it. His stained brown cardigan sweater bulged at the front buttons.

"We been down this street twice, eh?" The nasal voice came from the younger man in the rear seat. He was thin and wiry, with a sardonic expression permanently grafted to his face. He had the beginnings of a beard and mustache, but the light blonde of the stubble made him simply look odd. His hair was worn long, half covering his ears, and he kept pushing it up out of his eyes as he spoke. The two men in the front considered him a smartass and not worth the trouble, but the boss had told them to take him along.

"Shut the fuck up, Mike." It was the driver

speaking. "I'm headin' down where all the tourists park, see. Down past the marina. Best way to get there is down this street . . . so like I said, shut up."

In the passenger's seat, Sam laughed, short and crisp. "Give 'im a break, Bruno. He don't know shit."

Mike piped up again, the nasal voice at a higher pitch now. "All I'm sayin' is, we been past that Pier place three times already. The sonofabitch ain't here. Now we're drivin' around like idiots. We're gonna end up in trouble."

Sam half turned to look at Mike. "Kid," he said, "what I hear about this 'sonofabitch' is, he'll eat your lunch before you know it's breakfast time. Just keep it down and keep lookin'. Remember, black Explorer with Illinois plates."

The big white Expedition reached the foot of Manypenny Avenue, turned right toward the Coast Guard office, and passed by a small public restroom. To the left, a park and an adjacent parking lot marked the south end of the Apostle Islands Marina. The parking lot was full, with cars, trucks, and SUVs from all over the midwest. Sam shifted his bulk in the front passenger's seat, then pointed toward the end of the long row of cars. "Coupla possibilities down there."

"Yeah, I see 'em." Bruno accelerated slightly toward the end of the row. There were two Ford Explorers parked side-by-side, facing the marina. The nearest was dark blue, and had Michigan tags. The second was black. As they neared it, they could make out Illinois plates.

"Bingo! About damn time!" Mike was already opening the back door.

Bruno braked as Mike jumped out. "Christ, kid! At least let me stop! Dumb ass!" He shifted to Park, leaving the Expedition idling, and he and Sam got out to join Mike at the Explorer. In the back of the Explorer, behind the rear seat, there was a small, wheeled suitcase. Hanging along the right rear door was a black suit, a tie neatly draped around the stem of the hanger.

Mike looked at the suit, then stepped back. "Sure as hell don't look like no tourist."

"This is our guy." Bruno replied. "Gotta be. So where the hell is he?"

The three men stood by the Explorer for a few minutes, hoping its driver would return. Bruno looked down the line of cars back toward the public rest rooms; nobody even close to the description could be seen.

Sam turned and gestured toward the line of wooden dock fingers next to the lot. "Let's try this guy." He was pointing to an elderly man seated on a bucket near the end of one of the fingers. At his feet there was a small tacklebox and a plastic container with dirt and worms. He held a fishing rod in his hand and seemed intent on the red and white bobber floating in the water.

Sam walked out on the finger, gesturing to Mike and Sam to stay back. "How they goin' tonight?"

The old man turned slightly, not looking at Sam but acknowledging him with a nod. "Hardly nothin' all day. It's been like that the whole week." He pulled in the bobber and raised the line, looking with disgust at the sodden worm on the hook. He stripped off the old worm, dipped his fingers into the plastic container and took out a live one.

"Been here all day, then?"

"You betcha. This has been my spot for years. Ain't worth shit right now, but it'll come around." He double-hooked the fresh worm and tossed his line, sinker and bobber back in.

"So, do you remember seein' anybody at this truck?" Sam pointed to the parking lot. He motioned to Mike, who went and stood by the black Explorer.

"Looks like someone's there now." The old man was chuckling at his own wit.

Mike started to say something, but Bruno put his hand up. Sam pressed on, a short, forced laugh preceding his words. "Seriously, we're tryin' to find our friend and we just wondered if anybody's seen him."

The old man turned and looked back at the Explorer, then looked up at Sam. "If that guy was your friend, I think he ditched you. He parked there about five, went into town lookin' all important with his suit and tie. Then I seen him come back, running hard. Had all kinds of bags like he'd been shoppin'. He gets in that car, changes out o' that suit and into some new stuff. Looked like a damn tourist. Then he locks that thing and takes off on a run, just him and some new fishin' stuff. I betcha he's already out there, so if you're waitin' for him I'd plan on bein' here awhile."

"Whaddya mean, 'out there'?"

"I mean, if he went on one o' them charter boats, it had to be a special hire. They only go out usually half days and whole days, not late like that. He was runnin' tryin to catch some fool that agreed to take him late, I bet. Sure didn't have a boat of his own."

"So where's these charter boats?"

"Over there, through the park. City dock."

"Thanks. Hope they start biting." Sam turned and motioned to Bruno, and headed down the row of cars past the marina's Travelift, Bruno on his heels. Mike started to follow. Sam looked back and stopped. "Stay with the truck."

"Dammit, I'm comin'. I'm just as . . . "

Bruno stepped in front of him, hand up. "Kid, just do what you're told." Mike looked at the big man, then scowled and sulked back to the big white Expedition.

Sam was walking as fast as his bulk would allow. He puffed, "Goddam kid. He's a hothead, always lookin' to cause trouble."

"He'll take care of that himself, I bet." Bruno walked easily by Sam as he spoke. "He'll cross the wrong guy someday and that'll be the end of him."

"Sooner the better." Sam was breathing hard now . . . he wasn't used to this.

They walked past the marina office, along the shore of the harbor in front of some condominium units, and then finally past the small gazebo across the street from The Pier Restaurant. Turning right, they walked out onto the City Dock.

There were a number of boats in their slips, some with signs indicating that fishing charters could be had, others with ads for sailboat rides. A bearded man in a brown khaki coverall was watching one of the charter boats. He sat in a folding chair alongside the boat. Sam got right to the point.

"We're lookin' for a friend of ours, might

have gone out for a late charter. He would have been by himself."

"Lotta people go in and out. What did he look like?"

"Well, that depends. He could have been down here before, in a business suit, then come back later to go out dressed different."

"Yeah, I seen 'im. Strange duck. He was talking to Skip, left, and then came back with all new stuff. Probably don't know a fish from a muskrat."

"He went out with this Skip?"

"You betcha, a while back. Funny thing . . . real late in the day, and it was just him. Skip usually has three or four guys, but not this time. Guy's a big spender, eh?"

"So which boat is he on?"

"Sign's right there: *Blue Moon*." Mr. Khaki pointed to Skip's sign.

"Thanks." Sam pulled out a small note pad and a pen, writing down the information from the sign. He nodded to Bruno and the pair headed back toward the shore. "Gotta call Chicago."

Bruno reached inside his jacket and pulled out a cell phone, flipping it open. "What's the number?"

"Screw that. I'm calling from one of those." He walked toward a pair of pay phones alongside The Pier Restaurant. "When we're on one of these jobs, I don't want nothin' out over the air." He puffed along until he had reached the phones, stopped at the first and quickly dialed in credit card information. He pulled out his notepad and leafed back a couple of pages, then punched in a number and waited. "Bruno, watch for that dumb ass kid. He better've stayed at the truck."

"Yeah." Bruno looked back across the park toward the marina. "So who's this you're callin'?"

"Dunno, somebody in Chicago. They just gave me this number and told me what to say." He stopped, suddenly listening to the phone. "Yeah, uh . . . it's about the Perry contract." He listened intently for a minute, then spoke: "Your guy's out charter fishing." A pause, then, "That's what I said . . . What? . . . Name of the fishing boat's *Blue Moon* . . . No, I don't know what he's looking for."

Bruno looked at Sam. "Ask 'em what the hell we're doin' here."

Sam raised his hand, then made a slashing motion across his throat. He was listening intently now, then reached back for the pad and pen. "Wait a sec. Okay, go." He wrote furiously, then spoke again. "Okay, is this right? He's landing on this Madeline Island, about 10 o'clock? We take the ferry over . . . Okay, we'll meet him there." Sam hung up the phone.

Bruno adjusted his stance. "So what's the deal?"

Sam was already walking back toward the Expedition. "Let's go get dumb ass and the truck. We gotta catch a ferry. The Chicago guy says his boss is comin' in on a private plane, tonight, and we gotta pick him up." He quickened his pace as he puffed along the shore toward the marina, Bruno striding easily alongside.

July 25, 8:39 p.m. CDT

Blue Moon was running alongside Manitou Island, the old fishing camp off to starboard passing as they flew along. Jack was impatient. "Put some speed on!"

Skip half-turned, watching the seas ahead while answering. "This ain't exactly planing water. I'm goin' as fast as I can without pounding the hell out of everything. Notice how they're building up?"

"Just keep it going, then, but don't hold back. You get us to that place you pointed out. And I'm watching this map, so don't try anything."

"You'll get there." Skip was growing more desperate; he now knew without a doubt that he wouldn't live through the night unless something changed, and changed soon. He thought back to the dock at Bayfield, and his initial gut feeling as Jack had talked him into going out. He thought, "Dumb shit. Should have followed your instincts." Then his thoughts turned to the people on that sailboat. What had they done? Who had they pissed off this much? He started the broad turn as they passed little Manitou and began to run northeasterly along Otter Island.

Behind him, Jack was staring at the chart, then at the Islands. "Good boy. Just keep it going." *Blue Moon* roared on, closing the distance between herself and *Pipe Dream*.

July 25, 8:42 p.m. CDT

Paul drained the last of the tea, savoring its warmth as it slid down his throat. He'd talked Rich into a cup as well. Rich was using his more for a hand warmer than as a drink. He sat with both hands wrapped around the cup, fingers intertwined, and he looked up at Paul. "Have you decided where we'll head?"

"For tonight, nowhere. This stuff is still building up and anyplace would be a rough ride. You don't want that on Lake Superior, especially at night. I'll figure it out by morning, and we can get out of here." He put his empty cup down in the galley sink, then turned and slid open the companionway hatch. "I'll be right back down. I just need to check the anchor rode."

Rich watched Paul disappear above, then returned to his cup to pull the warmth from the tea into his hands.

July 25, 8:57 p.m. CDT

Skip turned the wheel slightly, and *Blue Moon* answered by swinging to Port. They were rounding the northeast tip of Otter Island, and Rocky and South Twin Islands were coming into view to the north. Behind him, Jack stood, looked at the chart, and then at Skip. "That the place?"

Skip didn't want to answer, but there wasn't much choice. "Yeah, that's it."

"Okay, keep heading in there. Where's your binoculars?" Skip was silent. After a minute, Jack pushed him hard. "I said where are your goddam binoculars?"

Skip bent and pulled the binoculars from their slot and handed them reluctantly to Jack. "Don't be there." He thought to himself, but straining to see in the waning light through the spray-spattered glass, he thought he could make out a sailboat, over along South Twin. Another, single worded thought: "Shit." He looked back to find Jack leaning out around the glass, binoculars to his eyes. It would be so easy, one push . . . Jack lowered the binoculars and raised the Beretta, glaring at Skip. The sudden hope vanished as quickly as it had risen.

Jack moved to the wheel, handing the binoculars to Skip. "Take a look." He said. "Is that a Tartan 37?"

Skip hesitated and was rewarded with another sharp jab to the ribs. He left Jack at the wheel, stepped to the side, and grudgingly raised the binoculars and looked. He could feel the bile rise in his throat as he recognized the profile. Stalling, he lowered the binoculars, then looked back to Jack. "Can't tell."

Jack's voice went low and very menacing. "You tell me now if that's them. Tell me wrong and you're dead right now, and from here I'll still get them if that's the boat. Then I'll get back in and do Char and her sister. Your choice. NOW!!"

Skip looked at his shoes, and mumbled, "It could be."

Jack returned to the side and raised the binoculars again, then smiled. "Got you, you little prick." He threw the binoculars to the seat and turned to Skip. "Pick it up. Head straight for that sailboat."

July 25, 8:59 p.m. CDT

Paul knelt at the bow, his practiced eye checking the chafing gear around the anchor rode. He had already made certain they stood well enough off the dock and the anchor was holding the bow steadily out into the channel. Satisfied, he rose to return below. The sound of an engine came to him on the wind and he looked to the south. Off the tip of Otter Island, he could see the powerboat pounding along, throwing great gouts of water and spray as she made for the anchorage. He watched for a minute, then went back into the cockpit. He started down, then stopped halfway to turn and watch the powerboat.

Rich sensed something in Paul's posture, in his hesitation. "What's the matter?" He said, standing as he put down his cup.

"Powerboat coming this way. Probably just a fisherman wanting to tuck in out of this stuff."

"Are you sure?"

"Yeah, that has to be it," Paul lied. He wasn't sure, but a nagging doubt was building in the pit of his stomach.

July 25, 9:03 p.m. CDT

Jack grabbed Skip by the arm. "I have to get my tools. You head for that boat and don't slow down. If I feel any change in our course . . . " He didn't finish the sentence. He gave Skip a hard glare and then turned and went below. Skip watched Jack disappear, thoughts racing . . . what to do . . . jumping is out of the question . . . I'd never survive it in this water . . . Wish I could warn . . .

Skip looked toward the companionway, then

back at his console. The radio . . . Skip turned the speaker volume down, very low. He gripped the microphone and keyed it, mouth close to the mike, almost whispering: "Sailboat at South Twin." He would usually give his call sign and vessel name, but there was no time. Listening, ear close to the speaker . . . no answer. Again, he keyed the mike. "Sailboat at South Twin." For the love of God, answer.

Aboard *Pipe Dream*, Paul was standing in the companionway, still watching the powerboat. The radio crackled to life. "Sailboat . . . South . . . " The voice was low, almost unreadable. It sounded like a whisper or interference of some kind. He turned and regarded the radio, reaching for the squelch control. Then again, this time clearer: "Sailboat at South Twin." Rich sat up, eyes wide. "Is he calling for us?" Paul put a finger to his lips, signaling for quiet.

Aboard *Blue Moon*, there was still no answer. Skip looked behind him, then keyed the mike again. "Sailboat at South Twin. If you're a Tartan, you have big trouble . . . " He saw a fleeting motion to his right before the pistol butt rendered him unconscious. Skip's form slid from the helm seat, his hand dragging the throttle down as he fell. The boat slowed and turned to port. Jack inspected the butt of his pistol, then withdrew a handkerchief from his pocket, clearing the end of traces of blood and hair. He looked down at Skip's still form, bleeding from the scalp. "Can't kill you yet," he said. "I might need you." He pushed Skip the rest of the way from the helm seat and took his place. Getting his bearings, he turned the boat back toward the distant form of the white sailboat, then pushed the throttle forward. The boat settled at the stern as the engine began to push the hull inexorably toward its target.

Aboard *Pipe Dream*, Paul needed no confirmation. The cryptic message cut off in mid-sentence and the sudden veer and slowing of the powerboat told the whole story. Somehow, they had been found. "Damn!" He yelled. "They're coming!" He jumped through the companionway to the cockpit, held in the preheat and checked the throttle, then started the diesel. Rich was near panic. "Oh, God, he's here! I'm dead! He's going to . . ."

Paul returned below, grabbing Rich by the arm and spinning him until their faces were close. "Dammit, Rich! Look at me! You want out of this? I need your help, now!! We have to let the anchor go and run for the rougher water. We'll be more stable than he is. We'll have a better chance than if we just sit here and wait for him! Now, get on deck! And stay low!" He sprang up back up through the companionway, then turned back to Rich. "Before you come up, look in the hanging locker, starboard side, just past the settee. There's a rifle and a box of ammunition. Get it and bring it up on deck with you, and like I said, stay low!"

On deck, Paul looked south. The powerboat was still coming in fast, still pounding through the waves. There wouldn't be time to do anything about the anchor. He went to the wheel, leaned down and revved the diesel. He left it running at idle speed and put the transmission in forward . . . "Gotta keep her off the dock," he thought as he went quickly forward. He reached into his pocket for the rigging knife he always carried, then knelt at the bow, looked back toward the powerboat and sawed away at the nylon anchor rode until it parted. The free end whipped out to disappear in the cold waters, while the cleated end snapped back and almost took the knife out of his hand. He felt a momentary sense of regret, knowing a 35-pound CQR anchor, chain, and rode were gone. A look back to the south told him the decision was the right one. The powerboat suddenly slowed, then resumed speed, accelerating toward them.

As Paul stepped quickly back to the cockpit, Rich was still fumbling around below, pulling the old 30.06 from the hanging locker and locating the box of ammunition. He had them now, but somehow holding the rifle gave him no comfort. He stood and lurched aft to the companionway and came halfway up. Paul was now bent over the stern, cutting the lines that held *Pipe Dream* to the dock. As the last line parted, Paul turned and quickly applied throttle, turning the wheel to starboard. They began to move away from the dock and into the channel between the islands.

Blue Moon pounded northward through the chop. With Skip unconscious, Jack wrestled with the helm and with his rifle. He had assembled it and put the magazine in it below, but now the seas were making it difficult to prepare or aim. The life vest was also binding, and he set the rifle down and quickly shed the vest. He picked the rifle up and dropped the folding window in front of him; he now had a clear look at the sailboat, and it was moving! Heading away from the dock! "Sonofoabitch!" he yelled, now keeping pressure on the wheel with his knee while he aimed. Through the scope, he could see a figure at the wheel. He also thought he could make out someone in the hatch. The image in the scope was bouncing, unsteady. This wouldn't be easy. He squeezed off two quick shots.

SPANG! Aboard *Pipe Dream*, Paul jumped at the sound. Jack's first round had struck the mast, just below the gooseneck. He heard a THUD and felt a spray of splinters as the second hit the teak toerail just aft of his port primary winch. He looked at Rich, kneeling in the companionway. "Give me that rifle!" he roared, making sure he was heard over the diesel and the wind.

"I . . . I'm trying!" Rich stuttered, his hands unsteady as he hefted the rifle up through the companionway.

"You have to come up! Just stay low when you do!" Paul was looking back over his shoulder, first at Rich, then back to the nearing cruiser. He could hear it over the diesel. He looked back to Rich, who had made it into the cockpit and was duck-walking between the seats.

Aboard *Blue Moon*, Jack noticed the seas lessening. They were entering the lee of South Twin Island. "Good," he said to himself, "Now it's steadier." He throttled back a bit, and then propped his knee back against the wheel. The sailboat was growing larger, and he could clearly see a second man, low in the cockpit. He noted the general profile and the receding hair . . . he was sure it was Perry. He checked the magazine, then raised the rifle. "Steady, steady . . . " the motion was still too much for good aim, but he couldn't let them get out in the rough stuff. His finger moved and with the motion came a sharp staccato burst as three rounds left the muzzle.

Paul was half-turned toward the oncoming boat. Before he saw or heard anything, he was pulled violently forward and to the side as one bullet tore across the front of his life vest, less than an inch from entering his chest. His hand still held the wheel, and his sudden lurch pulled the wheel around. As the second and third rounds smashed into the cabin trunk, *Pipe Dream* swung suddenly to starboard. Rich had just begun to stand, holding up the rifle toward Paul. The sudden turn threw him off balance, and he fell against the port lifelines. The rifle was knocked from his hand, and it arced out over the churning water, disappearing at last with a small splash.

On *Blue Moon*, Jack watched the sudden veer of the sailboat, and smiled grimly. "Showtime," he muttered, slowing *Blue Moon* to an idle. He raised the rifle once again, this time steady, this time intent on the kill. He could see the man who had been at the wheel trying to regain control and he could clearly see the second man. He now was half standing, half sitting, seemingly frozen in place like a deer in the headlights. He put his eye to the scope and centered in; now the features were plain, even in the dusk. It was Perry. "Game over, you little shit." He thought to himself. With the practiced calm of the sniper, he steadied his grip and began a slow exhale to ready his shot.

On *Pipe Dream*, it seemed to Paul that everything was happening in slow motion. He could see the powerboat, very near now, could see the rifle in the hands of the would-be killer. *Pipe Dream* had come to a dead stop; in the commotion, her transmission lever had been knocked back to neutral. The diesel was running too high, and the subconscious part of Paul that was still rational pulled back the throttle by force of habit. He could see Rich, not moving, staring in horror back to the powerboat. He couldn't stop it, couldn't move quickly enough . . . If he could only throw something in front of Rich, but it was too late, too late . . .

Jack had finished his exhale now, and the crosshairs in the scope were centered on Rich's head. He began to squeeze the trigger slowly, slowly . . .

He did not see the blood covered hand reaching up from the deck, pushing the throttle all the way up. As *Blue Moon* leapt forward, Jack was thrown backward, the shot he had aligned so carefully whizzing harmlessly into the overcast sky. *Blue Moon* was speeding directly toward the sailboat now, and as Jack struggled to stand, the bloody hand yanked the wheel hard over.

The sounds came simultaneously; the crack of the rifle shot and the sudden roar of the powerboat's engine. Rich winced at the first sound, throwing his hands up, but even as he did so the bow of the powerboat rose and she began to career toward *Pipe Dream.* Paul had regained his position behind the wheel, but now he knew it was over; they would ram him, and there was nothing he could do about it. He stood watching as the powerboat roared toward the meeting.... and then suddenly, inexplicably, she turned sharply to port. The turn was violent and uncontrolled; the stern was now toward them, and Paul made out the name *Blue Moon* as the boat continued its tight turn. The wake struck *Pipe Dream,* and she rocked as the powerboat spun out of control nearby. Finally, as if fulfilling a death wish, *Blue Moon* struck her own wake. The sudden change in the buoyant forces, coupled with the angular momentum of the turn, were her undoing, and she rolled suddenly back to starboard and then flipped completely over. Two figures were catapulted off the bridge. *Blue Moon* landed upside down, and her screaming engine suddenly stopped. The upturned hull rocked side to side for a minute and settled to bob steadily in the waves. One head, then a second, broke the surface near the hull.

Paul thought he would never breathe again; he exhaled loudly and then looked at Rich. "Christ, that was close! You okay?"

Rich was staring blankly at the overturned powerboat. "He . . . he tried to kill me . . . he was . . . he was this close . . ." He slowly stood and looked at Paul. "We have to get out of here."

Paul looked back to the men near the powerboat. One was floating, face up, a life jacket keeping him that way. He was still, eyes closed. The second was struggling, clawing at the rounded hull, trying desperately for a handhold. He was panicking, and Paul could see that he wore no life vest. Turning to the rail, Paul opened the case on his LifeSling, removed the long coil of line and pulled the sling out. He held the coils in his left hand, gripped the sling in his right hand and stood at the stern, preparing to throw. As he made ready, the man at the hull slipped beneath the waves. He surfaced again, gasping, grasping, and Paul threw the sling as hard as he could; it didn't quite reach. The struggling man submerged again, splashed briefly to the surface, and then disappeared. He did not reappear.

Rich was looking on in disbelief. "What the hell were you thinking?" he screamed, tears rolling down his face. "The sonofabitch was going to kill us both!"

Paul was hauling in the line, retrieving the sling. He didn't look at Rich. "One thing you learn out here is that there are no enemies when someone's in trouble at sea. We don't even know if it was the shooter."

"But suppose it was? You'd have him right here, where he could . . . "

"Could *what*? After a few minutes in this water, the best he could have done was shiver you to death. We could have picked them both up, tied them up and taken them back to Bayfield . . . then we'd have let the cops sort them out." He pulled the LifeSling in over the rail, laid it down on the seat behind the wheel, and put the transmission in forward. "Let's get that one." He turned the wheel and headed for the second man.

Rich was still nearly hysterical. "What if he's the guy?"

"Then he's the guy. We don't leave him in this water. Suppose he's a victim? How'll you feel knowing you let another innocent man die?"

Rich's breathing slowed; he looked sheepishly at Paul. "I . . . I never thought of it that way. But be careful of him. He might still have a gun . . . "

"He's out like a light, maybe dead already. Now get over here. I'm going to need your help." Paul had worked *Pipe Dream* to a position just upwind of the unconscious man, and had put her in neutral. As they drifted down toward the lone figure, Paul retrieved a telescoping boathook from the cockpit locker and extended it. He yelled to Rich, "Go and get the main halyard, just like I showed you when we raised the main. Release that sheet stopper and let it run." He watched as Rich pulled up on the stopper to free the halyard, then went to the starboard shrouds, unscrewing the headboard shackle from its stowed position. "Good man. You'll make a sailor yet. Now bring it across the boom and hand it to me."

Rich did as he was told, and Paul now held the shackle in his hand, the halyard slack as it arced up toward the masthead. Paul handed the boathook to Rich. "Use this and snag him to bring him alongside. You're gonna have to hold him there while I hook him up." Rich moved to the rail, then looked down. The unconscious man floated in his life vest, face up, within a couple of feet of the hull. His eyes were closed; there was a deep gash on his right cheek, and his hair was matted with blood.

Paul motioned to Rich. "Okay, now hook him! Work it in under that top tie on his vest."

Rich strained to work the business end of the boathook through the nylon web that passed just under the man's chin. At last, seeing the end of the hook under the web, he gave the handle a turn and the webbing was trapped in the hook. The motion of the boat in the waves made it difficult to hold the man steady against the hull, but he tried his best. Paul was bent low, fumbling around his feet; Rich saw that he had retrieved a mooring line and tied one end around his right ankle, the other end around the steering pedestal. "Okay," Paul said. "Hold him there." Paul passed the halyard outboard over the top lifeline. Then he crawled beneath the lower of the two lifelines, reaching downward with one hand, the other hand clutching the shackle. After several tries, a larger wave rolled them down toward the unconscious man, and Paul was able to grab the web of the vest. "Don't let go with that boathook!" he grunted. His other hand pulled the shackle downward, and after a couple of false starts he was able to secure the shackle around the web. He tightened it as best he could, until he was certain the threads were fully engaged; then he pulled himself back from beneath the lifeline and stood, shaking from the effort.

Rich was still holding the boathook. "What do we do now?"

Paul crossed to the starboard side and returned the sheet stopper lever over the halyard to its locked position. "Rich, I'm gonna winch him up. Grab the halyard and steady him as he comes up. When you can get his legs over the lifelines, you pull him in." He took three turns with the halyard around the winch on the cabintop, just aft of the sheet stopper. He took a final turn over the stripper and around the winch jaws, then retrieved a winch handle from a pocket along the seat. Seating the handle in the winch, he began to grind, first in one direction, then in the other as he realized he would need the lower gear ratio to pull the man up. The halyard tightened, then began to move upward toward the masthead. The shackle tugged at the webbing of the life vest until the man's full weight was resisting the pull. Paul bore down and exerted himself at the winch, and slowly, slowly, the man was lifted from the water.

Rich held the boathook in his right hand and guided the halyard with his left hand, keeping it from sliding forward along the hull. He reached out with his left hand and grabbed hold of the life vest as it rose to meet his grasp. He untangled the boathook from the webbing and threw it back into the cockpit, then held on to the unconscious figure with both hands. Paul was straining at the winch, and Rich began to coach him: "About another foot, that's it . . . 10 inches . . . 7 . . . just a little more . . . Okay! I think we can get him!" He began to pull the heavy body inward, the legs resisting as they struck the lifelines; then Paul was there, and the two of them wrestled the man into the cockpit. Paul went back to the winch, unwound the halyard from it, and raised the sheet stopper lever. The figure in the life jacket slumped to the cockpit floor.

Paul was panting with the exertion. "Get him below. I have to get us secured somehow." He opened the cockpit locker and retrieved a smaller anchor, an aluminum Fortress. It had several feet of chain and a nylon rode attached. He pulled the coiled rode on deck and secured the bitter end to a cleat at the stern; then he lifted the anchor over the stern rail and held it there, while he shifted into forward. As *Pipe Dream* gathered way, he eased the anchor into the water and then quickly paid out the rode, watching colored markers in the weave of the rode go by. They told him how many feet were out. He was doing quick calculations now; "About 25 feet, let's do at least 6 to 1 . . . 150 feet . . . there, that ought to do it. He snubbed the rode around the cleat and shifted to neutral, and *Pipe Dream* pulled the rode taught. After watching for a minute to assure himself the anchor was set, Paul took a locking turn around the cleat, pulled the throttle down to idle, and pulled up on the kill switch. The silence was sudden and welcome. He rose and went below.

Rich had pulled the man down through the companionway and everything below was soaked. As Paul stepped to the cabin sole, he almost slipped on the wet teak and holly. Rich, he could see, had already pulled the life vest off the unconscious man, who was sprawled in a sodden heap on the sole. Rich was standing, looking down at the still figure. "Is he dead?" he said, quietly, his eyes moving from the figure to Paul and then back.

In answer, the man shuddered and coughed. His lips were blue, and the blood on his cheek and scalp gave him an almost cadaver-like appearance, but he was alive. Paul knew it was important to warm him up. "Let's get those clothes off him. There are blankets forward, stowed under the starboard V-berth cushions. Lift the cushion, there's a hatch with a fingerhole . . . " Paul had bent to the man and was unbuttoning the shirt, struggling to pull it off. He decided it was better to work quickly and worry about the clothes later. He pulled out his rigging knife and began to cut the stubborn garments away.

In a few minutes, Paul had cut the man's soggy clothing away, and the blankets Rich had retrieved were wrapped around him. He was shivering uncontrollably, now barely conscious. Paul stood and went to the galley, where he had placed the man's wallet and the other contents of his pockets. "Let's see who we have," he said, opening the soaked wallet and leafing through the plastic sleeves until he found what he wanted. He read the Wisconsin Driver's License, looked at the photo and looked back to the shivering man. "Rich," he said, "This isn't the shooter."

Rich heaved a sigh. "Who is he?"

"His license says his name is Gordon L. Meyer. He lives right there in Bayfield."

"Sk-skip." The low whisper came from the settee; the man was conscious now, his eyes open. He still shivered as he looked at Paul.

Paul leaned down, put his hand on the man's shoulder. "Take it easy. You'll be okay, but you've got to warm up."

"Skip." The voice was stronger now, audible. "They call me Skip."

"Okay, Skip. For what it's worth, welcome aboard. We're going to get you warmed up and then we'll talk."

"W-Where is h-he?" Skip said, a quiver in his voice. "The g-guy who was a-after you?"

"Gone. Drowned. We saw him go under."

A shuddering sigh of relief escaped through Skip's lips, which were regaining some color. "G-good. N-never thought I'd be glad somebody bought it."

Paul was kneeling to look at Skip's wounds. "Yeah, well, if somebody did this to me I'd be glad to see him gone." He turned to Rich. "There's a first-aid kit in the head. Get it, and alongside in the same cabinet there's a roll of gauze." He turned back and began looking at Skip's scalp wound, gingerly moving the hair to expose the gash. Skip winced as he got too close.

"Ahhgh . . . He pistol-whipped me. First here," he touched his cheek, where the blood had clotted, "then he clubbed me over the head right after we saw you. I was trying to call . . . "

"We know. We heard you, and we started to make a run for it. It wasn't much good. We thought we were done."

Rich had retrieved the first-aid kit and the gauze and now handed them to Paul. "I saw some alcohol in there. I'll get it."

"Thanks. We'll need some water, too, and one of the towels." Paul continued to clear the hair from the scalp wound. "You're going to have a nice egg for a while. He clipped you pretty good."

"He was below, I guess after his rifle. I remember calling you . . . and then nothing. When I started to come to, I heard shots. Unnnhhh . . ."

"Sorry. I'll get something on this for you in a second."

"Th-thanks. Anyway, I was laying on the d-deck under the wheel, and he had that r-rifle. He was aiming. I was dizzier 'n hell, but I reached up and jammed the throttle forward."

"I thought HE did that. It looked like he was trying to ram us."

"No, it was me. The b-bastard fell back on his ass, but he started to get back up real quick. All I could think of was to put 'er hard over and throw him off balance again. Then I remember going in the water . . . then I woke up here."

Rich was standing over Paul's shoulder, holding a plastic bottle of rubbing alcohol and some towels. He had heard, and he regarded Skip with a new respect. "You saved us. You . . . you wrecked your boat and saved us."

Skip's eyes widened and went to Rich. "My boat. How bad?"

"Upside down."

Paul interrupted. "Don't worry about your boat. She's inverted, but she'll probably end up ashore over on Rocky the way the wind is headed. Might even be repairable or . . . you're insured, aren't you?"

Skip actually chuckled a bit. "Yeah," he replied, "up to my ass. The bank wanted more coverage than she's worth. I suppose with all the equipment, replacement cost would be higher. Ouch!"

"Just hang in there — I'm almost done." Paul had wiped away the last of the crusted blood and was cleaning the gash with a corner of one of the towels. He had poured alcohol on it, and it stung. "There. Rich, can you get some kind of dressing on this? Try a wad of gauze and one of those ball caps to hold it in place." He gestured toward a hook on the bulkhead, where several baseball style caps hung; most of the caps bore logos from various marine suppliers.

Rich took Paul's place and began to fashion a dressing from the gauze. Paul went to the quarter berth behind the nav station and pulled out a Richardson's Chartbook for Lake Superior. He laid it on the sloping desktop of the nav station and opened it to the sheet showing the western Lake.

Rich had finished with the dressing, laying it

as gently as possible across the wound and then doubling it back over itself. He reached up and took one of the hats, then fitted it carefully over Skip's head to hold the dressing in place. "How's that?" he asked.

Skip reached up, felt the hat and touched the top over the wound. "Good," he replied, "Feels as good as I could expect. My whole head hurts."

"That's no wonder." Rich said. "Paul, you got some aspirin?"

Paul looked up from the chart. "Excedrin. In the kit."

"Okay . . . what are you looking at?"

"Our next move."

Skip was sitting up now and he looked concerned. He pulled the blanket tighter, then spoke. "Not back to town. I'd bet there's more than one. We go back there, first thing that happens is everybody who knows me talks this all over town. Next thing you know, some new asshole is after us. Hell, this bastard knew about my wife!" He was speaking with the knowledge that he was involved in whatever this was. There was no denying it.

Paul regarded him, then the chart. "Okay, Skip . . . what do you think about Corny?"

"Corny?" Rich queried. "What's Corny"

Skip looked at Rich. "Cornucopia. It's a little town a few miles west, on the mainland. Nice little harbor, well protected. He's right. We're about, ummm, 26 to 28 miles away." He turned his gaze to Paul. "How fast can you go?"

"This southeaster, probably 7 plus with just the jenny." He laid the chart aside, and came forward to sit on the settee across from Skip. He looked at his watch. "It'll be real late when we get there — probably after 2 A.M. If there's no space and we can't raise the harbormaster, we can raft off one of the other boats 'til morning."

Skip thought a moment. His eyes rose to meet Paul's. "You think it's a good idea to use the radio?"

"Not as *Pipe Dream*, that's for sure. We'll make up a name, a common one. It's not legal, but somehow I'm not too worried about that right now." Paul got up and moved back to the companionway. "I'm going up and get us straightened out. Then, we'll head out. We can plan our next move on the way." He disappeared into the blustery darkness.

Chapter 7

MADELINE

July 25, 10:03 p.m. CDT

In the dark, the King Air 200 touched down on the Madeline Island runway. It had been an uneventful flight from Chicago, but as the weather worsened the pilot had indicated he was diverting to an alternate airport. He explained that it would be a difficult and uncomfortable crosswind landing at Madeline Island, especially as late as it was. Mansfield had blustered and bullied him into sticking with the original destination. Now, as he brought the plane to a stop in the headlight glare of the waiting SUV, the pilot was making a mental note: "Never fly this prick again."

Bruno, Sam and Mike stood by the Expedition as the plane came to a stop. Waiting until the engines shut down and the props had free-wheeled almost to a standstill, they walked toward the opening cabin door.

Almost before the steps were locked into position, Mansfield alit, travel case in hand. Closely following him was a trim, crew cut man in a crisp brown suit. As Bruno approached to greet Mansfield, the brown suit stepped between them and held up his hand, palm out. "Close enough. Who're you?"

"Uhhh, I'm Bruno. This is Sam. The kid's Mike." He gestured toward his companions; Mike's face grimaced at the term "kid."

Mansfield regarded them, then shouldered past the brown suit. He was direct, to the point. "Tollefson's guys. Tell me you found this guy Jack."

Bruno looked at Mansfield for a minute, then down at his shoes. "He, uh . . . he went out after 'em. He took a charter boat, one of the fishing ones. Left after six."

"So he knew where they went?"

"Dunno . . . We never talked to him."

Mansfield's face grew red. His eyes bored into Bruno's as he stepped very close and leaned into him, almost like a drill instructor. "So Tollefson sends me three more dumb shits! Like I don't have enough lately. Okay . . . how the hell do you know where he went?"

Bruno had backed up a bit at first but now stood firm in front of Mansfield. The big guy could intimidate all he wanted; Bruno wasn't buying it. "Like any decent investigator does. We talked around. Last place anybody saw him, he was on the fishing boat heading out."

Mansfield took stock of the man before him. Somebody with a little bit of guts for a change. No brains, maybe, but guts…. He decided to give him the benefit of the doubt. "Okay, okay . . . Tollefson was supposed to give one of you guys the keys to his condo. He said it's in Bayfield by some kind of marina."

"Yeah," said Bruno, "I got 'em."

Mansfield handed his travel bag to Bruno. "This is all I brought," he said as he walked past him toward the Expedition.

Bruno followed him, with the brown suit alongside. Sam opened the rear cargo gate, and Mike tugged on the handle of the front passenger's door. Sam barked at Mike "That's where he'll sit. Now get your ass back here. We gotta hurry — last ferry back to Bayfield is at 10:30."

Mike had the door open and was getting in. "For Chrissakes, I called shotgun . . . " A hand gripped his shoulder and yanked him backward; he sprawled on the ground, looking up at the brown suit. The man was grinning at him.

Sam gave his short laugh. "Send dumb ass back here. He's ridin' with the luggage." The brown suit reached down and grabbed Mike's collar, yanking him to his feet and shoving him toward the rear of the SUV.

Bruno handed the travel case to Sam, who put it and a glowering Mike in the rear section and slammed the gate. Sam and the brown suit then got into the rear seat, and Mansfield took the front passenger's seat as Bruno slid in and started the engine. Four doors closed with staccato "thunks" and Bruno wheeled the big SUV in a half circle, then accelerated away from the King Air and toward LaPointe and the ferry dock.

July 25, 11.47 p.m. CDT

Pipe Dream had cleared the sand spit on the southern end of Rocky Island, and now headed back northwest to pass west of Bear Island. They were almost on a dead run, with the genoa out to starboard but with no main; they were making just over 7 knots, sometimes almost surfing as they ran before a following sea. The ride was not comfortable and Rich had begun to show signs of seasickness. He had insisted on staying below, though Paul had told him it would not be as bad on deck.

Now, Paul could hear Rich below, and he knew the mal de mer was starting in earnest. "Rich!" he yelled to the companionway, "Get up here! Don't . . . " The retching noises told him it was too late. Rich had made it to the double sink in the galley. There would be a clean-up job when they got to Corny . . .

Skip moved past Rich and came up to sit on the port cockpit seat. He was wearing dry clothing borrowed from Paul and the shirt was a tight fit. He still had the hat pulled down on his head to retain the gauze. The red scrape on his right cheek looked angry but nowhere near as bad as it first had. He looked past Paul at the following seas, then forward to the big genoa. "Nice," he said. "She does real good in this stuff. Can't say as much for him." He nodded at Rich, still bending over the galley sinks.

Paul smiled. "Landlubbers — what can I say?" He thought a minute, then added, "I guess if I had his problems I'd throw up, too." He began to fill Skip in on what Rich had told him as *Pipe Dream* sailed on into the gathering darkness.

July 25, 11:53 p.m. CDT

Weekday nights in Bayfield were generally quite peaceful, and this one was no exception. There was a brisk, but warm, southeast breeze. At this late hour, just a few people strolled the City Dock area and the landscaped walk leading to the Apostle Islands Marina. A group of young men in their twenties and thirties exited a tavern, talking loudly in the manner of those under the influence as they walked toward the docks. With the tavern door ajar, the strains of rock music could be heard tumbling down toward the water, but as the door closed the silence returned. It was broken only by the occasional loud expletive, burp or laugh as the young men disappeared among the boats.

The row of condominiums that stood north of the marina was also quiet, but a second floor window oozed light from within. The shadow of a large man was framed in its glow, moving first one way, then the other.

The shadow's owner was walking back and forth, continuously moving as he peppered the three Minnesotans with questions. Bruno, Mike, and Sam sat on a long sectional sofa, untouched drinks on the side tables, watching Mansfield as he paced. Mansfield stopped again, this time in front of Bruno. "This Meyer guy, he's the one they said took the sonofabitch out. Right?"

"Yeah." Bruno had answered the same question before. He was tired, and just wanted to sleep. "On his charter boat, uhhh, *Blue Moon*. About six or a little after. I already told you."

Mansfield's gaze turned to Sam. Unlike Bruno, Sam was nervous; beads of sweat stood out on his forehead and his palms were moist. He kept rubbing his hands on his knees as he sat, waiting for Mansfield's question. When it came, it was yelled out, directly at Sam. "So, WHERE THE HELL ARE THEY NOW?"

Sam actually recoiled a bit, then recovered, nervously reaching up and pushing his thinning hair back over the top. He didn't look at Mansfield, but answered while looking aside to Bruno. "Don't know. We took the ferry over like they said, and met you, then came back here."

"And you didn't leave shit to watch the docks!" Mansfield was livid, eyes boring into Sam. "This dumb kid would have been better than nobody. Goddam incompetents."

The man who had worn the brown suit now stood at the kitchen counter. The brown suit jacket was off and hung in the closet; the white shirt was open at the collar, the striped tie loosened. The straps of the shoulder holster were in full view. He seldom spoke, but now he interjected, "Go check his dock. You said he had a place down at the City Dock. Go look and see if he's back."

Mansfield turned, looked at him for a moment and then turned back to the row of men on the couch. "Listen to Benjie. One Chicago guy, and he's the only one of you with any brains. Check the dock. Okay, one of you go check it out. Now."

Mike got up, smirking, and headed for the door. He'd had enough of this shit; now it was time for little walk. Mansfield didn't even look at him, but said, "Sit down, kid. One of these senior citizens here is going. At least that way I know they won't be off chasing the first piece of tail that walks by, or end up drunk in some bar."

Mike stopped and turned, the smirk giving way to petulance. "C'mon. I won't . . . "

"I said, SIT DOWN." It wasn't a request, but a command, and even Mike knew enough to obey it. He returned to the couch and sat.

Mansfield continued. "Find out if the boat's back. If not, ask around, see what you can find out. I want this shit over with. If the bastard's done, then that's good. If he's not, you have some real trouble."

If lights were powered by mood rather than electric current, the condo would have grown very dark indeed.

July 26, 1:51 a.m. CDT

Pipe Dream had been on a steady heading of 215 degrees magnetic for the past hour, since passing to the north of Sand Island. She had left tiny Eagle Island and its nearby shoals to port as she pressed steadily toward the southwest. In the cockpit, three figures sat talking while the autopilot maintained the course.

Rich had settled into a dull calm after bouts of seasickness. He was still well under the weather, but had taken Paul's advice to remain on deck, and it had helped. Skip had drawn him into a conversation about the past few days, figuring it would help him to get it all out in the open. Now Rich was describing how he had been able to locate Paul. "So when Gina said he was someplace on the upper lakes, I made up my mind. I thought they would never figure it out."

Paul's concern for Gina had taken over, and the edge in his voice let Rich know it. "You probably put her in danger, you know that? If they found you this easy, I'll bet they already have your cell records."

Rich wouldn't meet Paul's eyes. He sat, pale and drawn, looking at the cockpit sole. "I . . . I didn't think . . . "

"Damn right you didn't!" Paul emphasized his outburst by slamming his open hand on the seat.

Skip looked at the two, then ahead into the darkness. "So call her from Corny. Tell her what's going on and tell her to lay low." He stood, squinting off to port where the greater dark of the mainland could be made out. "Comin' up on Squaw Point."

Squaw Point was a broad headland that marked the eastern end of Siskiwit Bay. After clearing the point, they would head straight in to Cornucopia, which lay at the foot of the bay.

Paul stood with Skip, looking off to port and then back ahead. "Should see the entry lights before long. Let's figure our course in."

Skip thought a minute, then asked, "How fast are we goin'?"

Paul looked back at his instruments, which glowed a ruddy red in the darkness. "About 7 knots in this stuff. Sometimes more, but the wind'll lay down in the lee of the point."

"Okay," Skip answered, "There's only one entry light: a green flasher, two-and-a-half seconds if I remember. We stand on about half a mile after we make it out. That'll be about 5 or 6 minutes at this speed. Then we head about 180 straight down. That clears any problems. The bay's pretty much wide open."

"Nice to have the local knowledge along." Paul grinned, then turned back to Rich. "Rich, I'm sorry I was so . . . " He stopped as he realized he was talking to Rich's back. Rich was once more being noisily ill over the side.

July 26, 2:02 a.m. CDT

The Dewar's swirled over the ice as Mansfield slowly shook his glass. He hadn't slept. He was alone in the living room of the condo, lights down, curtains open. He stood at the window, looking out over the harbor and watching the flashing lights that marked the south entry to the breakwater. He stared a moment more, then raised the glass and let the Scotch temper his anger. It was all so simple, he thought . . . one damned geek with a conscience. It should have been easy. Those incompetent clowns. He should have been taken care of in Chicago.

He lowered the glass and watched the harbor scene a moment more, then turned away. There would be no turning back. It had taken too long to build, and this little shit wasn't going to take it all away. He walked back to the recliner, sat and leaned back. He brought the glass to his lips and took another drink. This was turning into a long night.

Chapter 8

CORNUCOPIA

July 26, 2.20 a.m. CDT

After spotting the Cornucopia entry light, they had sailed on as Skip suggested, then turned and made straight for the harbor. Paul had been impressed with Skip's knowledge, because the heading to the end of the breakwater from their turn was almost exactly due south. They had dropped sail on the way in, furling the big genoa as they started the engine. Now, the diesel hummed as they neared the entry. They had decided to take their chances on finding space and had not made any radio calls.

Skip stood at Paul's side. He gestured toward the green entry light. "That's on the end of a sheet-pile breakwater. The entry runs toward the southeast, but that breakwater turns and heads due west for its last three or four hundred feet. Round it and you'll be in the channel."

Paul throttled down the diesel, then replied. "Anything else I should know?"

"Yeah," said Skip, "They keep it dredged, but the west side's always deeper. Less chance of doin' any mud farming if you stick to the right. Remember, the first part goes right back east along the inside of the breakwater. You'll see the turn easy."

Pipe Dream cleared the end of the breakwater, the diesel idling, and slowly turned to port, heading back east and entering the channel. Looking forward, Paul could see the sheet piles along the inner side of the breakwater, and he made out the turn ahead. He approached it and then turned back toward the southeast; he could clearly see the channel, and he stayed to the right as Skip had suggested. Moving at a crawl, they entered the little harbor.

"Okay," Skip said, gesturing ahead. "You'll come to what amounts to a triple fork. Left is a basin behind some shops, but it's usually full with fishing boats and cruisers. Center one, forget it. It's where the Siskiwit river comes out, and it's shallow as hell. Little runabouts and stuff go in there, but there isn't more than 2 or 3 feet of depth most of the time. You want to head right."

Paul grunted in acknowledgment, noting the right channel appearing before him. Both sides of the channel were lined with sailboats and an occasional power cruiser. He swung *Pipe Dream* to starboard and shifted to neutral, coasting now along the lines of boats. There appeared to be no available open space, but there was a fairly long service dock to port in front of a large barn-roofed building. A "76" sign marked it as a fuel dock. "We'll tie up there for now," he said, "and if they want us to move, they'll tell us."

Rich was back on deck, apparently more comfortable now that they were out of the seas. Nevertheless, he looked about nervously, then asked, "So this is back on the mainland?"

"Yup." Skip didn't look at him; he was already rigging docklines and getting ready to step off as they neared the dock.

"How close to Bayfield is this?" A small touch of his past panic was creeping back into his voice.

"Close to 25 miles, but I doubt anybody'll think we're over here."

Skip opened the lifeline gate and stepped off, lines in hand, as Paul brought *Pipe Dream* alongside the dock. A small amount of reverse throttle tucked the stern in and brought them to a stop. Skip had quickly made bow and stern lines fast to cleats along the dock, and now Paul stepped forward, attached a third line at a midships cleat on the port rail, and stepped to the dock. He moved forward and brought the line around another dock cleat, and as he tightened it, the bow moved out until its line was taut. Skip took up the slack in the stern line, and Paul made his line fast to hold the boat in place. "Single springline will do for now," he said to Skip, "especially if we end up having to move."

"Makes sense. We probably need to . . . "

"Hello . . . it's kickin' up out there." The voice belonged to a thirtyish man who had emerged from the barn-roofed building near the fuel dock. He wore a light jacket and shorts, no socks, and a pair of shower clogs. "Don't get too many comin' in at this hour. I'm what passes for a harbormaster around here. My family lives in the barn. You're okay there for now, I guess . . . I got no place else to put you."

Paul regarded him as he approached, then rose to meet him and extended his hand, which was taken in greeting. "Paul Findlay. How much for the dockage? She's a 37-footer."

"Don't worry about that for now. We can settle up later in the morning. You folks'll want to rest up after plowin' through that stuff."

"Thanks!" Replied Paul. "Is there a pay phone around?"

The harbormaster gestured inshore toward what appeared to be small campground. "Down that way. There's restrooms and showers in the campground, and a walk down to the highway and east over the bridge will get you to a phone. Over there." He turned and pointed to a row of small shops along a gravel parking lot on the other side of the Siskiwit River.

"That'll do fine. We'll catch up with you in the morning, then."

The harbormaster flashed a quick grin. "I'm not goin' anywhere." He turned, then turned back. "By the way, my name's Dave. And you'll want this." He dug into his jacket pocket, then handed Paul a restroom and shower key on a chain and float, turned again, and went back to the barn house.

July 26, 2: 45 a.m. CDT

They sat silently for a time in *Pipe Dream*'s cockpit, collecting their thoughts and considering the situation. Paul looked first at Rich, who appeared to have recovered from his bout with seasickness, and then at Skip. He was glad they had been able to rescue the grizzled charter skipper, and now he was more than glad to have him here. As he looked, Skip shifted his position and then spoke.

"I need to call my wife. She's in Ashland . . . stays with her sister summers while I'm running the boat. That creep knew about her and I'm not gonna take any chances. Besides, she's gonna hear about this and I need to let her know I'm okay."

Paul thought a minute, then replied. "Yeah, and I definitely have to call Gina. That's my ex. She could be in danger from all this." He paused and glanced over at Rich, who averted his eyes. Paul looked back to Skip and resumed. "How about your wife? Can she be trusted not to tell anyone? She'll have to act like the wife of a man missing and presumed lost. If she doesn't, they'll know right away."

"Like I said, she's with her sister. She's got a different last name, so how would the press figure out . . . "

"They have nosy news people up here too. As soon as your boat's reported missing the bastards'll start looking for next of kin for reaction. It sells. They'll dig up where you live during the winter, and then they'll pick up on your relatives and your wife's relatives. It's just a matter of time. Maybe not that long if some Coastie gets a big mouth."

"Yeah, that's true. But she can do it. I'll tell her just enough to let her know how serious this is, and how important it is that she keep up the act. Guess I'll try her now. She stays up a lot of nights." Skip rose, looking at the growing light to the east, and stepped over the coaming, onto the deck and down to the dock, tossing "Back in a few." Over his shoulder as he walked off toward the pay phones.

Paul and Rich sat in silence for a few seconds before Rich heaved a sigh and spoke. "I never meant for any of this to happen. I didn't want to put you in danger, and certainly not Gina. It's just that . . . "

Paul cut him off. "It's okay. I know you didn't get up a few days back and decide to become a hit-man's target. Things are what they are and now we have to deal with them." He stood and fumbled in his pocket, pulling out a handful of change. " I have to reach Gina. Be back in a few minutes." The boat rocked slightly as Paul followed Skip into the night.

Paul collected his thoughts as he walked down the drive to Highway 13, across the bridge over the Siskiwit River, and then back to the small row of shops and the phones. Skip was already there, on the phone, and Paul could hear him across the gravel parking lot: "No, really, I'm fine. But I'm in a situation . . . Just let me finish . . . Char! Let me finish! Now don't interrupt. This is important. When they come to you and tell you that the boat is missing, or that they've found the boat but not me, don't tell them a thing. Not a word. You have to act upset, like I was really missing or gone. And don't even let on to your sister. Okay? . . . Because it could put you in danger . . . No. I've done nothing illegal, it's the people on the other side of this . . . yes, very. Now I know I can trust you. I always have and always will. Now I have to go. I'll be in touch when I can. Just remember that I love you and I will see you again . . . Soon. Now goodbye." Skip replaced the handset just as Paul reached the phones. "Well, that went as well as I could expect, I guess."

"Upset?"

"More than mildly. Her sister was out like a light, so that's a good thing. But she'll do it. She's strong and she knows now how important it is."

"Good. I hope my call goes half as well."

As Skip stepped away from the phone, Paul took his place. He dialed Gina's number in the Minneapolis suburb of Crystal, Minnesota, waited while the mechanical voice droned, and then fed the phone coins as instructed. One ring, two, three rings, and then the familiar voice was there, slightly slurred with the haze of a sudden awakening. "Hello . . . who is this? Do you have any idea what time it is?"

"Gina, it's Paul. Listen carefully . . . "

The voice was suddenly alert. "Paul? Where are you? Did Rich get in touch with you?"

"Gina, please listen to me. I can't talk just now. Get in your car and go the place we always used to go for breakfast. I'll call you there."

"You mean over at . . . "

"Don't say it. Don't say anything more. This is important. Just go and I'll talk to you there."

"But it's the middle of the night."

"Yeah, and it's a damn truck stop. They're open 24 hours. Just go."

"Paul. Why . . . "

"I'll tell you later. Just go now. Please!" Paul hung up, knowing Gina would slam the phone down on her end. He waited, recalling how long the drive should take. The place was a good ten minutes from her house, another five to get going and another five to park and go in.

He let twenty minutes pass and picked up the receiver. After all these years he still remembered that number. As he inserted the coins he wondered which name she was using. They had never actually divorced, but was she going by her maiden name, or . . . The voice in the handset said, "Willie's."

"Is there a Gina Findlay there? Might have just arrived?"

"Yeah, she's here. Just saw her walk in." The voice grew faint and said, "Gina! Phone call for you! You can take it by the kitchen entry." The voice grew louder again. "I'll put you on hold and she'll pick up the other line."

"Thanks . . . " He didn't get the word out before there was silence. A second later, she was there.

"Paul?"

"Good girl. I . . . "

"You know I hate that. Now why all the damn mystery? What's going on?"

"Gina, just sit there and listen. Wait for me to finish. Then you can ask all the questions you want. Okay?"

"Okay."

He proceeded to tell her as much as he dared about Rich, and his situation, and the danger they faced. She started to interrupt a couple of times, but each time he halted her and told her to let him finish. He ended by telling her, "That's where you come in. They may know by now that Rich contacted you, after this all started. It wouldn't take much for them to figure out our relationship, and then they'd likely try to use you to get to us. They may already be listening on your phone. That's why I sent you to Willie's."

"So what do I do?"

"Okay, this is important. I don't know if they're watching your house or not. Do you think you were followed?"

There was silence for a moment, then, "No, I didn't see another car most of the way over."

"Good, don't go back to the house. You need to get away from there and the only way I know how to protect you is bring you to me."

"C'mon, Paul, I'm not . . . "

"I'm serious. We have some nasty shit going on and you're in it, too."

"There was a lengthy silence; then she

asked, almost in a whisper, "How did you let this happen? I mean, I know it's Rich, but couldn't you just get him to the cops?"

"You weren't listening. There are evidently cops involved. Sooner or later they'd probably get to him unless he can make the whole mess public."

There was another silence, then an audible sigh. "So, how does coming to where you are protect me?"

"If you're with me, they can't grab you for leverage, can they?"

"I guess not. So what am I supposed to do for clothes?"

"Go shopping. You always loved that. But you need to bring more than clothes. Get yourself some camping gear, at minimum a good sleeping bag and a small tent. When you have everything, leave town. I want you to go up to Grand Portage and catch the boat out to Windigo on Isle Royale. Use the gear and stay there until we come for you."

"When will that be?"

"I'm not sure. It depends a lot on the weather. Just get going and get there as quick as you can." He paused, then added, "You still got a passport?"

"Yeah, if I can find it."

"Then you'll need to risk going back to the house to get it, but make it quick. No time for packing. If there are strange cars parked anywhere nearby, forget it. Keep driving and just get to Windigo."

There was a brief silence on the other end before she replied. "Paul . . . is this for real?" There was an anxious note in her voice, and it told Paul that she already knew it was very real indeed.

"Absolutely. Your life, and ours, may depend on it." He paused for a moment, then went on. "I never fell out of love with you . . . I hope you know that."

"Yeah . . . We just couldn't get the lifestyle thing worked out. I've never so much as dated since."

"I know. Me too. Now I have to go. I'll see you at Windigo. And don't tell anybody. I mean anybody."

"I won't."

"Goodbye, and be careful." He set the handset back on the hook, took a deep breath, squared his shoulders, and walked back toward the boat.

July 26, 9:14 a.m. CDT

Mansfield stood at the condo window, looking out on a gray and blustery morning. He could see the whitecaps beyond the breakwater and just one solitary sail in the distance. He sipped his strong black coffee, then lowered the mug and went back over his restless night. His anger had not abated, but he had controlled it for now.

He looked at his watch and then turned to walk to the phone. "Maybe he got the job done," he muttered to the empty room. He picked up the handset to dial his Chicago office number. The knocking interrupted that activity, and he replaced the handset and strode to the door, throwing it open to find Bruno and Sam. He glowered at them for a moment before snapping at them. "Well?"

Bruno looked Mansfield square in the eye. "We been there all night. That boat he took never came back in. The whole damned place is buzzing about some search — four or five other boats were headed out to look for the boat, and the Coast Guard's been out since way before daylight."

Mansfield's mind was racing as he considered the news. If this Jack was as good as they say, he was not about to leave any witnesses. And he sure as hell wouldn't bring the boat back here without the captain. "Maybe it's done. Go back there and keep an eye on things. If you find out anything new, you let me know."

Bruno replied, "You got it, we'll . . . " and was rudely cut off by the slamming door. He turned to go, shaking his head as he looked at Sam and said, "What a bastard. Glad we don't run into him much."

Inside, Mansfield returned to the phone and dialed his office number. On the second ring, Sherry picked with her standard greeting: "M&L Investments."

He didn't need to identify himself. "Any messages?

"Oh, Mr. Mansfield, let me check. How was your flight?"

He didn't answer and in a moment she said, "You have several phone messages, a couple of them from . . . "

He cut her off. "How about the mail? Any cards?"

"Cards?"

He was irritated now. "Just check!"

"Just a minute." He heard her put the line on hold; after no more than a minute she was back. "You got the usual assortment of client letters, bills, ads, but no cards. What's so . . . "

"Never mind. I'll check with you later." He

hung up and went to the table, uncorked his Dewar's and took a quick swig straight from the bottle.

July 26, 10.27 a.m. CDT

Sam and Bruno stood by the little Gazebo next to the land end of the City Dock, watching the activity as the locals discussed the missing boat. The wind was still fairly strong, although the clouds had lessened. Several boats had gone out to join the search for *Blue Moon*.

Sam looked away toward The Pier restaurant. "Damn kid . . . what's takin' so long? He gotta grind the coffee?"

Bruno kept his stare focused on the dock. "Relax. He'll be along."

"Like he was this morning? I had to drag his ass out of the sack. Asshole."

"And you weren't a little prick when you were his age?"

"Not like that I wasn't. I'd have had my ass handed to me quick, if I acted like this little shithead . . . and speakin' of shitheads, here he comes."

Mike was crossing the street from the Pier, a covered styrofoam cup in each hand, and one more balanced atop the cup in his left hand. He had a white paper donut bag gripped in his teeth. He walked heel-and-toe, trying almost too hard not to drop the balanced cup. As he reached Sam he looked at him and mumbled across the top of the bag. "Taig . . . the . . . fgggn' . . . cp!"

Sam grabbed the balanced cup. "Coulda made two trips, dumb ass."

Bruno relieved Mike's left hand of the second cup, and Mike took the bag of donuts from between his teeth. He glared at Sam. "You're usin' me for a damn gofer. I ain't no frikkin' gofer."

"Yeah, well, you look like one. Hairy little critter with buck teeth."

Mike's face grew red and he started to reply, but Bruno clapped a hand on his shoulder. "Let it go, kid. You'll keep them buck teeth if you just let it go."

At that moment, Bruno saw several people run over toward one of the boats that had remained. Something was happening. "Hold this, kid." He said, handing his coffee to Mike as he headed off down the dock. He reached the small clot of people and pushed his way closer; everyone was listening to a marine VHF transmission. He only made out catches of it, but it seemed certain that something had been found.

After a few moments, a white-haired man climbed from the boat to the dock and held up his hands, asking for quiet. "Here's what they say. They found the boat, upside down and up against Rocky Island a quarter mile north of the park dock. No sign of Skip or the guy he took out."

Someone called out from the middle of the crowd, "They think they made it ashore?"

"No, they looked. There were some campers down at the sand spit. Said they were already turned in and heard a boat, then they heard something like shots but they never saw anything. They thought it must have been backfiring."

A stout man at the front shook his head. "That Skip, he wasn't going to turn his boat over. With the wind like it was last night, shelter woulda been good up in there."

The white-haired man continued. "The Coast Guard's been asking if anyone else heard a radio transmission last night, sometime after 9 o'clock. They picked up something at that time, but they want to see if anybody heard it better."

Bruno turned and walked back up to rejoin Sam and Mike. He filled them in on what the white-haired man had reported, then pointed down past the Apostle Islands Marina toward the Coast Guard station. "I'm going down there and see if I can find out what they heard." He grabbed his coffee from Mike and set out along the path in front of the condos, toward the marina and the Coast Guard station.

Mike watched him go. "I coulda done it. Why don't you guys ever let me do nothin'?"

Sam chuckled. "'Cause if we sent you down there, the Coastie's would be laughin' too hard to tell you shit."

July 26, 11:14 a.m. CDT

The wind was still up; the slapping of unrestrained halyards against a few masts in Cornucopia harbor was grating on Paul's nerves. *Pipe Dream's* halyards had been carefully tensioned away from the mast, held off by bungee cords run to the uppers. It was a simple and common courtesy, not to mention a way to prevent the chafing that such slapping causes in the lines. Too many absentee owners didn't give it a thought.

The cacophony made Paul think back to his childhood. His mother had adorned their porch with numerous wind chimes, and he had not liked them any more than these larger nautical versions. Paul's father had even gone so far as to call the wind chimes "neighbor annoyers" but that brought only a withering look in return. The wind chimes remained long after Paul had left. When he'd sold the old house after his mother died, one of his last tasks had been to take them down. He wished now that he had kept at least one . . .

The slight shift as Rich stepped aboard brought Paul back to real time. They had plugged the bullet holes in the cabin with some white sealant and smoothed them as well as possible before someone started asking questions. They had picked up teak splinters and generally cleaned the boat up after all the confusion of last night. The wet cushions, soggy blankets and various articles of clothing were on deck, tied to lifelines to dry in the brisk breeze. Paul had found another change of clothing for Skip and then they had all taken turns at the shower. Rich was the last to wash away the last night's stress. "Better?" said Paul, shifting his legs to give Rich more room to step to the teak cockpit seat.

"Uh-huh. At least I feel halfway human again."

Skip stepped up and through the companionway, bringing a bottle and three cups. "Might be a bit early, but a little bracer will do us all good," he said as he put the cups on the seat and poured a finger of Black Bush into each. They all took a cup and each took a sip in silence; there was nothing to toast except survival. They sat for a while, slowly enjoying the Irish whiskey, the slapping halyards, and the whistle of the wind in their ears.

Paul took his last sip and set the cup down beside him. "Last check, this will lay down this evening. Our best shot is to head out of here sometime after midnight. The seas are supposed to drop to 2 feet or so by then."

Skip added, "Weather window's okay, wind'll be backing around west and falling. That should give us a broad reach all the way up. Nice to make it without throwing a bunch of tacks."

Paul grinned at the comment "I don't imagine you were always a gearhead. That's rag-hanger language if I ever heard it."

"Yeah, I sailed pretty much all my life. My dad had an old wooden ketch down in Manitowoc, and I kinda grew up aboard her. Later, I bought a C-scow and raced it all over. I haven't done much on cruisers like this, but I do know a sheet from Shinola."

Paul laughed at the crude pun, then turned to Rich. "Fate gave you another sailor to help out. Let's hope it's a sign." He turned back to Skip. "I have no idea how long it'll take them to figure out what they're looking for. When we leave here, we need the harbormaster to think we are headed down Duluth way. Then we'll head west, past the point and well out of view, before we make our turn and head northeast for Isle Royale."

Skip pondered that for moment. "Easy enough. I'll go ask him if he has any info on dredging down that way. With the lake levels like they've been, the smart boaters are checking before they head for most places."

"Okay, ask him about Barker's Island. That's a well-known marina and it'll give whoever's looking a nice wild goose to chase. I'd be willing to bet there's at least a couple T37s there."

Rich looked up. "What's a T37?"

"You're aboard one.   If they ask the Barker's Island people if there are any Tartan 37s in the marina, they'll be told that there are.   They'll waste their time checking them out. Every minute is worth something."

Skip got up and stepped to the dock. "Guess I'll go lay the groundwork."

July 26, 11:20 A.M. CDT

Bruno stood at the counter just inside the Coast Guard office door, talking to the rating behind the desk.

" . . . just a terrible thing about the *Blue Moon*. I knew the guy a little — went out with him a time or two. They ever find anybody?"

"Sir, I can't comment on that. They'll release the report when they have it ready."

"Sorry, I knew that. I just was hoping they'd found him, 'cause I heard some guy say he caught a radio call last night . . . "

"Somebody else heard the call?"

"Yeah, a guy that was talkin' down at the dock. Big fella, brown shirt and one of them captain's hats. I don't know what boat he was from. So you guys heard a call too?"

"Well, parts of it. It was broken up and we need to talk to this man and find out if he heard it any clearer. I'd go down to the dock with you but everybody's out on the recovery and I can't leave the station untended."

"What did the part you heard say? I'll ask him if it was the same call and bring him back here."

"Sir, I can't play the tape for you. If you'll just..."

"I know that, but just tell me some of what it was about. If it's the same message he'll come right over."

"Well . . . I guess it wouldn't be out of line to give you the general content. We're pretty sure it was the *Blue Moon.* The transmission was strange — it was almost a whisper — but we could make out the words 'South Twin' and 'Tartan' and something about trouble."

"What's it mean?"

"He was calling or referring to a Tartan, and I'd guess he was somewhere around South Twin Island. Since the boat was found washed up on

Rocky, that makes sense."

"What's the Tartan part?"

"That's a make of sailboat. Either he saw one or was calling for one. We've checked, and the ones docked here and at Port Superior and over in LaPointe are all accounted for. Sir, if you can just go and bring this guy back here, that'll do the most good right now."

"You betcha. I'm on my way." Bruno turned and left the Coast Guard office, heading back toward the marina and on toward Mansfield's condo.

July 26, 11:27 a.m. CDT

In Chicago, the coroner was completing his work, as the police interviewed the neighbors and the press clamored for details. His assistant handed him a clipboard. "Shit." He looked at the body, then back to the assistant. "The press'll have a field day with this one. I can see the headlines tomorrow. 'POPULAR ALDERMAN COMMITS SUICIDE'. The sensation rags'll put it different: 'SCIANNO SWALLOWS PISTOL.' I always wonder what drives 'em to it." Alderman Vincent Scianno had locked his door, finished off a fair amount of whiskey, and then put a .38 in his mouth. End of story, end of another life.

At the desk, a detective was bagging the paper that had been beneath the whiskey glass by the phone. It was just a single sheet, torn from a spiral binder. There was no spiral binder in the room. The sheet had just a few cryptic notes scrawled on it:

Ford Exp.

Minn pl

Bruno Mike Sam

The Coroner had finished his work, and the gurney carrying Vincent Scianno's body was wheeled out. Vincent no longer had to deal with Ted Mansfield.

July 26, 11:30 a.m. CDT

Bruno really didn't care much for Mansfield. He stood now, hands folded in front, as Mansfield paced the room in the second floor condo. "Bastard's really stuck on himself," he thought.

Mansfield stopped and turned to Bruno. "So they were calling a sailboat, a . . . what did you call it . . ."

"A Tartan."

"Yeah. But all they found was the damn fishing boat? And no bodies?"

"Not so far."

"Then he fucked it up. The famous mechanic fucked it up. Wait here." He left Bruno and went to the phone, picked up the handset and punched in a number.

Halfway through the first ring, a strange male voice said, "Hello."

"Who is this? I'm trying to reach Vince Scianno."

"Who's calling?"

"Just tell him he's got an important call."

"Sir, I need to know who . . . "

Mansfield slammed down the phone. "Shit, what now?" he muttered, picking it up again and dialing a second number.

Sherry's familiar voice came on the line. "M&L Investments."

"It's me. Any messages? Any more mail?"

"No . . . but there's some really bad news. It just came over the radio."

"What?"

"Alderman Scianno . . . I know he's . . . was . . . your friend . . . he killed himself."

"He WHAT? Jesus!"

"It's horrible. They said he shot himself. In his office. I . . . "

Mansfield slammed down the handset. There would be no cryptic card or any other report, even if the job was done. He'd have to take matters entirely into his own hands now to be absolutely certain. He banged his fist on the countertop in frustration. "Goddam chicken shit. Took the easy way out."

He picked up the handset again and punched the keypad. Three rings and then an automated answering system answered. "You have reached the Tollefson Boatyard . . . " He waited through the instructions until he heard, " . . . for Brad Tollefson dial 2 . . . " He punched the 2 and waited.

"Mr. Tollefson's office."

"Put him on."

"I'm sorry, sir. Mr. Tollefson is not available. May I send you to his voice m . . . "

"No voice mail. You find him and tell him he has an urgent call. Just give him this number." Mansfield looked down at the number card on the phone and read it to her. "Now you find him and have him get back to me right away. Tell him it is in regard to our very recent mutual accounting problem."

"I'll see what I can . . . "

"Don't see . . . do! This is extremely important and we can't waste any time." He hung up abruptly as was his habit.

In Duluth, Brad Tollefson looked at his assistant with questioning eyes. "Who was that?"

"He didn't say. He was sort of rude. He said it was . . . " She looked at her scrawled note. " . . . in regard to our very recent mutual accounting problem. Here's the number." She handed him the note.

Brad looked briefly at the note, then back to the assistant. "Marcie, why don't you take a couple of days off?"

"That's okay, I can stay . . . "

"No, I really want you to go home and enjoy some time with your family. You can pick up on things when you come back." He started to turn to his office door, then looked back. "And take your family to dinner. On me. " He retrieved his wallet from his hip pocket, pulled out a couple of fifty-dollar bills, and pressed them into her hand.

She blushed slightly, then smiled. "Well . . . okay! But I don't understand . . . "

He held up a hand, palm out, interrupting. " Just go and have a nice evening. You've been working hard lately, and this afternoon I just need some time to myself. Now go, and I'll see you in a few days."

"Should I put your time off on my calendar?"

"Just mark it as vacation. Two or three days max . . . I'll call if I decide to stay longer." Without another word, he retreated to his office and closed the door.

In the office, Brad sat heavily in his leather chair. He waited until he heard the outer door close as Marcie left the office, then looked again at the note. He knew without question who the caller was. Brad was a big man, an ex-football player, and he feared almost nothing, but Mansfield was another matter entirely. "Ruthless bastard." He muttered, and then he picked up the phone and dialed the number.

The phone at the other end rang only once and was picked up. The harsh voice rasped, "Tollefson?"

"Yeah, it's me, what's up now?"

"Our problem is still not solved. The expert who was going to handle it blew it. Your creeps aren't much better, but at least they have a line on it."

"Whaddya mean?"

"We know what we're looking for now. A sailboat. We don't know where it is yet, but I figure with a sizable cruiser like yours we should be able to get ahold of them pretty damn quick."

"Ted, I can't just head out. Have you seen the damned lake? It's kickin' up out there . . . "

"I thought you knew how to handle that barge of yours."

"I do. That's why I'm not heading out into this stuff. We have to wait for it to calm down a bit."

"The more time we waste sitting on our asses, the farther . . . "

"Ted, slow down. That's just it. They probably aren't going anyplace either. "

"So when will you be up here?"

"From the phone number, you're still at my Condo."

"Yeah. In Bayfield."

"Okay, I've made the trip a lot of times. Average in decent conditions is about 6 hours unless I push it, but . . . "

"Push it. Remember, your ass is hangin' out over the same fence as mine is."

"Okay, but fuel use will go through the roof."

"So what? Just get here. How soon can you leave?"

"Lemme check the forecast." Brad turned his chair to the marine VHF receiver on the credenza behind the desk, switched it on, and pressed the "WX" button. As he listened to the automated voice and waited for the open waters forecast, he looked at the framed chart of western Lake Superior on the wall above the radio. At last, the voice droned, " . . . open waters of western Lake Superior, Winds east-southeast 25 to 30 knots, waves 5 to 7 feet, becoming south 15-20 knots by 11 P.M with waves 3-5 feet. Winds shifting west by 2 A.M. 10-15 knots, waves 2 to 4 feet . . . "

Brad returned to the phone. "About the middle of the night. If I leave here around 2 A.M that gets me to Bayfield by maybe 7:30 or 8:00 in the morning if I average 16 knots or so, but that's pushin' hard. It'll still be a little sloppy."

"Okay. Be here." There was the characteristic click and abrupt end to the conversation, and Brad was left to wonder why had had ever started an association with Ted Mansfield.

He picked up an intercom mike and punched in a two-digit number, then keyed and released it. There was a tone, then a voice: "Fuel dock."

"I need you to bring *Valhalla* over and fuel her up. Make sure she's pumped out and the water tanks are full. Stock the fridge for about a week long run. And call the guys — tell 'em I need 'em on board by about 1 this morning." As he unkeyed the mike there was a brief tone.

"Got it." There was another tone, then silence. He hung up the intercom mike, rose, and walked to the Lake Superior chart on the wall. He regarded it in silence for a moment, then looked down and shook his head with a single word. "Damn."

July 26, 12:07 p.m. CDT

It had been a hectic morning, but Gina had done as Paul requested. She'd stopped by the house, run in and dug out her passport, and then left as quickly. There had been no sign of watchers. She'd parked on a side street and caught a little sleep, waiting for the stores to open. Then she'd gone shopping, and she had probably maxed out her Visa card doing it, she thought, but what the hell... she was at least getting new clothes out of it. She hadn't been particular. She had purchased underwear, two bras, shirts, pants, sweaters, a jacket, socks, a new pair of athletic shoes, toothpaste and a toothbrush, deodorant . . . She hadn't bothered with makeup. She had a feeling it wouldn't be needed on this trip. She had also bought a large backpack to put it all in, a small pop-up tent, and a sleeping bag. As an afterthought she'd bought a self-inflating air mattress and four D-cell batteries to power its built-in air pump. She didn't relish the prospect of sleeping on the ground.

At milepost 249 she crested the rise on I-35 and saw the vast expanse of the lake stretching to the horizon and the cities of Duluth and Superior on its shore. It was time for lunch. She would make her way to Canal Park next to the famous lift bridge for a quick sandwich at Grandma's Saloon. The popular restaurant was one of her favorites, and at least it had given her something to look forward to on this puzzling journey.

She had fought back flashes of the old anger on her way. Why did he have to drag her into this mess? Then, recalling the morning's phone conversation, she realized that he at least believed she would be in serious danger if she stayed at home. Her thoughts had then strayed back to the crux of the matter between them. He had wanted her to cruise with him, but she couldn't let go of a more normal lifestyle in spite of her love for him. She had enjoyed it at first but . . . Her thoughts were interrupted as she reached the Michigan Street exit that would take her to downtown Duluth and Canal Park.

July 26, 1:20 p.m. CDT

Paul left the old General Store to head back

down to the Siskiwit Bay Marina and *Pipe Dream*. He had bought some bread, sliced meat from the small deli, and some ice. Now, as he neared Highway 13, he shifted the weight of the ice bags to his left hand. There was no traffic on the highway. The strong wind that still blew from the east gusted as he made his way across and he reeled slightly as he adjusted his weight. He entered the gravel drive and walked past several boats on their cradles and turned to pass between the boat launch and showers. It was then a quick walk back to the north, along the east side of the marina between the finger slips and summer trailer homes, back to the fuel dock. Rich met him at the dock and relieved him of the ice, saying, "I could have gone with you to help lug this back, you know."

"They still don't have the foggiest idea what I look like. They'd spot you in a New York minute."

"So what's the difference whether they see me here or across the highway?"

Skip stood from where he had been sitting at the helm. "That's why we did the end-for-end this morning. With the bow headed out, if we see anything the least bit suspicious we can at least make a run for it. If you're up at the store it doesn't do much good, does it?"

Rich stepped aboard with the ice. "Guess not. I just feel like I should be pitching in more." He stepped to the companionway and then below to stow the ice.

Paul watched him go and then glanced over at Skip. "He'll get his chance. He'll get all he wants before this is over."

"Yeah, well, we have a lot of hours left before we head out. I hope they got it right and this starts to lay down tonight."

Rich glanced up at the scudding clouds. "They're higher and they've started to turn a little. We're getting on the back side of that low. By tonight it should flatten out, and there's supposed to be a shift west."

"Let's hope so. I'm on up here for another hour — then it's you."

"Got it. Anybody shows up that looks out of place, fire her up, yank the lines and get her off the dock." Paul had rigged both the bow and stern lines with looped hitches that could be easily released from the helm position. "Just make sure you haul them all the way in so we don't foul the prop."

Skip stared across at the small row of shops and the highway beyond. "I figure it has to be at least two guys traveling together. Anyone with kids is a sure no."

"Probably not," replied Paul, "but let's not take any chances. If they don't look right, we go."

July 26, 2:44 p.m. CDT

Gina finished her lunch at Grandma's Saloon, and stayed a moment to watch as a laker — a thousand-foot Great Lakes ship — entered beneath the lift bridge. She would normally have spent some time here, watching the ships come and go and enjoying the view, but today it was windy and the briskly moving air brought the chill of the lake with it. As the stern of the big ship receded toward the inner harbor, she turned and headed back to her car. She had more pressing business to the north and east.

She left Canal Park and made her way back to the expressway, turning right onto the ramp and accelerating to merge with the traffic as she began her trip along Minnesota's north shore.

July 26, 4:47 p.m. CDT

Paul sat behind *Pipe Dream's* wheel, absently watching the gravel parking lot beyond the small boat basin. During his watch, a number of vehicles had come and gone, disgorging families and couples into the small row of shops and just as quickly swallowing them back up with their souvenir purchases. Two vehicles had pulled in directly to the lot next to the fuel dock, but in both cases they were obvious tourists. A single black SUV had slowed and stopped, then turned in by the boat launch at the end of the channel. That had caused Paul to start the diesel, but he just as quickly shut it down when a man and two children got out to look at one of the boats that rested in the grass on a wooden cradle. Below, Rich and Skip had risen quickly when the diesel started, but when Paul motioned to them that all was well, they returned to the cabin below to try and nap a bit more.

Now he began to think ahead to the night that lay before them. He mentally ran through the preparations. The 50-gallon diesel tank had been topped off, as had the 90 gallons of fresh water storage. The waste holding tank had been pumped. They had food and beverage, and some ice to help keep things fresh when they were away from shorepower. The charts were folded to show the western lake, Isle Royale, and finally Thunder Bay. He had transferred key waypoints into the GPS. They would come in handy in the coming darkness.

Paul's thoughts were interrupted by the *crunch* of tires on gravel. Another vehicle was entering the drive to the harbor fuel dock. He sat upright, then reached down to the start button with his left hand while his right hand picked up the ends of the quick-release docklines. He looked over toward the sound and heard the burbling of a large V-8 engine, and when the grill of an old, rusted GMC pickup emerged from behind one of the summer trailer homes along the drive, he let out his breath in relief and put the docklines down.

As Paul collected himself, Skip emerged from below, his gaze first at the truck and then at Paul. "Trouble?"

"Nah . . . just one of the locals. This is gonna be a long evening."

July 26, 4:15 p.m. CDT

Interstate 35 had given way to US 61, and Gina had been enjoying the drive as much as she could, considering the knot in her stomach. It had nothing to do with the sandwich from Grandma's. She had turned off the radio, preferring instead to open the windows and let the air make its own music.

Her attention alternated between appreciation of the surroundings and an unbidden inner conversation. As she rounded a curve, the whole expanse of Lake Superior stretched endlessly off to her right; she couldn't help the small grin that spread over her face in spite of the situation. "Paul might be right," she thought as she looked at the blue vista. "I feel more at home here than I ever did in the house."

Forested land hid the lake again, and her thoughts turned back inward as she considered the past few hours. She fought back flashes of anger, reasoning that she didn't know the whole story . . . But why was she in this predicament? What had she done? She'd talked to Rich Perry, that was all. But now she felt like . . . well, like some kind of criminal. The anger rose again. Paul had a lot more explaining to do. She glanced to the right again as the trees thinned and the blue waters came back into view. Grand Portage was less than an hour away.

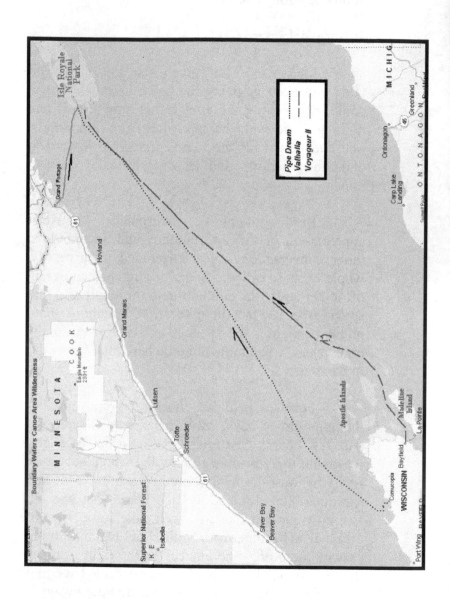

Chapter 9
BIG WATER

July 27, 1:34 a.m. CDT

It had been nearly an hour since the crew of *Pipe Dream* cast off her lines and motored her slowly out of Cornucopia. The wind had rounded to the west as predicted, and now blew at a steady 10 to 12 knots. Paul had talked with Dave, the harbormaster, that evening. He'd asked for dredging information and particulars about Barker's Island. If someone came looking, that might be enough of a red herring to send them scrambling over to Duluth/Superior.

Now, as the waves lessened and they'd gone far enough that a landbound observer would report they'd headed west, they altered course to head back to the northeast toward Isle Royale. Paul broke out the whisker pole and rigged it to keep the genoa full. Once it was set, he left Skip on watch above and went below to talk to Rich.

Rich was lying down on the port settee, but he was awake. Paul sat heavily down on the starboard settee as Rich sat up. "Okay," said Paul, "we're on our way. We'll put in at Windigo, on the western end of Isle Royale. Gina is supposed to meet us there. Then we head on up to Canada the next day. I'll feel a whole lot better when I know Gina is safe, for one, and also we need to try and make as much of the trip at night as we can. We can't help sailing all day today but a night run from

Windigo into Thunder Bay is our safest bet."

Paul rose and headed back up the companionway. Skip had engaged the autopilot, and *Pipe Dream* was moving smartly along through the night under main and poled-out genoa. Off to the north, the lights of a big laker were plain, but the ship was not a concern; she was headed toward Two Harbors.

July 27, 3:47 A.M. CDT

There had been no sleep at the Bayfield condominium. Mansfield had been pacing endlessly, waiting for reports on several fronts. Just minutes ago he'd been told that Tollefsons's cruiser should arrive in about 4 hours, and that had set him off on another rant.

"Jesus H. Christ!" he roared as Bruno handed him the note. "Who gives a shit about some little waves? Can't he get his ass here quicker that that?"

Bruno held a hand up. "Hey, I'm just the messenger boy. That's when he can get here. You keep yellin' like that, the neighbors'll have the cops on us."

"Fuck the neighbors! I'm telling you . . . " The ringing of the telephone interrupted him. He picked up the receiver and simply said, "Go."

Mansfield listened intently, then grabbed a

note pad and pen, and began to write down some information. He looked at it, and then said, "Okay. Go find out what she knows. Do it now . . . No, I don't give a shit if it's the middle of the fuckin' night. Who we got up there? . . . All right, get them on it. Tell 'em to call me."

He hung up, then turned back to Bruno. "They got Perry's phone records. After he got away, the only call besides Bayfield was to some woman named Gina Findlay. She lives in Crystal, Minnesota. That's just west of downtown Minneapolis."

July 27, 6:30 a.m. CDT

Gina was sitting in a small coffee shop, nursing a cup of French Roast and absently thumbing through a local advertising flyer. She had found a cheap motel near Grand Portage, but she hadn't slept well. She watched as a few people came and went. At this hour, most were either fishermen or those who were, like her, waiting for the ferry trip to Isle Royale.

One of the advertisements caught her eye. The company offered a fleet of sailboats for charter, and the ad featured a photograph of a young couple aboard a sailboat, obviously in love and having a wonderful time. She thought back to the first time that Paul had taken her aboard *Pipe Dream*. She had never sailed before that day, but in those few hours she had discovered why those who did were devoted to it. She had taken to it quickly, and Paul had been so pleased. Paul . . . her mind snapped back to the present. She put down the flyer and picked up a map of Isle Royale she had gotten when she reserved passage. She located the Windigo Ranger Station on the western end, tracing the route from Grand portage to there with her finger. It would be a two and a half-hour trip, and at last she'd see him.

She hoped the plan had not changed, but there was nothing for it now but to go as he'd instructed. Or perhaps he might have called back . . . She saw the pay phone by the front door, and opened her small handbag to check for change. She'd left her cell phone behind in the rush but she could at least check her answering machine for messages while she was waiting.

She rose and walked to the pay phone, picked up the receiver and dropped in fifty cents. She dialed her calling card number and then her home number. The phone rang once, twice . . . but before the third ring, when she could punch in her code and listen to her messages, she heard a click, then silence . . . but not silence. Someone had picked it up. Her hand involuntarily went to her mouth, and she could feel the cold sweat breaking out on her forehead. She waited a few more seconds, then said, softly, "Who's there?" From the other end, nothing . . . then she repeated, louder this time, "Who's THERE?" She thought she heard a background noise, a step perhaps. The anger took over. "What are you doing in my house? I'm calling the police!" There was an audible click.

Whoever had answered had hung up without a word.

She hung up and turned back toward her table, talking to herself as she walked, "Shit, shit, shit . . . what have you done?" She left money on the table to cover the coffee and a tip, picked up her jacket and the papers, and went back to the door. She paused for moment, slipped on the jacket against the morning chill, and walked outside to wait and think.

July 27, 6:42 a.m. CDT

"That was her." The balding man in the leather jacket had just hung up Gina's phone. He looked at the gray-haired man in the dirty Minnesota Gophers sweatshirt, then turned back to the machine. "I got the number on her caller ID. Gimme some paper and a pen."

The Gopher went around the corner into Gina's study, grabbed a sheet of paper from the tray on the computer printer, and a pen from a stand by the console. He brought them back to the living room. "Hey, Larry," he asked, handing over the pen and paper, "ain't they lookin' for some kinda sailboat?"

"Yeah, so?"

"So she's got a bunch of pictures over her desk. Some of 'em have a lady, prob'ly her, and some guy on a big sailboat."

Larry scribbled down the number from the caller ID, then pocketed the paper and followed the Gopher back to the study. There they were . . . several photos, some taken aboard, some from the dock. There was one in particular with the woman alone, standing at the wheel. She was looking back over the stern at the camera and smiling. Below, on the transom, was the boat name: *Pipe Dream.*

Larry headed back for the phone. "Gotta call this in. Keep looking for names."

July 27, 6:56 a.m. CDT

Coffee was flowing in the Bayfield condo. Bruno had just rousted Mike off the couch, where he'd been noisily snoring. Mike was standing, bleary-eyed and unsteady from the fog of sleep, and he was complaining loudly. "Geez, you ain't got no good reason to wake me up. There's nothin' goin' on . . . "

Bruno stopped him in mid-sentence, raising a clenched fist. "You wanna go back to sleep quick, smart ass?" Mike just glared at Bruno, shook his head and walked away.

The telephone rang and Bruno bent to the handset, but Mansfield elbowed by and picked it up. "Yeah . . . Who the hell is this? . . . Okay, It's about damn time. What have you got?" He listened intently, then motioned impatiently for a pen and paper. His motions became more agitated, then he said into the phone "Hold it." Looking up, he shouted, "Get me some goddam paper! And my pen . . . on the table!"

Bruno found a pad of paper on the kitchen counter, grabbed the pen on his way by and handed them to Mansfield, who snatched at them impatiently and sat down. Bruno turned away, thinking to himself, "If this fucker wasn't the boss, I'd . . . "

Mansfield just said "Go," and started writing. After a minute he put down the pen, then said, "Keep looking. Toss the whole place if you have to. I want the guy's name."

He slammed down the phone and picked up the pad, then got up and handed it to Bruno. "That was from this Gina Findlay's place in the Twin Cities. She isn't there, but they found the boat's name in pictures. It's *Pipe Dream.* Then she called, probably to pick up messages off her machine. They got the number she called from. Find out where it is."

Mansfield returned to the window. After a moment in thought, he returned to the phone, picked it up and dialed. He waited, looking at his watch. One ring, two, three . . . He heard the sleepy voice on the other end, then was uncharacteristically nice. "I'm sorry to get you up. This is Ted. Who can you find up around Bayfield, Wisconsin that has a plane we can hire? . . . No, I don't need to go anywhere. I'm looking for a friend's sailboat. He's out there on Lake Superior someplace but I don't know where . . . No, it's not an emergency. I just need to find him so I can go meet him on a big power cruiser . . . Yeah, a business deal. Kind of important that I find him today . . . Okay, here goes. It's a white sailboat, about 37 feet long. Name on the stern is *Pipe Dream.* It ought to be someplace between here and Canada . . . No, not that far. I'd say no more than 70 or 80 miles east or west, but most of the way north . . . Well, whoever you can get. If the other guy had stayed . . . Yeah, I feel kind of bad about that. I probably should have listened to him when he wanted to divert, but we landed okay. Tell him I apologize . . . Okay, when you find somebody, call this number." He rattled off the condo phone number, said goodbye and hung up. He looked for a moment at the phone. "Self-righteous prick." He said, and went back to the window to stare out over the harbor.

July 27, 7:12 a.m. CDT

It had been a long night in less than ideal conditions. Brad Tollefson stood on the bridge of his cruiser, a custom 53-foot design he'd built at his own yard. He was watching the "Red 4" buoy that marked his turn at Red Cliff Point pass to starboard. He sipped on black coffee and looked at the chart; about a half-hour and they'd be docked. He thought he might be able to raise the marina now, so he pulled the VHF radio microphone from its mount and keyed it, saying, "Apostle Islands Marina, Apostle Islands Marina, Apostle Islands Marina, this is the motor yacht *Valhalla.*" He released the mike and waited, but there was no reply. After 30 seconds he keyed the mike again and repeated the call, but still heard no response. He replaced the microphone as he mumbled to himself, "Still pretty early." He looked ahead as he altered his course to pass southwest between the mainland and Basswood Island. He boosted the throttles and the twin Detroit Diesel 450 engines raised their tone in response.

He'd thought about this situation all night as he pounded eastward out of Duluth. He now regretted ever getting involved with Ted Mansfield, but he was in too deep.

July 27, 7:40 a.m. CDT

Pipe Dream forged ahead, driving a foamy wave down her flanks as she split the cold waters. They had made the turn six hours ago and had made great time. Paul checked the GPS one more time and verified that they'd averaged more than six knots speed over ground. If the wind held, they'd reach Isle Royale by dark.

Satisfied, he turned and went forward to the companionway. Skip was dozing in the navigation seat to port, and Rich was standing at the galley. He'd found the old percolator and was now trying to hunt up some coffee.

Paul started down the companionway ladder, and Rich spoke as he moved forward to make room. "Show me where the coffee is, and I'll make a pot."

PAUL ?

~~Skip~~ reached the cabin sole and then reached over the icebox hatches to a sliding storage door outboard and forward of the propane stove. He used a fingerhole to slide the panel aft, reached in and produced a back-and yellow can of Chock Full o'Nuts coffee. He handed the can to Rich with one hand as he slid the panel shut with the other. "Three and a half scoops. Filters are in the same door."

Paul then opened a center panel behind the stove and retrieved two stainless-steel bent rods. Each rod had a clap and thumbscrew on one end, and he attached the clamps loosely to a rod that ran across the stove front. The bent parts of the rods extended over one of the burners. He took the percolator from Rich, placed it on the burner, moved the two bent rods in so they held the base of the percolator and then tightened the thumbscrews. He bent down and pulled a lever at the stove base, and the stove began to swing on its gimbal mounts. "Now you're ready to make some coffee. Know how to light it?

"Yeah, you showed me last night in Corny."

"Just remember you have to hit the safety switch first. Put in water right to the bottom of the basket. And three and a half scoops like I said."

At the nav station, Skip opened an eye and said, "Best idea I've heard in a while. Couldn't sleep any more anyhow, what with all the racket you guys were making." He stretched his arms, then gingerly felt the red slash on his cheek and felt under his hat for the bump and painful laceration he'd gotten from the hit man. "Gonna want some aspirin with it, though. Feels like I got hit by a truck."

July 27, 7:57 a.m. CDT

The Apostle Islands Marina had limited available accommodations for a larger power cruiser, but *Valhalla* was shoehorned in. The big cruiser was pulled in across the long T-shaped end of D Dock, its bow facing north to facilitate an easier departure. Brad Tollefson had shut off the diesels, and now in the breezy silence he watched four figures coming toward him on the long wooden walkway from the marina office. He recognized the lead figure instantly, and it gave him no pleasure. Ted Mansfield had a way of dominating any assemblage of people, and he did so now. He strode toward the boat, his shoulders squared and his jaw set, and even from a distance Brad could tell this would not be a pleasant day.

Directly behind him, Bruno's hulking presence was familiar. The old longshoreman and sometime local muscle had worked at the Tollefson boatyard for several years. He carried a pair of duffels and a briefcase. Sam was less familiar but he knew him by his shuffling gait and the effort with which he hauled along his excess weight and a single bag. Bringing up the rear was Michael, slouching along and looking bored and insolent. Brad had wished he could have found someone else besides his sister's kid, but on such short notice he'd had to make do. Michael was a veritable leech at the boatyard, collecting a paycheck and repaying his uncle's kindness with a poor attitude and irresponsible work habits. Brad had hoped teaming him with the no-nonsense Bruno might help, but the walk said it all: same Michael.

Mansfield stormed aboard and headed straight for the bridge. He elbowed a crewman aside as he entered and faced Tollefson. "It's about time. Let's go."

Brad was incredulous. "Go? We just got here! I haven't even had the chance to go take a piss, let alone turn around and leave."

Mansfield walked to Brad and stood nose-to-nose with him, his finger pointed at chest level. He spoke quietly, menacingly. "You just remember where your money comes from. It sure as hell isn't from doing boat repairs for a bunch of northwoods hicks. I can bring it all down around your ears if you keep giving me shit. Now, how soon can you get this thing moving?"

Brad looked away, took a deep breath, then looked back, hands outspread. "Gimme an hour, maybe two. My crew hasn't even had breakfast."

"Let 'em take all the time they want. They can eat in town. They're staying here."

"No, they aren't. It takes at least three

people to safely run this boat. You have to have that many to . . . "

"So you got your three guys from Duluth, the ones that came aboard with me. They can do it."

"No, they can't. The only one that even works around boats any more is Michael, and if you've been around him more than ten minutes you know he's useless."

"Then they get a crash course from your regular guys, but when we leave this place the only people on this boat will be you, me, and your three stooges. The crew stays here. Got it?"

Brad felt his anger building again, but one look at Mansfield's eyes told him it was a losing battle. His shoulders sagged and he finally replied, "Have it your way, but don't say I didn't tell you when something goes all to hell."

July 27, 8:40 a.m. CDT

The *Voyageur II* is a very workmanlike boat. Her aluminum hull and superstructure are gray against the blue waters she plys. The stubby pilothouse forward is all business, and the low passenger cabins aft are utilitarian at best. Her job is to ferry passengers to and from Isle Royale with stops, not only at Windigo and Rock Harbor, but all around the sprawling National Park.

She was now under way out of Grand Portage, Minnesota, headed for the western end of Isle Royale. There were 14 passengers aboard the 60-foot motor vessel. A family of five stood along the port rail outside the low cabin. Two young couples, honeymooners perhaps, sat inside with their backpacks, and four college-age men were talking animatedly about their upcoming trek across the island wilderness. The 14th passenger sat alone near the aft end of the cabin. The trim woman in the dark hooded sweatshirt, jeans, and Topsiders was lost in thought, and neither the engines nor the chatter of the young men interrupted it.

Gina was recalling her time with Paul. It had been so exhilarating, as if they had each found the perfect match. It seemed that nothing could change that, and when Paul announced he was buying the boat, she had been all for it. She knew that his lifelong dream was to cruise and write about it; finding the boat had been a start toward that goal for him. At first she had eagerly adopted the lifestyle, sailing with him, learning the ropes, and in general enjoying the whole experience. She became a good sailor, and was proud of that fact.

What she had not factored in was the amount of time he intended to spend pursuing his dream. She began to feel isolated, cut off from friends and family, as the cruises grew longer. She recalled the first conversations, her explanation of her feelings, his inner battles. She thought back to that final day aboard, when she'd told him she couldn't keep doing what he wanted. She had been crying but had remained firm: a change had to be made or she could not go with him.

After that day, they had gone their separate ways. She went back to the Twin Cities and managed to get her old job as a hotel manager back. He sailed, wrote, and earned enough from his submittals and a couple of novels to feed his obsession. They had come together again, however briefly, to be there for Rich when Meg had died. Otherwise he had stayed in touch, always, and in every conversation she could still hear the hurt. She had always wondered if he could hear hers as well.

She came back to the present, as she wiped a developing tear from her left eye. She dug into the pocket of the sweatshirt, retrieved a Kleenex, blew her nose, and passed her fingers along the corners of her eyes again.

She wondered how it would feel. She was about to see him again . . . aboard the boat. Had she changed? Had he? If either of them had changed, how? Now, there was all this trouble, and she had been drawn into it. She felt her emotions shift as she remembered the phone call. Her life had been violated, and she needed answers.

She decided to find some fresh air to clear her thoughts. She left her backpack on the seat, rose and pulled the hood of the sweatshirt over her head, and stepped out onto the sidedeck to watch the waters go by.

July 27, 8:45 a.m. CDT

Valhalla was still at the dock in Bayfield. Tollefson's normal crew members were going over procedures and equipment functions with Bruno and Sam; Mike was ignoring them and lounging against a bulkhead. Mansfield had been on the phone, seeking word on his search aircraft. Now, he was pacing the deck, barking at anyone in sight, and looking at his watch every minute or so. He finally went back up to the bridge, bursting in as Brad was pouring a mug full of strong coffee.

He flung himself into the helm seat as Brad watched. He rubbed his forehead, looked at his watch again and started fuming. "How long does it take these guys to teach somebody how to toss a line? Get their asses moving. We need to be out there now!"

Brad shrugged it off. "They'll be done in a while. I'd rather these guys at least have an idea where to be and what to do before we head out. And for that matter, you don't have any idea where we need to head."

Mansfield stood and looked at his watch yet again. "Between you and your crew and the dumb shit at the air service, all I'm doing is waiting. He was supposed to get a fuckin' plane in the air first thing this morning, and nothing's happened. The longer we wait, the more chance they get away somehow. I can't let that happen."

222

At that moment, Bruno walked in and announced, "I guess we're ready whenever." He turned to Brad. "Your crew wants to know — you gonna come back here for 'em or should they grab a rental and head back to Duluth?"

Brad thought for a minute, then reached for his wallet and pulled out a corporate credit card. He handed it to Bruno and guided him toward the door. "I don't know when we'll be back here, so tell them to use this. They can get a car rental down in Ashland. There's a little regional bus that will get them down there."

He closed the door behind Bruno and turned back to Mansfield. "Okay, as soon as they're off, we can get underway."

"Good. I'm gonna check on the damn plane one more time." Mansfield left the bridge.

Brad sat down for a moment, his head in his hands, then shook off the frustration and began to think about departing.

July 27, 9:23 a.m. CDT

Aboard the *Voyageur II*, Gina watched as they motored through the North Gap, between Washington Island and the main island, and passed by the wreck of the *America*. She had read about it on the way. In 1928, the 182 foot steamer had departed the Singer Hotel dock on Washington Island and had struck a rocky shoal shortly thereafter. She was fatally holed, and though her captain tried to beach her where she lies, she was lost. All passengers and crew made it to safety. She had become a major draw for recreational divers, and now a major effort to preserve the wreck was under way.

As the boat entered the long, fjord-like finger of lake that was Washington Harbor, Gina moved from the port side to starboard, craning to see ahead as she looked for the dock at Windigo. She didn't expect to see *Pipe Dream* there yet, but in a little over two miles she would know.

July 27, 12:54 p.m. CDT

The Cessna Turbo Skylane flew over the deep blue lake in perfect VFR conditions. Visibility was basically unlimited; the wind from the past day's storm had given way to low humidity and crystal skies. The pilot, Art Neimi, wore a plaid flannel shirt and a dirty and weathered baseball cap. His thin blonde beard had gray flecks that accented his grizzled look. He'd rather have been home, but his friend down in Illinois had called him with this unusual request. The money was right and he couldn't very well refuse it.

He'd been working at his hangar at the Gogebic Iron County Airport, replacing the left side tire when the call came. It seemed some wealthy guy from Chicago needed to locate his friend's sailboat so he could rendezvous with it aboard a big power cruiser. The rendezvous was supposed to be a surprise so he didn't want any radio calls. Instead, he'd pay premium prices to have the boat located by air and its position relayed to him. At the time he'd thought, "What the hell? It's his money." Art didn't understand the very wealthy and didn't want to.

Art's wife had not been pleased when he told her he was going up, but after he told her what the pay was like, she was more accepting. He didn't relish the thought of flying alone all day, so he asked his 16-year old son to come along. Faced with the option of another day of boring routine, Josh had eagerly agreed. He now sat in the passenger's seat, and as was often the case when he flew with his Dad, he was doing the flying. He'd solo next month, and this was great practice.

They'd taken off and head north-northeast, out over the lake and toward the western end of the Apostle Islands chain. They would start their search there and criss-cross the lake outward toward Isle Royale, looking as far west as Port Wing, Wisconsin and as far east as Ontonagan, Michigan. They'd participated in air-rescue searches before using the same patterns, but never in skies this clear. Even so, if there were very many boats out, it would be like finding the proverbial needle in a haystack.

Art spoke loudly to be heard over the engine. "We're looking for a white, 37-foot sailboat named *Pipe Dream*. We'll have to come in low and astern to have any chance of catching the names."

Josh stared ahead and flew on as he replied. "There are quite a few out — and probably more up the lake a ways. Look." He pointed to the north and west, and at least seven sails stood out.

"Okay — better let me take it when we make the passes." Art took the yoke and began a shallow bank, turning toward the nearest of the boats and beginning his descent.

July 27, 1:20 p.m. CDT

Valhalla powered through the wide passage between the end of Stockton Island and Michigan Island, headed northeast toward the tip of Outer Island. On the lower deck, Mansfield had assembled Bruno, Sam, and Mike to lay some ground rules.

"First of all," he told them, "when we catch 'em, don't kill Perry. I don't care what happens to anybody else, but I have to get Perry to talk. I have to be sure he hasn't left me any surprises before we get rid of him."

Bruno raised an eyebrow, shot a quick look to Sam, and asked, "So there's just him and this other guy?"

"I'm not sure. The woman might be with them if she's met them someplace, but she was way up in Minnesota somewhere. If she's with them, they're farther away than I think they are. The plane's finally up, so we ought to know soon."

Mike looked up from his usual slouched position and asked, "Is that boat worth any money?"

Mansfield was on him quickly, picking him up by the collar of his shirt and speaking directly into his now wide-eyed face. "You little piss-ant! You haven't got any fuckin' idea what's going on here, do you? If that boat shows up for sale after they disappear, what do you think happens then?"

"I . . . I . . . dunno . . . "

"Goddam right you don't! Boats have hull numbers and they are traceable. That boat needs to be on the bottom of the lake by tonight." He dropped Mike's collar and turned away; he had just decided that when the boat went down, the stupid kid would be aboard her with the others.

July 27, 2:20 p.m. CDT

With Art at the controls, the Cessna was climbing out from the last pass. They had looked at twelve boats so far, but they had seen nothing like the name *Pipe Dream* on any of them. They were now over the main shipping lanes and had seen two lakers and a salty — an ocean-going freighter — and several power cruisers as well. It was summer on Superior.

Josh opened a brown paper bag and pulled out two roast beef sandwiches. "Want any mayo on yours?" he asked.

Art looked over at his son. "Just put mine back for now. I'm too busy to eat." He started a slow 180 to head back west and a bit farther north.

July 27, 3:07 p.m. CDT

Gina was sitting on a bench on the lower deck of the Ranger Station at Windigo. She had checked in and told them she was meeting a friend on a sailboat and wouldn't be camping. Then, as the day wore on, she began to wonder if she might have to change that assessment.

She'd stepped off the *Voyageur II* and into a pristine natural paradise. The air was so much fresher here and everything seemed so unspoiled. She had taken a paved walkway up the hillside to the ranger station, an earth-toned structure that blended wonderfully with the surroundings. The building had a low deck across the front, and on one end there was a raised, octagonal turret-like observation area. It housed the rangers' office, an interpretive center, and a small general store with essentials for the many hikers and campers who came each summer.

She looked out across the inner end of Washington Harbor. At the dock, it was less than a half-mile wide. Beaver Island neatly divided it just to the south and west. Two boats — one sail, one power — were swinging at anchor near the island.

The air was chillier now. She reached into

her backpack and pulled out a red windbreaker, then stood and pulled it on over the sweatshirt. She sat back down, her back against the rail, and put her backpack on the bench. She brought her feet up and lay down with the backpack serving as a pillow. The day had been a long one and it was only getting started.

July 27, 3.18 p.m. CDT

Josh was checking the gauges. He looked over at his Dad. "By about 3:30, we'll be at our limit. We'll have enough to get back plus reserve, but that's it."

"Yeah, I know." Art was pleased that his son was being thorough. He'd trained him well. "There are a couple more up ahead. Looks like the closer one is headed toward Isle Royale. We'll finish these two and call it a day." He started his bank and descent to pass over the near boat from astern.

Aboard *Pipe Dream*, Paul had been watching the small plane as it passed astern heading west about a thousand feet up. He'd thought little of it, but a change in the engine sound brought his head around, and he saw the plane turning back and descending toward them. "Rich! Skip! He shouted. Get below, stay out of sight!" The two men quickly clambered below; Skip pulled the companionway hatch closed behind him.

Art leveled the Cessna out at around 150 feet. Josh was at the side window, staring intently below, and when the plane was just astern of the sailboat, Art dipped the wing to give Josh a better look. He watched as they shot past the stern, then turned back to his Dad. "Could be the boat. There was a P in the name but I couldn't see the whole thing well enough. One guy, waving at us. How about another pass?"

"Okay, one more and then we head for home." Art pulled back on the yoke climbing out and turning to go around again."

Paul waved as the plane passed, hoping it was just somebody shooting pictures. He watched it climb out, and then saw that it was turning, perhaps coming back for another look. "Stay below! He shouted. "I think it's coming around again."

Art made the return loop and banked into the descent again. Josh pulled out a set of binoculars for a better look, and was now back at the window. This time, Art dropped a bit lower and brought the nose up just a bit, slowing as much as he dared. As they passed over, Josh brought the transom into the field of view of the binoculars. He pumped a fist, yelling, "That's him! *Pipe Dream*! You can call your guy now!" Art quickly noted the position, the time, and the heading, as Josh wrote them down.

Paul watched as the plane climbed out. This time, it turned to head off to the south-southwest. That second pass had confirmed for him what he already suspected. They had likely been found and their position would be reported. He called out,

"Might as well come back up. I figure we've been spotted."

Skip and Rich moved back into the cockpit. The three men sat in silence, looking ahead as *Pipe Dream* continued her way toward Isle Royale.

July 27, 4:17 p.m. CDT

Art was thumbing the key on a small handheld marine VHF radio. He'd tried calling several times, but they were apparently still outside of the limited range for the little transmitter. He made the call again: "*Valhalla, Valhalla, Valhalla,* this is *Pinpoint.* Over." There was only silence in reply. He glanced over at Josh, who was again flying the plane. "Keep this heading until we get them. They were gonna be over toward the Apostles somewhere."

Josh looked at his Dad. "I always thought you weren't supposed to use marine radios in the air."

"You're not, but as long as we don't call ourselves an aircraft, how will they know?"

Josh just nodded and gave the instruments another scan. This was a lot better than yardwork.

July 27, 4:35 p.m. CDT

Mansfield was simmering again. He sat alone in a padded chair on the deck aft of the bridge, sipping still more Scotch and staring at the Outer Island Light. His frustration was growing by the minute, since *Valhalla* had been doing lazy circles here for almost two hours. Brad had convinced him that charging out into the lake without knowing which way to go might actually put them farther off the mark once *Pipe Dream* was located. Still, to him it was like being stuck in a traffic jam. Even if you had to take a much longer route, moving in any direction was preferable to just sitting. He was contemplating what to do when he found Perry, until his thoughts were interrupted as Bruno stepped from the bridge.

"Mr. Mansfield! It's the plane. They found the boat!"

Mansfield got up and pushed past Bruno, through the door and into the bridge. Sam was writing on a pad as he and Brad listened intently to a slightly broken transmission. " . . . at about forty-seven forty-four north, eighty- . . . " There was static, then it picked back up. " . . . eight west. Heading was about 58 magnetic."

Brad waited, then keyed his microphone. "*Pinpoint, Valhalla*. Say again the longitude. Say again the longitude. Over."

The reply was clearer now. "Longitude eighty-nine twenty-eight west. Eighty-nine twenty-eight west. Over."

Brad waited then grabbed the paper from

Sam. *"Pinpoint, Valhalla.* Confirm forty-seven forty-four north, eighty-nine twenty-eight west, heading five-eight magnetic. Over."

From the speaker, a crackle, then, "Roger that."

Brad replied quickly. "Thank you, *Pinpoint. Valhalla* clear, back to Sixteen." He hung up the mike and pushed the red priority button that moved the VHF from Channel 68 back to a dual watch on Channels 16 and 9.

Mansfield moved to the Lake Superior chart that lay under plexiglass on the navigation table. "So where is it?"

Brad took the paper, moved to stand by Mansfield, and traced from the longitude and latitude scales on the top and side of the chart with his finger. He stopped at a spot west-southwest of Isle Royale. "Right about here. That puts them . . . " He stopped, moved his other hand up and spread his fingers between that point and Isle Royale, then moved them to a distance scale at the bottom of the chart. " . . . uhhh, about sixteen miles or so out. That means we won't reach them before they get to Isle Royale, assuming that's where they are headed."

"Can't you get this thing moving fast enough?"

"Ted, we're almost 50 miles from them right now. Even at my best speed, there's no chance.

Look, I know you're impatient, but we can still get to them before they hit Canada. If the woman went to Grand Portage and they are headed for Isle Royale, I bet she's gone over to Windigo. That's where they're going."

"Good, then we'll catch them there."

"Not a good idea. There's a ranger station there, campgrounds, all kinds of people at this time of year. We'll need to wait them out. If we stay outside the Washington Harbor entrance . . . here," he pointed to the islands west of the entry, "we'll be able to see them if they try to leave."

Mansfield took another sip of Scotch, rolled it around in his mouth and swallowed. "Good. Let's go." He turned on his heel and went back out on deck as Brad throttled up and keyed a heading of forty-four degrees magnetic into the autopilot.

July 27, 7:45 p.m. CDT

A solitary figure stood on the dock at Windigo, gazing down the long finger of Washington Harbor toward the open lake. It had gotten cooler still, so Gina had moved back down to the dock to catch what little warmth she could from the lowering sun. The light lasted well into the evening at these latitudes, but the warmth retreated much sooner. She had decided to give them until 9:00, but sooner or later she would need to sleep.

She sat in silence for a while, lost in a

jumble of thoughts, until she saw a mast approaching down the long channel. She stood to watch it, hoping it was *Pipe Dream.* She also dreaded that it might be *Pipe Dream.* Her inner conflict raged on as the approaching boat grew larger. When it veered to the right and tucked itself in behind Beaver Island, she exhaled loudly, then turned to walk back up the paved way to the ranger station.

July 27, 8:20 p.m. CDT

There was still some daylight left as *Valhalla* charged on toward the western end of Isle Royale. She was now perhaps a half an hour away, but she had not overtaken any boats since early in the passage.

Brad was mulling over their options for arrival. Based on Ted Mansfield's intent, they could not go in to the Windigo dock. Staying outside the harbor entry seemed the best bet. They would need someplace where they could anchor and yet see the entry, and also the areas around the islands to the north and south. He looked at the Isle Royale chart and decided on a position just north of little Barnum Island. They could anchor there, less than a mile from the harbor entry. From that position, they would be able to watch both the North Cut at Thompson Island, and the South Cut at Grace Island. Any boat trying to slip past would have a hard time doing so. Brad also knew that the charts and GPS readings did not always match in this area and that anyone trying to move out at night would have to be very cautious indeed.

He turned to a book rack by the helm and pulled out an almanac, leafing through it to find the date. The moon would be going down by 2 a.m. and he thought they might try slipping past sometime after then.

Mansfield was sitting in the left-hand helm seat, looking intently ahead with the ever-present Scotch in his hand. Brad spoke aloud. "About a half-hour from now, we'll put in here. We can see the whole thing from this position."

Mansfield thought for a moment, then looked over to Brad. "Are you sure there'll be a lot of other people in there? I want to get this over with."

"Bet on it. It's July, it's nice weather, and the place'll be hopping. There'll be the usual hikers and such, and you get other boats, and a lot of times you'll get whole Boy Scout troops."

"Yeah." said Mansfield. "That damn Boy Scout Perry would fit right in." He returned his gaze to the bow as *Valhalla* neared Isle Royale.

July 27, 8:40 p.m. CDT

The light was starting to fade a bit, but there was plenty to show the beauty as *Pipe Dream* passed between the points that marked the beginning of Washington Harbor. They had veered slightly northward and had come in on the north side of Washington Island, then continued inbound between Thompson and Grace Islands to the entry. Paul and Skip were continuing their running conversation about the history of the place, and just now Skip was citing facts about the wreck of the steamer *America* that lay off to port.

"Opened her bottom on one of the rocks that sticks up through here," he was saying, "But they got everybody off okay."

Rich was getting cold, but he didn't want to go below. He turned to Paul. "How far to the dock?"

"A little over two miles in. We should be there in twenty minutes or so." Paul looked up at the sails, felt the dying breeze, and went on. "Time to start the diesel and roll in that jenny." He pulled the shift lever up to neutral position, then leaned down to the engine controls and gave the diesel a few seconds of pre-heat. He advanced the throttle a hair and pushed the start button. After three cranks the diesel thrummed to life. He stood, looked back over the transom to assure that cooling water was being ejected with the exhaust, and then turned back to find Skip and Rich already furling the genoa.

Skip was grinning as he hauled the furling line. "Figured you wouldn't want to do it all."

Paul grinned back at him, and at Rich as he tended the sheets. "You guys'll make a crew yet."

With her jib furled, *Pipe Dream* motor-sailed on toward the waiting dock as her crew prepared to drop the main.

July 27, 8:57 p.m. CDT

Brad had brought *Valhalla* in to the south of Washington Island, but seeing no other boats ahead of them, he decided to use the waning light and idle through a narrow channel between the eastern end of Washington Island and the tiny Booth Island. That would lead straight to his intended anchorage just north of Barnum Island. As they cleared the narrow passage and looked to the east-northeast, he thought he saw a light down in Washington Harbor. "Could be them," he thought, "but maybe not." He glanced at the radar but there was too much ground clutter to pick out a sailboat that far in.

Mansfield had gone below to talk with Bruno about dealing with Richard Perry. Brad knew this could not end well. By night's end, he could very well be complicit in the deaths of some innocent people. He knew that Mansfield intended to kill Richard Perry, and the others as well, and then sink the boat in deep water with the bodies aboard. If he didn't try to stop it he'd always have to carry his share of the guilt. He'd be an accessory to murder at the very least. If he did act to stop it, that action would have its own drastic effect. He would be brought down with Mansfield's whole house of cards, and would spend a very long time in prison. He would lose his family, his business, his friends . . .

The waypoint alarm on the GPS sounded, signaling they were near their anchorage for the night. Brad checked the depth sounder and looked off to port at Barnum Island. He turned the boat into the wind, shifted to reverse, and applied some throttle until motion had stopped. At that moment, Mansfield burst in. "What are you doing now?" he asked, his face in its perpetual scowl.

"This is where we drop the hook and wait. Look." He pointed toward the Washington Harbor entry, visible in the gathering gloom. "From here we can see both cuts and the harbor. If they try to sneak out we'll see them."

Mansfield looked Brad straight in the eye, "Better be right."

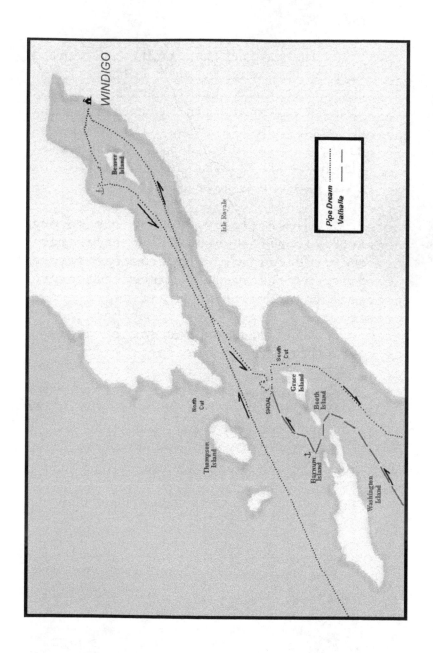

Chapter 10
WINDIGO

July 27, 9:02 p.m. CDT

As *Pipe Dream* neared the Windigo dock, Paul saw a woman walking quickly out onto it. The stride, the spring of the step, and the familiar profile brought his heart to his throat. Gina. He almost shouted out her name, but thought better of it.

Skip had pulled a set of fenders from the cockpit locker and had rigged them fore and aft of the starboard boarding gate that was formed by a single top lifeline between two stanchions. Docklines were rigged at the bow and stern. Skip now stood near the open boarding gate with the bow line in his hand, ready to step to the dock. Rich was behind him with the stern line in hand.

Paul angled the bow in toward the dock, then put the helm over and applied a little reverse power. Skip stepped neatly to the dock. Rich followed, stepping by Gina with a mumbled "Hi." Skip quickly made the bow line fast to cleat, then walked aft to help Rich.

Paul let the diesel idle for a few seconds, then leaned down and pulled up on the kill switch. In the pristine silence that followed, he could hear his own heart beating. He retrieved another dockline, and tossed the bitter end to Skip. "Let's set a single spring line." He walked forward to make his end fast at a midships cleat on the toerail.

Skip brought the other end around the same dock cleat that held the bow line, pulled it in and cleated it. *Pipe Dream* was secure at Isle Royale.

Paul's head was swimming. She was right here in front of him and he had no words, none at all. He stepped silently to the dock, walked to Gina and simply stood, regarding her with questioning eyes.

Gina returned his gaze for a long moment, as tears began to well up in those familiar eyes. Her shoulders begin to shake with the beginnings of weeping. He reached out to pull her to him, to comfort her . . . but she stepped back and slapped him hard across his left cheek.

He recoiled, startled, his hand rising to to his cheek. Then Gina's voice hit him like a hammer blow. "All these years, all these years, and then when I see you it's like *this*?   What have you got me into?"   She seemed to turn the volume up a notch as she continued, "They were in my house. Some bastard was in my HOUSE! Do you have any idea what that *feels* like?"

"Gina, that's why I wanted you to . . . "

"Wanted me to WHAT? Leave everything and come running up here . . . forget I have a life?"

Paul was over the shock, and now his own anger began to rise. He had to make her understand. "It's because I value your life above anything else that I called! Didn't you *listen* when I called? These people are serious! They want to kill Rich, and believe me, they'd have tumbled to you one way or another whether I'd called you or not!"

"If you had just . . . "

"Just what? Let Rich try to survive on his own? He'd already called you anyway, but regardless, I'd be helping him. We can't change what's happened. But we can sure as hell do our best to keep all of us alive!"

She stepped back, looked at Paul, then at Rich, then back to Paul. She started to sob, deep wracking sobs, and Paul stepped forward to enfold her in his arms. She didn't resist this time, and she buried her face in the space between his shoulder and neck as the tears came in torrents.

They stood that way for a time. Rich turned away self-consciously and walked to the far side of the dock. Skip busied himself by tidying up the boat. He stepped aboard and went below.

Finally, Paul and Gina separated. She accepted an offered Kleenex from Paul and dabbed at her eyes. She looked again into Paul's eyes and a slight smile played over her face. Then she said, "Come with me." She turned and took Paul's hand, and led him across the dock to Rich. He couldn't meet her gaze, but she reached out and took his chin in her hand and turned his face toward her. "We're here," she said, "we're here for you, just like you'd be there for us." She leaned forward and kissed his cheek. Then it was Rich's turn to cry.

Skip had put water on the stove for hot tea. He could hear the water in the kettle starting to hiss a bit over the propane flame as he reached into the sliding doors over the fridge to get the tea bags. He felt the shift in the boat as they stepped aboard, and soon Rich, followed by Gina and Paul, stepped down the companionway stairs. Skip squeezed in close to the galley stove to let them pass.

"Gina," said Paul, "this is Skip. I'll let him tell you why he's here."

She extended her hand and Skip took it, almost bowing from the hip. "Pleased to meet you, even if we could have asked for better circumstances." He released her hand and tuned back to the galley. "How many for tea?"

After the kettle had whistled and four mugs of tea had been properly steeped, they sat around the lowered saloon table. The mugs were set on coasters to avoid leaving rings on the teak surface.

Skip told his part of the tale, from his first glimpse of the hit-man in Bayfield to his rescue by Paul and Rich. Gina listened in amazement. Her expression clouded as it went on. As Skip finished, she turned to Paul. "I'm so sorry!" she said. "I never realized just how serious this all is."

"Well," replied Paul, "it's serious enough

that we need to get off this dock. We can tuck in behind Beaver Island. There are a couple of other boats swinging over there now, and I doubt that anybody will try anything when there are witnesses."

Skip sipped his tea, put it down, and asked, "You figure they know what this boat looks like?"

"Yeah. Remember the plane? And Gina said she called her house from Grand Portage to get her messages, and somebody picked up. They were there." He turned to Gina. "Do you still have pictures up? I mean of us and the boat?"

"Yes. I never could bear to take them down."

"Well, I'm pleased, but right now I wish you'd been pissed at me enough to trash those pictures. They know exactly what we look like. The guy in the plane probably had the whole description."

They sat in silence for a while, finishing the tea. Then Paul rose to go on deck. He looked at them and said, "Let's get over there and drop the hook." He slid open the companionway hatch and went up, as the others got up to follow.

July 27, 9:07 p.m. CDT

Mansfield had poured himself another glass of Scotch. He was staring into it now, remembering the first time he'd been involved in a "removal." There had been a chance — just a chance — that one of the public officials involved would get cold feet and turn against him. He had asked for help and had gotten some advice: take care of the details yourself. He did so, arranging the hit so it would look like the target had walked in on a convenience store robbery. The small-time street thug he had hired to do it was never caught, because afterward Mansfield had invited him to go fishing on Lake Michigan. That had been hard, killing the thug, but once it was done Mansfield had felt a sense of power he'd never experienced before.

He swirled his Scotch and took a sip, thinking to himself, "If I'd handled it personally from the start this time, I wouldn't be here on this goddam boat." He turned to the window and stared out onto the gloom.

July 27, 9:47 p.m. CDT

Paul finished backing down against the anchor. He waved to Skip, who made the rode fast and coiled up the excess on deck. With the big CQR anchor lost at South Twin, Paul had brought out his "lunch hook," a Fortress FX-16 aluminum anchor with 20 feet of chain and 200 feet of half-inch nylon rode. Paul pulled the kill handle and shut off the diesel. In the sudden silence, they looked about them at the forested hillside to the north and Beaver Island to the south. This was a good, sheltered area, and it would also be very difficult for anyone to spot them in here at night.

"What now?" Gina said, not looking at Paul, but over his shoulder at the darkness along the shore. She paused for a moment as if about to speak further, then released her breath in a long exhale.

"We have preparations to make. Let's get 'em done before we rest. It's . . . "

Rich interrupted. "Rest? Christ, there are people after us, probably right out there," he pointed down the entry, "people trying to kill us! How can we rest?" He was getting agitated again. It seemed at times that keeping him calm was a full-time job.

Paul continued, ignoring Rich's outburst. "....it's important that we be alert. We're going to have to leave in the middle of the night, I'd say 2:30 or 3 a.m. or so . . . after the moon is gone. If anybody's out there, they'll be tired, too. Seeing us from a distance on a dark night like this is going to be tough, and without lights we may be able to slip past. Soon as we're out of this channel we turn north and scoot up the North Cut at Thompson Island."

Skip spoke up. "We'll need good waypoints in the GPS if we're going to make that run back up between the big Island and Thompson in the dark. It's tough enough in daylight."

"Yes, but I've heard the charts and GPS positions don't match up to well around here. We'll still need to be very cautious. And it'll be tougher still if the wind comes up on our nose. "

"We're SAILING out?" Gina turned as she spoke.

"It's a south wind right now, light as it is. It should carry us right back out and then up past Thompson Island. If they don't see us, they still might hear us. My old Westerbeke is a great engine, but it sure isn't the quietest thing around."

Rich joined the conversation, "Won't the sails make us easier to spot?"

"We'll just roll out some of the genny. We should ghost along nicely. Then after we're on the main lake, we'll put 'em all up and run like hell."

Nobody spoke for a while. Paul cleared his throat and continued. "We have no idea if they are waiting out there, or what kind of boat they may have. We'll need to take a close look as we get near the points. We also need to leave ourselves some options. Just a sec."

He went below and returned with a folded NOAA chart. He sat down and pulled out a small flashlight, turned it on and illuminated the chart on the seat beside him. He put a finger on the chart and said, "We're here. We're tucked in northwest of Beaver Island, across the channel and west of the dock. If they come in to the dock they might not see us over here, and there are the other anchored boats nearby to confuse the issue."

They all looked to where Paul was pointing. He then moved his finger away from their anchorage, along a line down the center of Washington Harbor and trending toward the south shore. He explained as he traced the course, "I figure we'll do best about centered, with this breeze, but when we get close to the end I'd like to hug the south shore. It'll give us a good view and, if they are hidden west of Thompson Island," he pointed to a larger Island to the north of the Washington Harbor entry, "we might spot 'em."

Rich was skeptical. "Aren't we trying to go north?" he asked.

"Yes. Normally we'd stay right and then take the North Gap. But before we make the turn, I'd like a better idea what's out there. And then, there's this for a contingency plan." His finger moved to the smaller Grace Island, south of the entry. "If we think we're spotted and they're coming for us, we'll be close enough that we might able to duck in behind here through the South Cut and maybe have time to get ashore. There's a campground on the east end of Grace. If there are any people there, they'll think twice about coming for us."

Skip looked at the chart again. "That's also good for another reason. Depends on what kind of boat they have. If it's a smaller boat it won't do us much good, but if they have one of those big jobs they'll draw four or five feet. Look." He pointed to the area north of Grace Island. There were rock outcroppings there, some just below the surface. "They'll have to skirt around those. That would give us a little more time if we can put those between us and them."

Everyone fell silent for a few minutes, then Paul continued, "Okay. Anybody out there watching for us probably has radar." He pointed up to an object suspended on a line near the starboard spreader. "That radar reflector has to come down. A sailboat isn't a very good target without one."

"Maybe so," said Skip, "but your mast makes a pretty good target at close range. Any ideas how we mask that?"

Paul thought for along moment and then turned to Gina, saying, "You remember where I keep the chute? The cruising spinnaker?"

"Under the V-berth, isn't it?"

"That's the place." He patted her hand, then continued, "Have Rich help you. Pull it out and get it up on the foredeck."

Skip looked over at Paul and Gina, questioning, "What have you got in mind?"

"The chute's in a sock," said Paul, "so we hoist it but leave the sock down. Then we tie the bottom of the chute down tight to the base of the mast. That'll cover the mast top to bottom and dampen any bounce they get off it."

Rich, confused by the terms, asked, "A sock?"

Paul replied, "Yeah, that's a kind of sleeve that pulls down over the sail to keep it from filling when you hoist it. Then when it's all the way up you pull on another line and the sock goes up so the sail can fill. In this case we leave it down."

Skip nodded and said, "Okay, that ought to work. And if we hang some stuff off your forward toerails it'll help mask the hull a bit."

They all stood in silent agreement and went about the business of readying *Pipe Dream* for the coming night. Gina and Rich went below and found the cruising spinnaker. They opened the forward hatch and fed the sail up to Paul. Paul attached the shackle of the spare jib halyard to the head of the chute; when Rich and Gina rejoined him on deck they began hoisting the chute in its long sock up into the night.

Skip stood on the starboard deck where he'd found the small looped halyard that held the radar reflector aloft beneath the spreader. He hauled the reflector down, detached its clips from the halyard, turned, and took the reflector below.

The chute was at almost full hoist now. Paul stopped when top swivel was still a few inches below the halyard's exit sheave. He didn't want the chute to foul the genoa furler when it was time to sail. He wrapped the halyard three times around the mast-mounted winch and then secured it to a cleat below the winch. Paul held out the free end of the halyard to Gina, saying, "Come here and help me with the line. Rich, grab the chute and pull it down tight."

Gina knelt beside Paul as Rich stepped to the mast. He grabbed the sock with his hands and began to pull downward but Paul said, "No, wrap your arms around the whole thing so you can pull on the sock and the sail inside it all together." Rich adjusted his grasp as he was told and began to haul down again.

Paul handed the free end of the halyard to Gina. "Here," he said, "take several wraps around it while Rich holds it down." She did just that. When she'd finished Paul took the bitter end from her and passed it back through the topmost wrap, then brought it back to a cleat low on the mast. He looped the line under the cleat and then took his locking turns.

"Okay," he said, "that'll do it. You can let go now." Rich released the sail and it stayed tight against the mast in its sock.

Skip had come back on deck with towels and blankets and had been forward tying them off to the lower lifelines, where they now hung down to mask the bow. Finished, he stood and walked back to stand with the others at the mast. He looked up at the spinnaker in its sock, then back toward the bow, cleared his throat and said, "That's about as good as we're gonna do. She won't be invisible but this'll keep the signal down."

Everyone fell silent for a few minutes. Then Paul reminded them, "Okay, rest is the priority. I'll take the first watch. It's almost 10:30, so I'll wake somebody at 1 a.m. Gina, how about you?"

Skip protested. "I can take it. Let her get some rest."

"This is no time for false chivalry. The fact is, nobody's tried to kill her in the last few hours, and she's probably better rested than any of us."

Skip grinned at the gallows humor, then motioned to Rich. "C'mon, let's get some sleep."

Rich flashed a rueful grin. "I'll try, but it's gonna be a tough sell. My mind keeps racing . . . "

"Trust me," said Paul, "You'll be asleep before your head hits the cushion."

They all returned to the cockpit, and Rich and Skip continued their way below. There was some shuffling, a word or two and then silence. The moon had stooped lower and was now just above the trees. On deck, Paul and Gina regarded the scenery, the night, and each other. "You too." Said Paul, softly, motioning her below. "You have the next watch."

"If you don't mind, I'll stay here awhile. I couldn't sleep anyway. This whole thing is so unbelievable . . . "

"Yes, it is, but believe it. You need your rest as much as any of us, in spite of what I said awhile ago."

"I was never very good at doing what you wanted. Why start now? Besides, I kind of like it up here. Maybe I'll sleep in the cockpit."

"Suit yourself. But it's going to get pretty cold. This is Lake Superior, not inland in Crystal." Paul sat behind the wheel, and Gina sat on the starboard seat with her back against the cabin. The moon continued to drop; the air grew heavy with the evening chill.

July 27, 11:32 p.m. CDT

Paul was right. It had gotten colder. Rich and Skip, exhausted from the ordeal, were asleep below. Gina had remained on deck with Paul, sharing their first quiet moments alone in several months. She now sat beside him at the wheel, silent but regarding him with those eyes that used to hold so much love. He was uncomfortable in that steady gaze. He was sure he knew what was coming. He was wrong.

Gina dropped her gaze, reached down and

took his hand. "It's just like you, you know. You put sailing first, friends second, everything else third . . . but I think I understand now. There's something about this place, about the boat, that I never saw before, could never share with you before. It's magic. Even in this situation . . . " As she reminded herself of their predicament, her breath caught and the tears came again. It wasn't fear. She genuinely loved this man, this aggravating, undependable man who would put himself on the line for others. She slid down, put her head on his shoulder, and turned to bury her face in the wool sweater.

Paul's hand crept up to caress the dark hair that now bore a hint of gray. It had been a long time since he had held her like this. His left arm pulled her shoulders to him, and they sat in silence as the moon dipped lower behind the pines that loomed on the shore.

July 28, 1:40 a.m. CDT

Valhalla swung easily on the anchor. She was lying just off little Barnum Island with her bow pointed east-southeast. The Washington Harbor entrance was visible at about 40 degrees to port. The moon was low on the horizon. Soon what little light there was would be gone.

July 28, 2:30 a.m. CDT

Pipe Dream came to life. They had each had a chance to catch a little rest, but the time had come to act had come. The moon was gone, and the darkness would hide their movement as well as they could expect. Skip was at the bow, hauling in the anchor rode. Rich was ready at the starboard jib sheet.

Paul lifted his face to the night, felt the breeze. "We have a little southerly right now. We'll use it to ghost out of here with no engine noise."

Rich looked back at him, "Just tell me when."

"Hold it until Skip says the anchor's up."

From the bow they heard the clank and rattle as the chain came aboard. Skip called back, "We're clear. Let me get this out of here before you bring 'er out." In a minute, Skip came back along the side deck, the lightweight Fortress anchor in one hand, the chain draped in a loop over one shoulder, and the large coil of rode over the other.

Paul reached out to take the anchor as Skip stepped down into the cockpit. He noted the neatly coiled rode and the fact that there was nothing trailing behind on the deck, and remarked, "Should have asked for some help. You really do know your way around a boat." He turned to Rich. "You'll have to get up for sec. The anchor goes in there." Rich stood and moved away from the starboard seat. Skip opened the cockpit locker hatch, and then he and Rich stowed the anchor and closed the hatch.

Rich moved back to the seat and picked up the genoa sheet as it tailed off the winch. He looked back at Paul. "Okay to bring it out?"

"Bring it out slow. We'll use about two thirds of it."

Rich began to haul in the sheet, and Skip kept a little tension on the furling line to make sure it didn't foul itself on the drum. The sail began to unwind from the forestay, and as soon as the wind began to fill it, it started unfurling on its own. Skip increased his tension on the furling line, then gripped it firmly and stopped it when the sail was around 70 percent out. He cleated the furling line, and Rich passed the sheet up over the stripper and into the jaws of the self-tailing winch.

Paul was clearly pleased, "I told you guys you'd make a crew yet." He asked Rich to bring the sail in a bit. Rich grabbed the winch handle, put it in its socket on the winch top, and slowly turned it, the winch pawls clicking in the night, until Paul said, "Good."

The sail was drawing well now, and they could hear the ripple of water along the hull as *Pipe Dream* gathered way. They cleared the western tip of Beaver Island and continued down the reach of Washington Harbor toward the main lake.

Skip moved to the port side, looking alternately ahead and at the shore, barely discernable in the darkness. "Running like this without lights — the Coasties would have our lunch if they caught us." He paused, then continued. "Come to think of it — what if we let ourselves get caught by the Coast Guard?"

"They'd just turn us over to the police if we tell them what's going on. From what Rich says, there's no telling how far up it goes, so we stay with the plan. Let's get him to Canada and from there he can get it worked out. Short of catching this Mansfield guy and turning him in, that's our best bet."

Gina was below at the nav station. Her attention was focused on the GPS chart plotter display and the moving icon that represented *Pipe Dream's* position. She called up to Paul, "Steady ahead. Looks good so far." She'd done this often when she'd sailed with him before, and it only made her more aware of how much she missed it.

They continued with very little conversation for over a half-hour, the boat slowly sailing west-southwest along the wide channel. As they got nearer the entrance, Paul brought the helm over to head toward the southernmost point as they had planned.

Skip was staring ahead, then moved forward to take a better look; then he turned back to Paul. "There's someone out there, a single anchor light. He's almost dead ahead. I make it about a mile down, maybe just off Washington Island."

"Yeah, I see him." After the terse reply, all was tense silence aboard *Pipe Dream*

July 28, 3:17 a.m. CDT

Valhalla's bridge was silent. The faint glow coming from the instruments, the radar display, and the idle chart plotter screen was the only illumination, and it cast Mansfield's face in a chiseled, bas-relief effect as he stared out into the darkness. He took another sip of his Scotch, and wrinkled his nose at it. It wasn't his usual Dewar's.

Brad Tollefson was half asleep in the armed swivel seat behind the helm. Sam was snoring on a settee to port. Mike was nowhere to be seen. Bruno was keeping watch as instructed. He was alternating between standing outside and watching from the enclosed bridge. He had just come back in. He stamped his feet and rubbed his shoulders with crossed arms, "Fuckin' cold out there for July."

Brad stirred and stretched, "What did you expect? We're in the middle of Lake Superior."

Mansfield stood and peered intently through the glass. "What's that?" he said, putting down his Scotch and heading for the side door. He opened it and leaned out, staring into the darkness, and then leaned back in and motioned to Brad. "Gimme those binoculars."

Brad retrieved the Steiners from their pocket

by the helm, then stood and walked to the door. Mansfield snatched then impatiently out of his hand and then leaned back out and raised the binoculars to his eyes. He watched for almost a minute, then handed the Steiners roughly back to Brad. "Something moving out there." He said. "What do you think?"

Brad took Mansfield's place at the door, raised the binoculars, and peered into the darkness. He scanned across the Washington Harbor entrance, once, twice. On the third time, he stopped his slow scan as he pointed the binoculars toward the southern shore. He saw a shift in the shadow against the backdrop of the dark land and the slightly lighter water. There *was* motion, and though he couldn't see any running lights he suspected it might be a sail. He watched to be sure, then turned to Ted. "Might be something."

"Might be something? It *is* something. I bet it's a sailboat. Don't they have to have lights on at night?"

"Yeah, everybody does."

"Then it's them. They wouldn't be out there with no lights unless they don't want to be seen. Let's get over there."

"Ted, we can't be sure. If we wait 'til . . . "

Mansfield interrupted that thought in his sudden rage. "Goddammit, start this fuckin' boat!"

He turned to Bruno, then to Sam, who was rising from the settee, rubbing his eyes. "Go find that kid. I want everybody up here."

Brad turned the key and, one after the other, the big diesels thrummed to life. He hit the anchor light switch on the panel and then the navigation light switch. "Let's get that anchor . . . " he stopped, realizing nobody was listening. He turned to Ted. "I need these guys out on deck while I get the anchor up."

Ted regarded him coldly. "Just raise it and get this tub moving."

"I said I need somebody out there. They need to work the deck wash hose to get all the mud off the chain. And also to free things up in case the damn windlass jams. My regular crew all know what to do without being asked. Why the hell did you put them off the boat in Bayfield?"

Mansfield turned and spoke, his voice a growl. " Fewer witnesses."

July 28, 3:22 a.m. CDT

Pipe Dream had reached the point that marked the Isle Royale end of the South Cut. Paul and Skip were watching the anchor light in the distance and debating whether they should make the turn and head in behind Grace Island. Then, across the water, they heard the roar of a big diesel starting and soon another. The decision had been made for them.

Paul put the wheel over to take the boat to port. He shifted to neutral, hit the preheat for a few seconds, and started the diesel. There was no benefit to remaining silent now. He shifted into forward gear and pushed the throttle forward until the engine was running at around 2500 rpm. *Pipe Dream* surged forward. He shouted at Rich and Skip, "Furl the sail!"

The sail was quickly wound tight around the forestay and the sheets secured. Rich stared off to starboard, toward the light. As he did, he saw running lights come on and the anchor light go off. "Are you sure it's them?" he said, his face white in the night.

"Why else would they start up at this hour? And that's a big sucker from the sound of it." Paul was grim, intent on his course.

Skip emerged from below, a flashlight and the chart in hand. "We need to make for this area." He illuminated the chart and pointed to the north shore of Grace Island. To the north and west, between their current position and the big cruiser, there was an area of rocky shoals, and just west of the shoals, a tiny island. He moved his finger to a point just north of the tiny islet. "If we head here, they'll have to head out and around those shoals. When they do, we can curl around to the south and get behind it. That ought to at least buy us some time."

Paul's eyes moved from the chart to the water ahead, as he strained to see. "Turn the light out. I have good night vision but not with that on." His vision sharpened and he could make out the point off to port and the tiny island just to starboard. "Watch the depth sounder. The board's up, but we still draw a bit over four feet. Yell if it hits ten." He turned the wheel, swinging the bow to starboard and toward the small islet.

Skip glanced at the island, then tuned on the flashlight for a second to steal another quick look at the chart. "Good idea. He's got to bring that big mother all the way around, and then he has to deal with rocks too. He won't be able to use his speed."

"Yeah, provided he draws more than four or five feet." As he finished the tone of the diesels in the distance changed from a low idle to a steady hum. A searchlight beam came on at the bow of the cruiser, aimed in their general direction.

Rich had been standing by the companionway, but he sat down quickly on the port side, seemingly trying to put more distance between himself and the lights. "Shit!" he said through clenched teeth, "Here he comes."

July 28, 3:29 a.m. CDT

On *Valhalla's* foredeck, Bruno stood with Sam and watched as the windlass hauled up the anchor, waiting as instructed to clear any jams if necessary. The rode and chain disappeared neatly below as the big Delta anchor finally rose to the bow roller. Sam trained the stream from the deck wash hose at the chain and anchor as he'd been told, and they watched as the mud sloughed off and the chain disappeared below, dripping but clean. Bruno stepped forward and retrieved the retainer pin on its lanyard, and placed it through the holes to keep the anchor aboard.

He rose to head back aft, motioning to Sam. "That's got it. Let's go." As they began to move back toward the safety of the main deck, they heard the engine tone rise and they had to adjust their footing as the boat began to move forward. They stepped over the low rail and down into the well in front of the lower deckhouse, just below the bridge.

Bruno reached beneath his jacket and found the cool metal in its holster, then pulled it out. The Smith & Wesson .357 revolver was an old gun, but he preferred it for its lighter weight and power. He checked the cylinder; he'd probably need it soon. Satisfied, he reached back beneath the jacket and replaced the revolver in its holster.

Sam watched as Bruno checked his gun, then shuffled off toward the lower cabin to retrieve his own. Bruno watched him go, then set out to find the kid and get him on deck. "Little pain-in-the-ass," he said to the night.

On the bridge, Mansfield was red-faced, exhorting Tollefson to close in on the sailboat.

"Goddamit!" he screamed. " They're right there! Get us close and we can keep them from getting away. I gotta get that fuckin' Perry aboard. Get this thing moving NOW! Ram the sonofabitch if you have to and we'll haul their asses out of the water!"

Brad left the throttle where it was, looking at the chart in the red glow cast by the navigation lamp. "I'm not taking chances in here. There are rocks. We have to go down a way and come back to stay off them . . . "

Below, Sam had come back to the foredeck with his gun. He picked up a handheld spotlight and flashed it out into the night. The powerful beam caught a flash of white in the distance, and it was moving to starboard.

Above, Mansfield saw the distant sailboat slide by in the beam of light. "They've changed course!" he screamed at Brad. "They've changed course. Get over there! Speed this tub up!"

Tollefson, now angry himself, shot back. "You haven't heard a goddam word I said! We go in there, we'll . . . " Mansfield's sudden sucker punch caught him flush on the jaw, and he stumbled back and sat down heavily on the deck. At that moment, Bruno entered the bridge.

"You guys seen . . . " He stopped in mid-sentence. Tollefson was sitting on the deck, stunned and looking up at Mansfield. "What the fu . . ."

Mansfield pointed to Tollefson. "He moves, cold-cock him!" He stepped in front of Brad and to the wheel, looking out ahead, and pushed the throttle levers forward, The sudden roar of the engines was followed by a lurch as the big cruiser began to gather way.

Tollefson struggled to get up, reaching for the back of the helm seat and beginning to rise. "No! You can't . . . " Bruno's pistol butt came down across the back of his head, and he slumped to the deck, unconscious and bleeding.

Mansfield concentrated on the sailboat ahead. Below, Sam had recovered from the sudden motion and was now training the searchlight on *Pipe Dream* as *Valhalla* quickly closed the distance between them.

July 28, 3: 35 a.m. CDT

The crew of *Pipe Dream* had been watching as the big cruiser began to head for them, waiting for it to change course and go around the shoals; they'd decide what to do next when the other boat had committed to that.

Skip broke the concentration. "Once he's turned away, if we tuck in close as we dare we might be able to keep . . . " At that moment, the note of the diesel engines increased to a loud roar. The searchlight faltered for a moment, then returned.

"Jeezus! What the hell is he doing?" shouted Paul, frozen at the wheel and staring in awe as the cruiser accelerated and sped straight for them . . . and toward the rocky shoal.

"Wonder what he draws?" Skip was watching the accelerating cruiser. He could see that whoever was driving was not that familiar with large powerboats. "He's put on way too much speed and his stern's down!"

At the wheel, Paul could feel Gina's fingers gripping his arm tightly. Her voice was pitched high with fear. "Oh, God," she said, "they're going to ram us!"

July 28, 3:37 a.m. CDT

On *Valhalla's* bridge, Tollefson lay unconscious behind the helm seat. Bruno was to starboard, his revolver in hand, braced against the frame of the open doorway to the deck. Mansfield stood in front of the seat, gripping the wheel and glaring ahead as the once-distant sailboat grew larger in the spotlight. He was talking, chewing on words as if they were a tough steak: " . . . been fucking with the wrong people. Little punk-ass bean counter . . . This is what happens when . . . " At that moment, *Valhalla* struck the shallow rocks.

The rending, tearing sound was quickly followed by the change in pitch of one of the diesel engines operating at full throttle with no load. The starboard diesel still ran but lay on its side, dislodged from its mounts. Its prop and shaft were gone, and a large portion of the bottom with them. The boat's forward motion was halted so quickly that Bruno was flung forward against the door frame, his left arm caught between his body and the structure of the boat. He heard, rather than felt, the bones snap. The gun was jarred from his right hand and bounced on the deck, then slid to the base of the helm console. Tollefson was caught by the helm seat base before he could slide farther forward, but Mansfield hit the wheel hard and bent forward over it far enough to hit the top of the console with his head. The deck seemed to rise, then fall back and start to tilt to starboard. Within seconds the starboard diesel coughed, sputtered and then stopped with a loud bang as water entered its air intake, causing it to seize and throw a rod through the block. Only one diesel was running now, and it quickly sputtered and then stopped as well, leaving an eerie silence

July 28, 3:38 a.m. CDT

Aboard *Pipe Dream,* Paul was frantically searching for a way to evade the onrushing cruiser when they heard the crunching, grinding sound and saw *Valhalla* rise up, then settle and stop. Across the water they heard the change in the pitch of one of the diesels, followed quickly by an explosion of some kind. They watched in stunned silence for a moment. Then Rich stood, gaping. His mouth began moving silently. Then his repeated phrase grew louder with each iteration: "Holyshit-holyshit-holyshit — HOLYSHIT — HOLY SHIT!" He pumped his fist in the air and began to laugh or cry. Paul couldn't tell for sure which.

They heard the remaining diesel aboard the cruiser stop. In the surreal silence, Skip turned to Paul, gestured with both hands toward the scene and said, "Stupid bastard — ran his damn boat right up on the rocks. How dumb can you get?" He looked at the cruiser, now settling visibly at the stern and listing well to starboard, then continued. "She's going down and fast. Must have ripped her bottom clear out."

Gina stood beside Paul, still gripping his arm. Paul took one hand off the wheel and encircled her shoulders with it, pulling her into a sudden hug. All he could say was, "I'll be damned."

July 28, 3:41 a.m. CDT

Valhalla's decks were now steeply inclined as she listed and settled toward the stern. Mansfield had been stunned by the impact and had fallen and slid across the deck toward the injured Bruno. He shook his head to try and clear his vision, then rolled to his hands and knees in an attempt to get up. While he groped around for support his hand found an object, familiar in shape. It was Bruno's gun. He grabbed it, stood falteringly with one hand braced against the tilting console, and looked at Bruno. The big man was still standing, but his left arm hung limp and useless. Mansfield began to shout, "What the hell…"

"You stupid asshole — you wrecked my boat!" Brad Tollefson had been jolted back to consciousness. He sat on the sloping deck, clutching the helm chair for support. His scalp was bleeding, but his eyes were focused on Mansfield with a look of pure contempt. "I told you about the shoals! I told you!"

Mansfield pointed the gun at him. "Shut the fuck up. How do we get this boat off the goddam rock?"

Tollefson began to laugh, an ironic grin spreading across his face in the red glow of the navigation lights. "Off the rock? She'll be off the rock soon and on the bottom. In minutes! That's what you did, you dumb shit! You ripped her bottom out!"

"Shut up and tell me where the lifeboat is."

"I have an inflatable life raft, in a canister on the aft deck. By the look of things you'll never reach it. We can get in life vests, but in this water we'll be damn near frozen before we can get ashore."

"So where are the life vests?" The deck shifted under them and Mansfield could feel the boat moving, even shifting just slightly astern. The movement lent urgency to his voice. "Hurry it up!"

Brad was trying to stand, still using the helm chair for support. He heaved himself up, clutching the back of the chair with both hands. He nodded toward the starboard side settee. "Over there. Cabinet underneath, the door says PFD on it. Should be a bunch of 'em." He reached back, gingerly touching his scalp and feeling his wet stickey blood.

Bruno moved down along the bridge interior to the settee. He went to one knee, crying out in pain as his broken left arm hit the top of the seat. Under the seat edge was a tilt-out door marked "PFD storage." He opened it with his good right hand and pulled out one of the orange safety vests. He looked at it and said, 'How'm I supposed to get this on with my fuckin' arm broke?"

Mansfield stumbled and slid down the deck and grabbed the vest from Bruno. Without a word, he began to put it on himself, and as he did so he moved to the higher door to port and struggled through it to the outer deck. Bruno watched him with contempt as he left, and then pulled out two more vests. He tossed one to Tollefson, then stood staring at the other.

"Here," said Brad as he sat and slid down the sloped deck toward Bruno. "Let me help you get this on." He took the vest and slowly raised it up Bruno's left side, trying not to put pressure on the arm as he slipped the webbing up and over the shoulder. He was almost successful.

Bruno flinched as Brad moved the vest past the break. "Unnnnh!"

"Sorry."

The spasm of pain subsided. Bruno looked over at Brad, shaking his head and glancing at the bleeding scalp wound. "Sorry about that. You and me go back years, but he said I was goin' to prison if I didn't do what he wanted." He looked to the port side door where Mansfield had gone. "Miserable asshole, ain't he?"

"You don't know the half of it. Wish I'd never gotten involved with him." As Brad finished the sentence the stricken cruiser began to slide backward off the shoal, settling as she went. She was going down. He helped Bruno get his good right arm in, then secured the front snaps and ties. "That'll have to do. Let's get on deck." He grabbed his own vest and began putting it on.

Bruno reached into the compartment and took out two more vests. "You seen Sam? Or that kid?"

"Take those. If we find them they'll need 'em." Brad didn't tell Bruno that he suspected Sam was already in the water, having gone overboard with the impact. He also knew that Michael had been sulking in one of the aft cabins below. Since he hadn't appeared to whine about the situation, he was likely unconscious, maybe worse. Either, way, the kid probably wouldn't make it; Brad wondered how he'd break the news to his sister if he survived the night.

They struggled up across the tilted deck and through the door to the port side deck, following the route Mansfield had taken. They found him there as well, staring out into the night with the revolver in his hand. The stern of the boat was fully submerged already and they could hear air being forced out of hatches and doorways from below as the sliding, sinking movement astern gathered speed. As if to emphasize the moment, the remaining lights flickered out as the rising water engulfed the battery banks.

"Okay," said Brad, staring down at the black water, "stay aboard until the water's up to there." He pointed over the side, to the open port just below them. "When it reaches that port, we'll need to jump. We have to get clear so we don't get snagged on anything."

They watched the water nearing as the doomed boat slid backward and downward to meet it. The forward part of the hull was making a scraping sound as it slid from the rocks beneath it.

They waited until they could wait no more. Then Brad yelled, "Go!" He helped Bruno crawl up and over the rail. The big man groaned in pain, then fell the short distance to the water below. Brad quickly hauled himself over as well and flung himself outward as far as he could. The jolt of cold upon hitting the 40-degree water was electric, even in July. The shock left him gasping for breath. He found Bruno floating beside him, grabbed at the life vest strap, and began to kick away from the boat, pulling Bruno with him.

Mansfield waited longer. He stood, watching the two men below him moving away. Swearing softly to himself, he soon realized he was not in control of this particular situation. It was an unwelcome feeling, but there was nothing left to do now but jump. He quickly hauled himself over the rail and dropped into the water with a gasp.

July 28, 3:47 a.m. CDT

Pipe Dream's crew stood in silence, watching intently as the big cruiser slipped backward into the waiting water. They were around five hundred feet from the stricken boat, and there were still lights on aboard it.

Paul pointed toward the eerie scene, still dimly lit by a few lights. "Look. On the deck, just aft of the bridge. There's somebody out there." As he finished the thought, the lights flickered once then went dark. In the darkness, the shadow of the white boat stood out as a dark gray shape against the night. They could hear a hissing sound along with a slight grinding.

"Must be a huge hole," Skip said quietly. "That's air being forced from belowdecks. Lotta water comin' in quick." The dark gray shape of the superstructure sank lower and grew smaller. In less than a minute, all that remained above water was the top of the bridge and its electronics mast, although they could no longer see it, and that was slipping away fast.

Paul shifted into forward, then gave the throttle a boost. "We'd better get over there quick."

Rich tuned immediately, his face white, his eyes wide. "NO!" he shouted. "We're clear, we can go! They can't get us now! What are you doing?"

"We have to try and pick up . . . "

"NO! Call somebody, they'll get anybody left out there!"

"Rich, they won't make it at all if we leave. By the time anybody gets here the hypothermia will do them in. We'll pick up anybody we can, then take them in to Windigo."

"Are you crazy? They were going to kill us!"

Paul was angry now. "Sit down and shut up! Like I said when we picked up Skip, all they could do now is shiver you to death. We can tie them, if necessary, but we don't leave anybody there to die. What if it's another Skip?"

Rich looked sheepishly from Paul to Skip. He mumbled, "Sorry . . . " then sat down and put his head in his hands, as Gina moved beside him to put a comforting arm around his shoulders. Paul lowered the throttle to an idle as they neared the shoal, then shifted to reverse and gave the diesel a short boost of power to stop *Pipe Dream* at the scene.

July 28, 3:50 a.m. CDT

Brad and Bruno floated in the icy water, their speech already quivering from the cold. They looked toward the approaching sailboat, and Brad raised an arm to wave feebly, try and attract attention. "They g-get closer, t-try to yell," he told Bruno.

Bruno was beginning to shiver visibly. "C-can't do m-much with this arm, b-but I c-can shout."

Fifty feet away from them, a jumble of teak deck furniture floated in the darkness. A forearm was wrapped over the top of a slatted table, a head low in the water behind it. The other hand, on the end of the table, still gripped a revolver. Mansfield watched the approaching sailboat, trying hard to ignore the numbing cold and thinking out his options.

July 28, 3:54 A.M. CDT

Aboard *Pipe Dream,* Skip had the spotlight on deck and was now scanning the area. He halted for a moment on some flotsam, perhaps deck furniture; seeing no motion, he moved on to his right, scanned past something and quickly returned the beam to it. "There!" he shouted, and Paul looked down the beam of the light. He could see a

276

raised hand, and he thought he could hear a cry over the idling diesel.

Paul raised the shift lever to engage forward gear, and *Pipe Dream* began to close the distance to the figures in the water. "Two of 'em! Drop the stern ladder — it's calm enough, so we can bring them aboard that way."

Off to port, Mansfield pulled his head lower to the water behind the shielding furniture, watching the sailboat as it made its way toward Brad and Bruno. The boat slowed and then swung its bow toward him. He could see figures at the stern of the boat, the spotlight on the two others on the water. He began to kick, slowly pushing his hiding place ahead of him toward the bow of the boat.

Paul brought *Pipe Dream* to a halt, her stern near the two men in the water. Skip had the stern ladder down, and was now standing on the rung closest to the water, gripping the stern pulpit with one hand. His other hand held the boathook. He extended it to the floating figures, and a hand took the end as Skip hauled back to bring them to the ladder.

In the water, Mansfield had reached the bow. He released his floating refuge, and now began to make his way quietly aft along *Pipe Dream*'s port side.

Aboard, all hands were focusing their attention at the stern. Skip now had Tollefson's top life vest tie in hand, but Tollefson said, "H-help him f-f-first. His a-arm is b-broken." Skip released his hold on Brad's vest and took Bruno's instead, pulling him toward the ladder.

Skip looked at the big man, saw the blue cast to the lips and the shivering. "Can you get your feet up? There are two steps under the water. Get your feet on them!" He pulled, and could see the effort in Bruno's face; Tollefson was behind and pushing.

Amidships, in the water along the port side, Mansfield could hear them now over the idling diesel. He made a mental note. "Steps in the water."

At the stern, Bruno had found the lower step with his feet. Skip was hauling him up with Brad trying to help from in the water. "Annnghh!" Bruno cried out as a wrench of his broken arm brought a new wave of pain even through the numbness of the cold. Paul reached over the pushpit rail to help, and they slowly brought Bruno up the steps, then to the teak taffrail on the aft end of the cockpit. He urged Bruno to step up. "Can you get a leg up and over the rail?" He patted the top bar of the stainless steel-pushpit.

Bruno stood shivering and looking at the rail. Slowly, laboriously, he raised a leg and managed to get it up and over while Skip and Paul supported him. He grabbed the backstay with his good hand and stepped down to find the inside of the taffrail. "Okay," said Skip, "almost home. Turn

as you go over and bring your other leg across."
Bruno did as he was told, wincing in pain but
determined, and soon brought his other leg into the
cockpit. They helped him step down and move
forward.

Skip turned his attention back to Tollefson,
still in the water. Paul motioned to Rich. "Check
him for weapons."

Rich hesitated, but Bruno grunted "L-lost it
w-when we h-hit them r-rocks."

"Check him anyway." Paul said, and then
turned back to help Skip with Tollefson. Rich
began to search the shivering Bruno, and Gina
moved to assist him.

Along the port side, Mansfield remained
still. He could hear the conversation at the stern as
Tollefson was being helped aboard. "Bring him
up," said a voice, and yet another said, "Here, grab
this rail." Then a third, quivering: "G-got it. J-
jeezus, it's c-cold . . . " He listened as they got
Tollefson over the rail and into the cockpit. Then
the voices seemed to move forward a bit. Mansfield
was shivering violently now, but he doggedly
finished his way to the stern. He passed the
exhaust. The smell of diesel exhaust was strong and
warmer water from the engine cooling system
splashed him, but he was at the ladder. He gripped
the ladder rail with his free hand, revolver in the
other, and struggled to find the lowest step with his
feet.

Brad Tollefson sat shivering in *Pipe Dream*'s cockpit as Skip and Paul, seated to each side of him, searched him for weapons. "I d-don't have any." He said. The he looked back to starboard, toward the shoal, "Th-that was my b-boat. Stupid s-sonofab-bitch sank her."

"Was he driving?" said Skip, nodding across toward Bruno.

"N-no. It was that goddam M-mansfield."

Rich looked up sharply. "Mansfield was aboard?"

"Y-yeah. He was c-calling all the sh-shots."

Paul looked at Tollefson, then back over to Rich. "Wonder where he ended up."

"R-right here!" The voice from the stern was a shivering snarl, and they turned to see Ted Mansfield at the stern rail, leveling a revolver at them. The look on his face was one of pure malevolence, as he turned his gaze to Rich. "Hello, Rich. He sneered. "You're h-hard to t-track down."

"Ted, I . . . "

"Shut the f-fuck up!" roared Mansfield. He was shaking almost uncontrollably but he managed to keep the gun trained on the cockpit. He stepped slowly over the pushpit, then sat down heavily to port behind the wheel. He waved the gun at Bruno. "G-go check and see if they have any g-guns." He turned to Gina, motioning again with the revolver. "Get me a fuckin' b-blanket or something. I'm f-freezing."

Bruno glared for moment at Mansfield; then, broken arm notwithstanding, he rose and made his way below. Gina looked to Paul, who nodded; she got up and followed Bruno.

Mansfield stared at Rich in silence. Gina returned shortly with a blanket and held it out to him, and he grabbed it roughly and used one hand to work it around his shoulders, never taking his eyes off Rich. Finally he spoke. "Now . . . Tell me what you wrote down. Everything."

Rich wouldn't meet his eyes. "I didn't . . . "

"Look at me, goddam it! What the hell did you write down? And don't tell me nothing. You always wrote everything down . . . damn anal retentive prick!"

Rich looked slowly up, swallowed hard, and then sighed. His shoulders slumped and he motioned toward the companionway. "It's all there. In my sport jacket pocket."

Mansfield didn't take his eyes off Rich as he yelled to Bruno, "Look for a sport jacket while you're at it!"

"Goddam," came the voice from below, "it's

slow goin' with this busted wing. Hurts like hell. Jeeez . . . "

"Get down there and help him look," Mansfield said, gesturing to Brad with his gun hand, "and while you're at it see if they have any dry clothes. I'm still frozen."

Brad glared back at Mansfield. He started to say, "You sunk my goddam . . . "

"Just do it!" Mansfield roared. He watched as Tollefson stood and made his way below; then he turned his attention back to Rich. "We'll see what's in that jacket. Then we'll figure out what comes next."

Paul felt the hair on the back of his neck stand. This man intended to kill Rich, and probably all of them. He thought for a minute, then spoke, "Look, if you kill him, or any of us, you won't get back anywhere safely, not with this boat."

Mansfield looked at Paul, then at Skip and then back to Rich. He seemed to resolve some inner dilemma as he glanced up at the mast and then back to Paul. When he spoke, his voice was firmer now, most of the shiver gone. "I think you're just trying to buy time, but in case you're right, where can we go? I don't want any big cities. Someplace small, out of the way."

Gina had been quiet for some time but now her anger came to the surface. She looked

Mansfield straight in the Eye and replied, "How about hell?"

Mansfield bristled at the comment. He glared at Gina for a long moment and turned back to Paul. "Keep a leash on this bitch and answer my fucking question. Where can we go?"

Paul shot back, "Why the hell should we go along with you? You're planning to kill us anyway."

Mansfield slowly turned the gun until it pointed directly at Gina. When he spoke it was a low, menacing snarl, "If you want to watch her buy it first that's fine with me. You've got one minute to start with some answers."

Paul looked at the gun, which was still aimed at Gina. It couldn't end here. Not like this. They needed time. He took a deep breath and then replied, "Okay. Just leave her alone. There's always Canada, or back down to Bayfield."

"Fuck Bayfield. There's too much going on there, over that asshole that missed." Skip looked up at him with the comment. Mansfield continued "I'm not going to Canada either. Too much shit with that. Someplace small, stateside."

Paul paused, his eyes on Gina. He didn't look back at Mansfield when he said, "Well, the closest is probably Grand Portage."

"Show me where that is."

"Skip," said Paul, turning. "Where's that chart?"

"The one we had out is just Isle Royale. You need the chart for the whole lake."

Skip rose to go below; Bruno was blocking the way, the Chicago gun in hand. A dirty sport jacket was draped over his good arm behind the gun. "Found this in an old duffel," Bruno said, "and we found this sport jacket. That what you wanted?

"Yeah," said Mansfield, motioning at Skip, "let him through. But watch him."

Bruno moved back below and Skip followed. There were some shuffling noises, and then Brad Tollefson came up the companionway stairs holding a sweatshirt and a pair of pants. He'd changed into some of Paul's clothes himself, and they were obviously too tight but they were at least dry. He threw the sweatshirt and pants to Mansfield and sat heavily on the port seat.

Skip came back up after a minute, unfolding another chart to half-width and handing it to Paul. He turned back, found the flashlight they'd been using, turned it on, and trained it on the chart as Paul spread it out on his lap. Paul used his fingers to point to the options. "We're here," he said, pointing to the western end of Isle Royale, "and this is Grand Portage." He moved his finger to the left and upward.

Mansfield looked for a moment, then responded. "No, too damn far for Benjie to come. He's still in Bayfield. How about over here?" He held the gun steady on Paul with one hand, and with the other he pointed to Eagle Harbor, on Michigan's Keweenaw Peninsula.

Paul looked at the chart and thought quickly. Eagle Harbor could be a sleepy little port, especially mid-week. If they went there, he knew, Mansfield's chances of getting away with this would increase. He also knew that Mansfield was not familiar with the area. He cleared his throat and spoke. "There are a couple of reasons that's not a good place."

"What reasons?"

"Well, for one, it's a really treacherous entry. You have to line up on range marks, and if there's any fog, it can be nasty. For two, the place gets a lot of tourist business this time of year. It'll be really crowded, and I'd guess you don't want that." Paul stole a glance at Skip; Skip's expression told him, "Good one."

Mansfield looked over at Tollefson. "Is that right?" Tollefson looked from Mansfield to Paul, then back, and nodded almost imperceptibly.

"Okay," said Mansfield, "What about here?" His finger rested on Copper Harbor.

Paul had been to Copper Harbor several times. He knew it was a busy place in the summer and that the anchorage and the new dock facilities would be active. Another ferry, the *Isle Royale Queen IV*, made daily trips to the other end of Isle Royale from the port. It would be hard to hide a crime from witnesses, and he doubted Mansfield had ever been there. He'd have to lie convincingly. He steadied himself and said, "It's a lot better than Eagle Harbor. It's quiet and out of the way, and there is a good anchorage."

Mansfield thought for a minute, then looked toward Tollefson, but saw only his back. He turned and leveled the gun at Skip. "Is he being straight with me?"

Skip glanced at Paul and then looked straight into Mansfield's eyes. "I've been in and out of there several times. It's like he says. A good place to duck into in a storm, but not a lot going on." Skip saw Tollefson turn slightly and raise an eyebrow at the comment, but nothing else was said.

"So how hard is it to get to by land?"

"When you get there, you can call your guy in Bayfield and tell him to come over and go straight up U.S. 41. It ends there."

"Okay, we make for there. Get this thing going." He picked up the sweatshirt and pants with his free hand and stood. Looking at Bruno, who had come back to the companionway stairs, he said,

"Watch 'em. If anybody tries anything shoot her first. I have to get out of these wet clothes." He pushed past the big man and made his soggy way below.

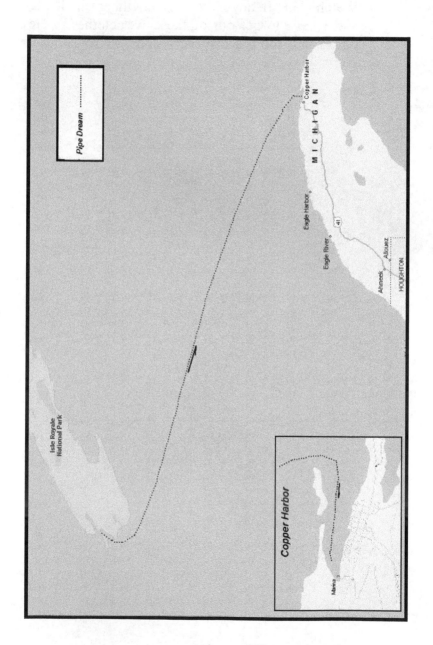

Pipe Dream

Isle Royale
National Park

Copper Harbor

MICHIGAN

Copper Harbor

Eagle Harbor

Eagle River

41

Ahmeek

Allouez

HOUGHTON

Marina

Chapter 11
COPPER HARBOR

July 28, 4:23 a.m. CDT

Pipe Dream was underway, headed east-southeast. She was close-reaching under genoa only, with Paul at the helm. Skip was next to Paul on the starboard side of the helm seat. Ted Mansfield sat to port, watching everything closely. He had changed into the pants and sweatshirt and had a dry blanket wrapped around his shoulders, but the revolver was visible in his right hand. Bruno sat on the starboard side, forward against the bulkhead. Tollefson had helped him get into a change of dry clothes as well. His broken arm was now in a makeshift sling; Gina had wrapped magazines around it with duct tape to form a crude splint. It had hurt too much when the sling pulled it tight against his body, so she'd put a dry life vest back on him to help pad the arm. She sat aft of the big man on the same side. Tollefson was on the port side, his head now wrapped and bandaged. Rich sat between him and Mansfield.

Under constant threats from Mansfield, they'd put away the sail and the clothing they had used to mask the boat from radar, and then motored carefully out through the South Cut between Grace Island and Isle Royale. Once they were on the open waters, they'd turned off the diesel and unfurled the big genoa. Mansfield had pulled Rich's notes from the sport jacket pocket, looked them over, and stuffed them into his own pocket. He'd been silent for a time, but he was alert and vigilant with the gun. Everyone aboard knew he'd shoot without hesitation if anything was tried.

Gina still sat just aft of Bruno, who held the Chicago gun at the ready. She regarded him and then said quietly, "How can you do this? We saved you. You know that. And I helped with your arm." She looked at the splint and sling.

"I'm really sorry, but I ain't going to prison for anybody. I'm locked in. I got no choices."

"Yes, you do!" she said, her voice rising, "You . . ."

"Shut up! Just shut up!" Bruno said suddenly, his eyes going from Gina to Mansfield and back. Mansfield had looked up at him when the subject was raised. "Like I said . . . no choice." Gina knew he'd do whatever Mansfield told him to do, and she dropped the subject.

July 28, 7:47 a.m. CDT

Daylight had come, bringing with it a change in the breeze. It had eased, then clocked steadily around and picked back up until it was blowing steadily at 11 knots from the west-northwest. *Pipe Dream* was now running wing-on-wing, the genoa poled out to port and the main boom held to starboard with a preventer rigged to the rail. Gina had taken over at the helm for Paul, who sat beside her on the starboard aft seat. On her opposite side sat Mansfield, willing himself to stay alert, with the gun at the ready. Skip was on the starboard deck forward of the cockpit, tending the preventer in case a jibe was necessary. Bruno stood in the companionway with the gun in his good hand; he could steady himself more easily there. Rich was below, sitting in silence and desperately trying to think of a way to survive the day. Tollefson lay asleep on the port settee.

Gina had found herself falling quickly back into habits she'd developed so long ago. Her eyes shifted from the sails to the water in a practiced sailor's regular rhythm. Her keen senses told her as much as the instruments did about the wind at her back; she was watching the main for any signs of back-winding, and making small helm corrections to prevent it. As she realized how quickly it had all come back to her, she admitted to herself how much she'd missed it. "Damn," she thought, "If we can get out of this . . . "

The thought was interrupted as Bruno mumbled, "I gotta hit the can." He turned to go below, but Mansfield stopped him.

"I want you up here with me. Just do it over the side."

"Come on, I got this busted arm."

"So? You only need one hand. Just do it."

Bruno glared at him, then made his way into

the cockpit. He went up and over the coaming to stand at the port rail.

At the helm, Gina felt the breeze freshen at her back. She looked up at the main to see a faint ripple at the trailing edge . . . and perhaps a chance to do something. Her right foot moved over to nudge Paul's left foot, and he glanced up at her. She looked at him and rolled her eyes up at the main, then forward to Skip.

Paul looked back at her, a question in his eyes, and again her foot tapped against his, her eyes rolling. He looked up and forward, and then at Bruno along the port rail, who was tucking the gun into his makeshift sling and fumbling at his fly with his good hand. Paul's eyes sharpened as he looked back to Gina, nodding ever so slightly. "Just might work!" was his unspoken reply. He stood and cleared his throat.

Forward, Skip looked back at Paul, who had his hands to starboard, hidden from Mansfield's view. Paul was making a gesture by using his left thumb and forefinger to form a closed ring, then pulling with his right as the ring opened, his eyes rolling up to the mainsail. Skip realized quickly what he wanted, nodded to catch Paul's eye, and slowly reached down and released the snap-shackle that held the preventer.

Gina waited until she was certain that Skip had released the shackle. She stole a glance to port, where Bruno was relieving himself over the rail; she looked back up at the sail, felt the wind, and then very lightly turned the wheel to starboard.

Mansfield felt the slight change in direction, then looked at Gina and started to say, "What the hell are you . . . "

Several things happened in a fraction of a second. Before Mansfield could complete his question, the aft edge of the mainsail was backwinded. Then it suddenly filled on its forward side as *Pipe Dream's* stern moved through the wind. Without the restraint of the preventer, the boom slammed sharply across the boat, striking Bruno and knocking him overboard. In the uncontrolled jibe, the boat lurched as the boom came over and Mansfield, who'd tried to stand, was thrown off balance. Paul lunged across behind Gina, desperately trying to reach the gun. Mansfield's right hand convulsed as Paul struck his arm, and the gun fired a wild, unaimed shot, the bullet going through the companionway opening and through the bulkhead forward of the galley. Down below, the slowed round struck Rich in the left arm just below the shoulder. Rich cried out in pain. Tollefson woke with the gunshot, rising up and grunting, "Wha . . . "

Paul had fallen as the gunshot sounded, and now Mansfield regained his balance, leveling the gun at Paul and Gina. "Goddammit!" he screamed. "I oughta shoot you all right now! Is that what you want? Goddammit!"

'Look," said Paul, sitting slowly up, hands raised, and motioning back to Bruno, "we have to go back and get him. We can't just let him . . . "

"You should have thought about that before you pulled that stunt. Fuck him, keep going."

"He'll die."

"Yeah, he'll die. Keep going, and get this boat straightened out."

Paul looked back over the rail. Bruno's still form was visible in the water; he had the life vest on under the splint and sling, and Paul knew he'd stay afloat. He also knew that hypothermia would kill Bruno if he was not recovered. They'd failed to wrest control from Mansfield, but still, he'd never think of abandoning anybody if there was a chance. He looked Mansfield in the eye and said, "I'm going back. Shoot me if you think you have to."

He slowly stood and then started to turn the wheel, but stopped as Mansfield gripped Gina's left arm and put the gun to her temple.

"I don't have to shoot you," growled Mansfield. "Not yet."

Paul looked back once more, then at Gina. He returned the boat to her prior course, then called to Skip. "Let's bring it back over and rig the preventer again." Then to Mansfield, "Now let her go."

Mansfield held the gun to Gina's temple for a long few moments, then removed it and released her arm. Gina looked back at him, not with fear, but with complete contempt and loathing. She moved from behind the wheel, still staring at him, and she didn't take her eyes off him as she backed down the companionway to help Rich.

Skip had brought the boom back to starboard, secured the preventer, and was now back in the cockpit. Mansfield felt uncomfortable with both men in the cockpit with him, and no help. He trained the gun on Skip. "Get some ropes. You aren't going to give me any more shit."

Paul nodded to Skip, who rose and opened the starboard cockpit locker. He retrieved several smaller lines from teak pegs on the forward end of the compartment, and flung them over on the port seat.

Mansfield rose and said to Skip, "Turn around, slowly."

Skip looked back at him, then turned and faced forward. Mansfield brought the gun sharply across the back of Skip's head, and Paul yelled, "Hey!" as Skip crumpled to the cockpit sole.

Mansfield quickly turned the gun and trained it on Paul. "Now you tie him, and tie him up good. I know knots. Don't try to pull anything."

Paul looked at the revolver, then at Mansfield's face, and finally to Skip's unconscious form. He engaged the autopilot, stepped forward and picked up two of the lines Skip had retrieved and bent to the task. When he had finished, Mansfield knelt, the gun still on Paul, and checked the knots and the tightness of the bindings. Satisfied, he stood and told Paul to lift Skip to the cockpit seat.

Skip was not a small man, and Mansfield called Tollefson to come up and help him. It took them several minutes to wrestle Skip onto the seat. By the time Paul lifted his feet up to complete the job, Skip was beginning to regain consciousness. He opened his eyes and tried to move, then muttered foggily, "What the hell . . . "

"He made me tie you." said Paul. Sorry." He patted Skip on the shoulder.

"Get up," said Mansfield. "If she's done with Perry, you two are gonna tie them both up. Get those ropes and get down there."

Tollefson went below as Paul reluctantly picked up the remaining lines. He turned to the companionway. "Gina," he said, "how're you doing with Rich?"

"I think his bleeding has stopped," she replied. "I'm wrapping it now."

Rich added weakly, "Yeah, I think I'm okay.

Christ . . . "

"Enough small talk," growled Mansfield, "tie them both."

As Paul stepped below, Mansfield followed with the gun at his back. "Him first. Where he is. Then her, up front."

They tied Rich, with Tollefson securing a line around his ankles and Paul working the arms. He was slow and careful because of Rich's injured shoulder, which brought more cursing from Mansfield, but at last the job was done. Paul helped him to lie on the settee, then moved forward as Mansfield checked the knots, always with an eye on Paul. Then Paul helped Gina onto the V-berth forward, tying her as gently as he could without Mansfield objecting. He whispered as he bent over her to tie her wrists. "I'm so proud of you. That took a lot of guts. We'll get out of this somehow..."

"Hurry it up!" Mansfield was almost spitting the words. He was on the edge and Paul knew it. He worked quickly then, finishing Gina's bindings. As he made the last knot fast, Mansfield told him to come back aft, then told him to move into the head to port. Mansfield then moved past him, going forward and checking Gina's knots. He turned back to Paul. "Okay, back up on deck. You and I will finish this trip."

Paul glared at him for a moment, then

moved out of the head compartment and aft past Tollefson, who had slumped to the port settee again. As he reached the companionway Mansfield followed, his gun still at Paul's back.

July 28, 3:14 p.m. EDT

Pipe Dream pressed onward toward Copper Harbor in the afternoon breeze. Her unusual deck crew sat silently, Mansfield with his gun always ready, Tollefson back in the cockpit and staring off at the horizon, and Paul thinking hard about possibilities. Skip was conscious, but he had not spoken as he lay tied on the starboard cockpit seat. The only noises from below had been an occasional grunt from Rich when he shifted his weight and his injured shoulder sent a new round of pain through his body. Paul was thinking furiously about possibilities. He was certain this would not end well unless something were to change.

They had passed into the Eastern time zone. They were crossing the shipping lanes and far off on the horizon Paul could see the white pilothouse of a huge laker, moving upbound toward Duluth. He knew from experience that the distance would close very quickly, and he thought to himself, "Maybe . . . "

As a plan formed in his mind, he turned to Mansfield, "Look, I have to go. I'm sitting here with my back teeth floating."

"Okay, but do it below. No more of that rail

shit."

Paul rose to go below, glancing as he did at the remote VHF microphone by the helm in its Velcro retainer. Pushing it down into the retainer to depress the push-to-talk thumb switch just might work. He stooped low as he passed Skip, whispering, "Stick your legs out a little." He continued below and to the head with Mansfield behind him, gun in hand.

Paul made a little small talk while he was below, asking Gina and Rich how they were doing. They both replied that they were okay, and Mansfield barked at them all to shut up. Paul headed back to the helm. As he entered the cockpit he looked at Skip. His legs now stuck out a few inches, just forward of the helm.

As Paul moved past Skip, he feigned a trip over Skip's protruding feet, stumbled at the helm and reached out to catch himself in the fall. As he did so, he jammed the remote VHF microphone down into its retainer. He risked a glance at it as he stood back up. He was certain it was keyed and that his radio was broadcasting. He only hoped the microphone was sensitive enough.

He stood up and moved back to the helm, sitting down on the starboard side behind the wheel. The microphone was directly in front of him. Somehow, he had to get Mansfield closer.

They sailed on for a time, and Paul watched

the laker grow larger as it approached. The dark hull was visible now above the horizon, well within VHF range. The big ship would pass astern but quite close. That was all he needed. He reached up, pointed to the instruments, and said, "Look, I've got to show you something if it's just going to be the two of us on deck when we get to Copper Harbor."

"What?"

"You have to be back here to see it. Somebody has to steer and the other one has to watch the depth."

Mansfield got up and moved to the port side of the helm seat. "Okay, show me." The gun was leveled at Paul's chest.

"This," Paul said, "is the depth sounder. Anything under 8 feet or so and I get nervous. You'll need to call it out as we go in."

"That all?"

"Well," said Paul, now thinking hard, "I just wanted to say that I have to hand it to you. Even though I know you're likely going to kill us, I have to at least admire what you've been pulling off."

Mansfield was partly angry, partly flattered. His ego had to hear the rest. "How so?" he asked, eyes leveled at Paul's.

"Rich Perry told me what he'd found. He

told me why you want him dead. I mean, when he started telling me some of the names in your book, I couldn't believe it. You have everybody in there. You're laundering money from all kinds of illegal activities, and the payoffs you've been pushing to Chicago officials, state and federal officials, cops, media people — wow! I've never seen anything like it, except maybe in the movies, and you actually did it! Maybe there ought to be a movie called 'The Ted Mansfield Story.' Or maybe 'M&L Investments: The Ted Mansfield Story.' How about that?"

"You won't live to see it if there is."

"I know, but just from that book in your safe-deposit box, a good screenwriter could make an academy award winner. Think about it!"

"I've heard enough of your bullshit."

"Okay, but you're going to have a tough time hiding this. I mean, *Pipe Dream* is a fairly good-sized boat and she's federally documented so you can't just change the name and sell her."

"Not a problem. When we get to this Copper Harbor, you're going to join your friends. I'll go ashore and call Benjie. He's supposed to have two more guys with him in Bayfield by now. When they get here, they'll take this boat out with all of you aboard. You're gonna disappear without a trace."

"Oh, so these guys of yours know how to

handle a Tartan 37?"

"Shut up."

Paul did so, looking back now at the laker passing about a thousand yards astern. As he did, the clear air was split with five short blasts from the laker's horn. Tollefson looked up quickly from his port side seat, recognizing the signal for danger, but he stayed silent.

Mansfield's head jerked around toward the noise "What the fuck is that?"

"That's a greeting. Wave, but keep your gun out of sight. Somebody could have binoculars on us." Paul leaned down, picked up his air horn and raised it. "I have to answer, or they'll think I'm some kind of a stuck-up prick." He gave five short blasts of his own horn, then put it away. Tollefson stared at him for moment, and Paul could see the inner conflict raging behind those eyes; then the eyes went back to the horizon without a word. For the first time since *Pipe Dream* had left Isle Royale, Paul felt a hint of hope.

July 28, 3:40 p.m. EDT

The Coast Guard Seaman was on the phone with his superior. He'd made it to his E-3 grade without ever hearing anything quite like the recording he had received from one of the big lake ships, and he wanted to be certain he handled it properly, "Yes, sir," he said, "Right away, sir." He hung up, turned to his console and called the laker on Channel 22, where they'd been instructed to stand by. He asked them to keep monitoring the other transmission on Channel 16. They were instructed to relay any new information promptly. Then he finished typing the message transmitting the audio file to his Commander, and clicked on "send."

July 28, 6:55 p.m. EDT

Pipe Dream was near the entrance to Copper Harbor. Mansfield held his pistol at the ready while Tollefson worked the lines and Paul secured the mainsail to the boom. As the last tie was secured, he motioned with his free hand. "Get down here and take us in. You find a place to anchor this tub and then we settle things." If anything, his voice had an even harder edge on it than before.

Below, Rich cried out in pain as he shifted and pressure was put on his wounded shoulder. Skip had been hauled below and put on the port settee, still tied, as they neared their destination. Mansfield didn't want anything the least bit suspicious showing on deck. "Hold on." Skip spoke just loudly enough for Rich to hear him over the thrum of the diesel. "If I read your pal right, it's gonna hit the fan soon. Just lie there and keep quiet."

"O-okay," Rich replied, "but watch Mansfield. He'd just as soon kill us all."

"I know. Just keep your chin up.   If the whole thing with the freighter means what I think it means, he's in for a surprise."

On deck, Paul had returned to the cockpit. Mansfield now sat on the port side by Tollefson, his pistol leveled at Paul as he stood behind the helm. Paul pushed the throttle forward and turned the wheel as *Pipe Dream's* bow swung to starboard.

Mansfield looked up sharply, his brow furrowed.   "I said anchor! Where do you think you're going?" His eyes stayed on Paul, and he extended his gun hand menacingly.

Paul maintained the turn. He knew that if they were to have any chance at all, they had to get nearer to the little marina. "Look," he said, "the last thing you want is to draw attention.   Nobody anchors out here, because the holding ground's bad and the swells make it untenable. Everybody goes in toward the launch area on the west end of the harbor. If we try anchoring out here, we'll have every set of binoculars around on us.   They'll wonder what kind of idiots we are." He risked a glance at Tollefson, who remained silent and stared ahead.

Mansfield thought for a few seconds, then stood and looked ahead toward the launch area and dock. There were some people over there, but not many. He swore under his breath, then looked back at Paul. "Okay, we go in and check it out, but don't make a move unless I tell you to." He waved the gun toward the companionway and the people tied below. "If she means anything to you, you'll do exactly as I say."

Paul brought *Pipe Dream* down the passage toward the small marina and launch facility on the western end of the harbor. He could see just a few cars near the modern building by the docks, and a couple of people walking along the piers. There were several smaller power cruisers and one sailboat at the marina. Off to port there were two larger sailboats at what were, apparently, private docks. Other than that, there was little to give him hope that his plan had succeeded.

Along the shore to the north, two men fished from a green-hulled Old Town canoe. Ahead, and coming down the center of the harbor toward the east, there was a young couple in a two-person sea kayak. They were paddling smoothly and in unison. The woman, in front, smiled and raised one hand to them, then resumed her paddling strokes. Astern, a small fishing boat was motoring along toward the pier, two men working to stow their gear in tackleboxes.

Mansfield grunted, "Stop the boat. Now. We anchor out here." Paul responded, shifting to reverse and applying power until *Pipe Dream's* progress was halted.

As *Pipe Dream* slid to a stop, the young kayakers were just off to port. They dug their paddles in and slowed, and the young woman called out, "Did you guys just come in off the lake?"

Mansfield moved close behind Paul, the gun at his right kidney. "Careful." He whispered through clenched teeth.

Paul forced a smile as he looked at the young couple. "Yes," he said "From Isle Royale." As he looked at them something was just not quite right. It didn't fit.

The young man spoke up now, "That's quite a trip, isn't it?"

Paul suddenly realized what he was seeing. Under their life preservers, there was not the usual Spandex or recreational gear. He had a sudden hope as he recognized what it must be: Kevlar vests . . .

"POLICE! DON'T MAKE A MOVE!" The shout came from behind them, on the starboard side of the boat. The two "fishermen" in the Old Town canoe had worked their way in as the kayakers attracted attention. They now sat with guns drawn, one aiming at Paul and the other at Mansfield.

Mansfield, startled, looked to the canoe. He said, "Look, I'll..."

"DROP YOUR WEAPONS!" It was a female voice but one with commanding authority. It came from the pleasant young woman in the bow of the sea kayak; she and her partner each had their pistols trained at *Pipe Dream's* cockpit. Paul slowly looked back around, and at the stern, two more men sat close by in the little fishing boat, their guns drawn and aimed.

Mansfield took stock of his situation, then slowly raised his hands, the gun suspended by the trigger guard and swinging like a pendulum from one finger. He extended it slowly over the side and let it fall into the water as Paul raised his own hands and exhaled in relief.

July 29, 12:42 a.m. EDT

Pipe Dream lay beside the dock at Copper Harbor. Paul had spent the last few hours helping the authorities sort everything out.

At first, Mansfield claimed he was the victim of a kidnapping. He said he'd been on a pleasure cruise from Duluth and that these other people had sunk the cruiser and taken them hostage. He told them to ask Brad, expecting Tollefson to back him up, but that had nearly resulted in the two men coming to blows despite the police presence all around them. Then, when Mansfield heard that the authorities had the entire cockpit transmission on tape, he clammed up and demanded to call his lawyer.

Paul told them about Bruno going overboard and about the sinking of the cruiser off Isle Royale. He also told them about *Blue Moon* and assured them that Skip had done nothing wrong.

Brad Tollefson confirmed the rest and told of Sam and his nephew, Michael, likely lost with *Valhalla* at Isle Royale.

Rich and Skip were questioned briefly and then sent down U.S. 41 for medical attention in Hancock. Police detectives and two FBI agents accompanied them so they could continue the questioning and Paul insisted that Gina go with them to be checked by the doctors. He politely declined the offer to go with them, saying he need to stay with the boat . . . Yes, the boat. He looked at *Pipe Dream* now in the glow of the halogen lights. She was an absolute mess. She had splintered sections of toe rail, bullet holes in the fiberglass of the deckhouse, blood stains all over and a general disheveled appearance that made him wince. He uttered a single word into the night air: "Shit."

EPILOGUE

September 27, 3:37 p.m. EDT

Pipe Dream had made her passage from Chicago, riding the Lake Michigan swells through the Straits of Mackinac into Lake Huron without incident. She then ran south, leaving Lake Huron to cross beneath the Blue Water Bridge and pass Port Huron and Sarnia on her way down to Lake St. Clair. She put in briefly north of Detroit, then continued down the Detroit River and into Lake Erie. Late September on Lake Erie could be tricky. This was the shallowest of the Great Lakes; fall winds at times raised heavy, confused seas, but this day was perfect. The Tartan 37 surged ahead under main and poled-out genoa as she sped eastward.

In the cockpit, Paul reflected on the events of the past two months. After extensive questioning, and with Skip's corroboration of their accounts of those eventful days, it was finally over. Neither Rich nor Paul were facing any charges in connection with the death of the assassin. Mansfield had decided to plead guilty, and in an effort to lessen his sentence, he had decided not to go down alone. The Chicago news had been filled with high-profile arrests. The charges being filed would result in newsworthy trials for months.

The body of the Chicago hit man, Jack, was found under the dock at Rocky Island two weeks after the incident. Sam's body was never found; Michael's was found in the sunken *Valhalla* and returned to his family for burial. Miraculously, a sport fisherman heading to Isle Royale had spotted something afloat the afternoon of July 28, and had recovered a man from the open lake. He was suffering from advanced hypothermia and had a broken arm and a severe concussion, but he received excellent first aid from the men on the boat. He was taken ashore and transported to a Duluth hospital. He eventually made a full recovery, in time to work with authorities in sorting out the chain of events. He would certainly spend some time in prison, but not as much as he'd feared. When Paul heard that Bruno had survived, a burden was lifted from his conscience.

After a short hospital stay, Rich Perry had returned to the M&L Investment offices at the request of the board of directors. All but one of the board had been completely uninvolved in Mansfield's scheme, and they looked to Rich to save what was left. With Sherry helping him, he had salvaged the company's legitimate business and retained a majority of the clients. The company's name was changing, and so, it seemed, were Rich's fortunes.

Skip got an excellent settlement from his insurance company and had replaced *Blue Moon* with a new and slightly larger boat. The insurance company was reluctant at first to pay the full amount of loss, but supposedly they had gotten a call from someone with some clout in the Chicago financial community. Skip never knew for certain, but he suspected it had been Rich Perry who placed the call and got things moving for him.

An extremely grateful Rich had helped Paul bring his boat down through the lakes to Chicago, where he had taken care of the repairs to *Pipe Dream*. He even took the time to visit her and Paul often at the Larsen Marine yard in Waukegan as the work was expertly done. When she was whole again and Paul was ready to leave, Rich was there to see him off.

Snapping his mind back to the present, Paul looked at the waters ahead, then considered his situation. *Pipe Dream* would reach the east end of Lake Erie, where he would have the mast unstepped and lashed on deck for the trip through the Erie Canal to the Hudson. Once there, the mast would be stepped and *Pipe Dream* would be free to head down the coast, perhaps to the Caribbean . . . and a return trip via the same route would put them back on the Great Lakes in June. There would be new adventures on new waters and something more to write about.

The sun was behind now, slowly lowering as the day wore on. The fine breeze and the gentle following sea matched Paul's mood. He looked about him again, then leaned back, one arm behind his head. With the other, he reached over and patted *Pipe Dream's* coaming. "What could be better?" he said to the boat.

"Tea's ready!" said the voice from below. Looking to the companionway, Paul smiled as Gina came up, bringing his tea and her own warm, answering smile. She handed him his tea, switched hers to her right hand, and sat down beside him, nestling into the crook of his arm.

"THIS could be better!" Paul said, to no one in particular.

Here ends the first adventure.

ABOUT LAKE SUPERIOR

Lake Superior is the largest of North America's Great Lakes. The lake has had prior names; the original name was given by the Ojibway, who called it Kitchi-gummi, or "Big Lake." You may recognize the term from Henry Wadsworth Longfellow's famous "Song of Hiawatha", although he spelled it "Gitche Gumee." As French explorers arrived and began their travels in the region, they dubbed it "Le Lac Superieur" because it lies to the north or above the other lakes. That name, translated to English, still stands today. What they did not know at the time is that "The Superior Lake" is in fact just that — the largest fresh water lake on earth. Russia's Lake Baikal contains a greater volume of water due to its extreme depth, but Lake Superior's surface area tops it and all others.

Lake Superior is home to Isle Royale National Park, a pristine wilderness accessible only by boat or seaplane. It lies nearer to the Canadian shore, but the international boundary passes to the north. Isle Royale is actually a part of the State of Michigan.

The U. S. States of Minnesota, Michigan and Wisconsin and the Canadian Province of Ontario form Lake Superior's 2,726 mile long shoreline. At the lake's eastern end, the St. Mary's River carries its waters down and into Lake Huron. Ships must traverse the famed locks at Sault Ste. Marie, more commonly called "The Soo." The locks draw tourists by the thousands each summer. The twin ports of Duluth, Minnesota and Superior, Wisconsin lie 350 miles away at its western end. These ports, along with the Canadian port at Thunder Bay, Ontario, ship North American products to worldwide destinations. Smaller, specialized ports around the lake deliver iron ore for the steel mills along the lower lakes.

The lake is famous for its deep blue water and its unrivaled shoreline scenery, but perhaps its greatest recent claim to fame is a darker moment: the loss of a great ore carrier, the Edmund Fitzgerald, in a horrific November 1975 storm. The tragic event is memorialized in song by famed Canadian singer and songwriter Gordon Lightfoot. His "Wreck of the Edmund Fitzgerald" is a haunting reminder of the power and fury that lie beneath the beautiful face of this Queen of all lakes.

Lake Superior Facts

- Water surface area: 31,700 square miles

- Volume of contained water: 2,900 cubic miles

- Water surface height above sea level: 600 feet

- Length: 350 miles

- Breadth: 160 miles

- Average depth: 483 feet

- Greatest depth: 1,332 feet

- Summer water temperature: 46 to 48 degrees Fahrenheit (8 to 9 degrees Celsius)

A GLOSSARY OF NAUTICAL
AND SAILING TERMS

This glossary is offered to those readers not as familiar with the nautical world as some may be, to help in understanding some of the terms and expressions used in this story.

Aft - - - - - - - - - - - - -   Toward the stern or rear of a boat.

Backstay - - - - - - - - -   A part of the standing rigging of a sailboat. The backstay runs from a point at or near the top of the mast to the stern of the boat, stabilizing the mast against movement forward.

Boom - - - - - - - - - - - -   A horizontal spar, projecting aft from the mast, to support the lower edge of the mainsail.

Bulkhead - - - - - - - - -   A dividing wall or partition on the interior of a boat. Bulkheads often serve as part of the structure of the boat, lending it strength.

Chainplate - - - - - - - -   A strong metal fitting attached to the hull structure, used to transmit tensile force from the shrouds into the hull.

Cockpit - - - - - - - - - -   Exterior secure seating and

helm area on a boat, most
usually found astern but
sometimes amidships.

Cockpit locker - - - - - - - - A storage compartment,
usually in the aft portion of
the boat and accessed
through a hatch in the
cockpit.

Dead reckoning - - - - - Navigation performed
without benefit of electronics
or other outside means of
position determination. It
involves logging estimated
positions based on the course
and speed over time from a
last known position. Many
mariners still keep dead
reckoning positions as
backup, in case of instrument
failure.

Deck - - - - - - - - - - - - The horizontal walking
surfaces on the exterior of a
boat.

Draft - - - - - - - - - - - - The distance from the
waterline to the deepest part
of a boat's keel or rudder.
Draft is an important figure
to know, especially in shoal
areas.

Fender - - - - - - - - - - - A cylindrical or spherical
plastic or rubber cushion tied
along the hull of a boat to

protect it from impact damage at docks and piers.

Foot - - - - - - - - - - - The lower horizontal edge of a sail. For instance, the boom holds the foot of a mainsail.

Fore, forward - - - - - Toward the front or bow of a boat.

Forestay - - - - - - - - - A part of the standing rigging of a sailboat. The forestay runs from a point at or near the top of the mast to the bow of the boat, stabilizing the mast against movement aft.

Furler - - - - - - - - - - - A mechanical device with a foil that surrounds the forestay and a drum at its base, used to furl a forward sail or jib attached to the foil neatly around the forestay when it is not in use.

Galley - - - - - - - - - - - The food preparation area or "kitchen" of a boat.

Genoa, genny, jenny - A large forward sail or jib. A jib that extends from the bow to a point aft of the mast when in use is referred to as a Genoa jib because it was reportedly first developed in Genoa, Italy. In common usage, the name is usually

shortened to Genoa or
Genny. (Jenny.)

GPS - - - - - - - - - - -   GPS is an acronym for
Global Positioning System, a
modern satellite-based
navigational system that
provides great accuracy and
reliability for mariners and
travelers in general.

Halyard - - - - - - - - - -   A part of the running rigging
of a sailboat. A halyard is
used to raise a sail.

Heel, heeling - - - - - - -   Under sail, forces generated
by the wind against the sails
resolve into a forward
driving force and a lateral
force that attempts to tip the
boat to the side. The lateral
force, by design, is resisted
by the ballast and keel, but
some degree of tipping
usually occurs. That is called
"heeling."

Jib - - - - - - - - - - - -   The forward sail in a sloop
rigged boat. It is attached to
the forestay.

Keel - - - - - - - - - - - -   The heavy structural member
that forms the bottom center
of a ship. In modern
sailboats, the keel is actually
a fin or foil that projects
downward from the bottom
of the boat. It provides

directional stability and resists movement to the side, and it also works with the sails to provide a degree of lift. In cruising sailboats, much of the ballast weight is contained in or suspended from the keel.

Knot - - - - - - - - - - -   In nautical terms a knot is a measure of speed, representing one nautical mile per hour. The name is derived from the old method of measuring speed through the water. A line with a resisting board or "log" on one end and knots in the line spaced at equal distance was used. The log was thrown from the stern, and the number of knots in the line that were pulled over the rail over a given time were counted while a glass timed to 28 seconds was turned. The distance between knots was 47 feet, 3 inches, and the number knots over the rail during that time provided the ship's speed.

Lazy-jacks - - - - - - - -   A trademarked system of lines used to contain a mainsail atop the boom as it is lowered. Most similar systems are now called lazy-jacks as a common term.

Luff - - - - - - - - - - - -   The luff is the forward or
leading edge of a sail. When
the word is used as a verb, it
describes the condition
where the sail is too close to
the wind and air passes
equally over both sides of the
sail, causing the leading edge
to flutter. This condition is
called "luffing."

Lunch hook - - - - - - - -   In nautical jargon, a lunch
hook is simply a smaller
anchor, used instead of the
primary anchor when
stopping for a limited time
only.

Mainsail, main - - - - - -   The aft sail on a sloop-rigged
sailboat. Its forward edge or
luff is attached directly to the
mast, and its lower edge or
foot is attached to the boom.

Mast - - - - - - - - - - - -   The primary vertical spar in a
sailboat.

Nautical mile - - - - - - -   This the standard measure o
distance at sea. The nautical
mile was first developed to
roughly represent one minute
of longitude at the equator; it
has been standardized to a
distance of 6,076 feet.

Nav - - - - - - - - - - - A truncation of the word 'navigation', often used by sailors to describe items such as a 'navigation station' (nav station) or 'navigation aids' (nav aids).

Port - - - - - - - - - - - The side of the boat to one's left when facing forward. A useful mnemonic in remembering the difference between port and starboard is that the words 'port' and 'left' each contain four letters.

Preventer - - - - - - - - A line or tackle rigged when sailing downwind, to prevent the boom of a sailboat from slamming violently across the cockpit if the mainsail becomes back-winded.

Rode - - - - - - - - - - - The braided or woven line attached to an anchor or anchor chain.

running rigging - - - - Lines on a sailboat that are used to hoist and control the sails. Running rigging includes, among other things, the halyards and sheets.

Sheet - - - - - - - - - - - A line attached to a sail, used to adjust its angle to the wind while trimming.

Sheet stopper - - - - -   A levered mechanical line
                           clamp used to restrain
                           running rigging.

Shrouds - - - - - - - - -   stainless steel or composite
                           supporting wires, rigged at
                           the side of a mast and
                           extending to chainplates. The
                           shrouds prevent lateral
                           motion of the mast. There are
                           often two shrouds per side:
                           the upper shrouds extend
                           from the chainplates upward
                           to the outer end of the
                           spreaders and then to the
                           masthead. The lower shrouds
                           extend from the chainplates
                           to the inner end of the
                           spreader at the mast.

Sloop - - - - - - - - - -   A single-masted sailing
                           vessel, characterized by a
                           triangular headsail or jib, and
                           a mainsail, rigged to the mast
                           and boom.

Sole - - - - - - - - - - - The horizontal walking
                           surfaces on the interior of a
                           boat.

Spar - - - - - - - - - - - Any of the rigid rig
                           components of a sailboat,
                           such the mast or the boom.

Spreader - - - - - - - - - A horizontal rigid rod or tube
                           extending out to the side

from the mast, holding the upper shroud away from the mast. This enables the mast and shrouds to form a structural truss, increasing strength.

Stanchion - - - - - - - -   A vertical post supporting rails or lifelines along the side of a boat deck.

Standing rigging - - - -   The wire rope components of a sailboat rig that support the mast in place, preventing both lateral and fore-and-aft movement. Standing rigging consists of the shrouds, forestay and backstay.

Starboard - - - - - - - - -   The side of the boat to one's right when facing forward.

Step, stepped - - - - - - -   The condition of support at the base of the mast. A mast that ends on the deck is called a 'deck-stepped mast.' One that passes through the upper deck and is supported at its lower end atop the keel is called a 'keel-stepped mast.'

Topping lift - - - - - - - -   A line providing vertical support, usually to the boom

Traveler - - - - - - - - -   An adjustable track allowing a lateral change in the deck attachment point of the mainsail sheet. It allows rapid and precise mainsail control.

Trim - - - - - - - - - - - -   The shape of the sail required to optimize movement of the boat. A sail is said to be trimmed when it is developing its best power for conditions. A change in wind direction or velocity will require a change in trim.

Topsides - - - - - - - - -   The sides of the hull from the waterline up to the toerail. The term 'topsides' is often misunderstood and taken to mean 'deck', because a sailor below may say, 'I'm going up topside.' He really means he is going on deck.

Vang - - - - - - - - - - - - -   A tackle or rig used to pull the boom downward to help shape the mainsail.

V-berth, vee-berth - - - -   The forward berth in a boat. It derives its name from its shape, since the hull sides narrow to a V shape forward.

Winch - - - - - - - - - - - -   A mechanical device to provide added power when raising or trimming sails. The sheet or halyard is passed around the drum of the winch multiple times and a handle is used to crank or "grind" the winch and apply mechanical advantage.

Windlass - - - - - - - - - - A windlass is similar to a winch, but it is mounted on the foredeck and is often capable of handling both rope and chain. It is used to provide power for raising the anchor. Some windlasses are powered by the boat's electrical system.